Back on Course

Full of Running #2

back on course

GRACE WILKINSON

First edition

Copyright © 2018 Grace Wilkinson

Also by the author

Comet in Summer

Confetti Horses

Eventing Bay

The Loxwood Series

chapter 1

'Do you know what you're doing for Christmas?'

Freya's arm stops its clockwise motion, the wooden spoon she's holding resting in the cake mixture. Her dark eyes meet mine, and she frowns before blowing out a breath with a laugh. 'Sybil. It's September.'

I lean over the farmhouse table to dip my finger in the cake batter. 'So?'

'So can we at least not think about the horror of the holidays until *after* the event season's over?'

'What's so bad about Christmas?' I ask, licking the raw mixture off my finger.

Freya picks up a lemon and starts grating the rind into the bowl. 'What's so great about it?'

I shrug. 'Decorating the tree. Putting up decorations. Playing games. Watching movies. Presents.'

'Okay,' Freya says quickly, putting the lemon and grater down. She holds up a hand and starts counting my list off on her fingers. 'A tree's nice. Stripes will attack any and all decorations' - I glance at the Dalmatian, his large figure seated beside me, and think I can't imagine him ever doing something destructive, but don't disagree out loud. 'There are three of us, and I'm an only child, so games don't really happen.' She pauses. 'What was the next one?'

'Movies.'

'Yeah, movies. You know I don't really watch much TV. Then presents, well, there's nothing I particularly want, and it's not like any of us can really afford to buy much, anyway. We've already said that we won't be doing presents this year, other than a token.'

But you just bought an FEI pony, I think desperately. Some months ago, Freya sold Diamond, the spotted pony she brought up through the ranks herself, and bought Battersea, an eventing pony who's won medals at the European Pony Championships as part of the Great British squad. As shocked as I was that Freya was parting with her beloved gelding, I was even more shocked that her family could afford a pony like Leo, as Battersea is known. And since then I've deduced that the purchase called for various loans and financial help, but still. Freya is a talented rider, anyone can see that, but I can't get my head around parents spending a small fortune on a horse when they can't afford to buy Christmas presents.

'Yeah,' I say, voice unconvincing, 'I guess you're right.' Something else Freya said, other than the mention of money, nags at me, tapping against my subconscious like a woodpecker pecking a tree, but I ignore it. 'Hey, have you heard from Diamond recently? Well, his new owners?' I ask as my eyes fall on a photograph held up on the fridge by magnets. It's a picture taken during a dressage test, and as a rider I would guess the combination is in the middle of an extended trot across the diagonal. As always, Freya's position is perfect. She is sitting square, hands together and elbows softly bent, heels under her seat, legs loose but on, staring straight ahead. Diamond exudes the same cool confidence, his ears pricked, spotted coat glossy, right fore reaching out so it is straight like a ballerina's leg, his left hind reaching under him and bending at the hock.

Diamond was a wonderful pony, but he was never going to make it as an FEI pony, as a team contender. I still never thought Freya would part with him, though. She hasn't mentioned him much since he left, but I do know he's gone to a good home, where he'll teach another young girl the basics of eventing.

Freya shakes her head, looking more morose than she did a moment ago. 'No, not since that message when he arrived. Not that I expect them to update me every week.'

'No, of course not,' I agree, doing my best to sound reassuring. 'I'm sure he's fine.'

'Yeah.' Freya grates more lemon rind into the cake batter, the two of us silent in the small cottage kitchen.

It is neither big nor fancy, but Freya's home is the kind I've always dreamed of living in. The thatch cottage has low ceilings and exposed beams, with wooden floorboards and walls of white stone. The furnishings are all old and cosy, the amenities semi-functional at best, and there are draughts and creaks everywhere, but the house is perfect. In the kitchen, where we're sitting, the oak table has gaps down the length of it that are filled with dust and crumbs, an Aga has been switched on for the first time since summer began, and a dog bed in front of it is covered in a tartan blanket. Pictures cover the fridge, mostly of Freya and Diamond, and more competition photographs and rosettes line the piece of furniture against the back wall.

Up until a few months ago, I didn't live in the country at all, but a terraced house in Cambridge. And now I *do* live in the country, something I've always wanted, and my pony - *ponies*, I correct myself - are just down the lane. But while our semi-detached cottage is picturesque from the outside, with its red bricks and diamond windows, it doesn't have the same homely feel inside that Freya's does. It's also smaller, and the absence of a good mudroom like the one here in Willow Tree House means it's hard to keep from traipsing dirt all through the open-plan ground floor, but I'm not complaining. Though I still wish the move to the country had been with Dad, too, and not under the circumstances of a divorce.

'D'you think he's okay?'

It takes me a moment to realise what Freya is talking about, my train of thought rolling through mudrooms and divorce papers. I sit up straighter and frown, hoping my best friend doesn't realise I lost concentration. 'Diamond?'

'The girl, Hettie, really seemed to like him,' Freya goes on, my distraction clearly not noticed. 'And she's only little, but she rode well, and her mum seemed like she'd be looking after him…'

'I'm sure he's fine,' I say confidently. 'You can always send them a message and find out.'

Freya pulls a face. 'Maybe. I dunno, I don't want to hassle them.'

'He's your pony,' I say.

'That's the point, he's not. Not anymore.' This is the closest Freya has come to discussing Diamond's departure - *really* discussing it, not just speaking the black-and-white facts - since it took place, and I wonder if I should say more, push the matter further, but Freya stops me, speaking before I can continue the conversation. 'Oh, I almost forgot, did you see this week's *Horse & Hound?*'

I shake my head. 'Why?'

Freya puts the lemon and grater down and turns towards the cluttered surface of the buffet. 'Here.' She pulls an already well-read copy of *Horse & Hound* from a pile of magazines - which are *all* copies of *Horse & Hound* - and chucks it towards me. 'I marked the page.'

I flip the magazine open to the page with a folded corner, and see a report on Blenheim. I'm about to ask Freya what I'm looking at, but then I see it.

Rose. And Paddington. The chestnut gelding is flying over a

skinny, his knees around his chin as Rose looks ahead for the next fence.

Freya dips her finger in the cake batter, then turns to open a cupboard. 'Good picture, huh?'

'Yeah,' I say, admiring the familiar horse, and feeling giddy at the thought of not only knowing this person, but getting to have lessons with her.

A cake tin clatters as Freya drops it onto the wooden table, and Stripes jumps up with a bark, mistaking the sound for somebody knocking at the door. 'Stripes,' Freya says in a firm voice, and the Dalmatian lowers his body to rest his head on his forelegs.

'Anything else interesting in here?' I ask, flipping through the magazine.

'Nah, not really. Except a horrible article on how loads of people are taking old horses to kennels and slaughterhouses because it costs too much to retire them or put them down. It says something like fifty per cent of people think it's acceptable.' Freya gags and pulls a face. I've never known her even eat chicken, so the thought of a horse going to the knacker's yard is enough to drive her crazy. 'It's just so wrong.'

'Yeah,' I agree, putting the magazine down. Awful as it may be, I can't really stand to read about the topic.

I glance at the fridge again, at the many pictures held up by magnets, and my eyes linger on my favourite. It's from a Pony Club camp a couple of years ago. Freya left everyone for dead in a fancy dress competition when she dressed up as Cruella de Vil, enlisting Diamond and Stripes as her Dalmatians.

Diamond, the pony that was not only unproven when she got him, but in terrible condition. How she could bear to sell him eludes me.

'Anyway.' Freya blows out a breath, looking down at the bowl. 'Let's focus on cake.'

It's only September, but already the evenings have started to get chilly. The sun no longer rises at four in the morning, but the perfectly reasonably hour of six thirty. Days of T-shirts and shorts are gone for now, but the month is an unpredictable one where weather is concerned, and we could still find ourselves in a fleeting heatwave yet before the end of the event season. But for now it's cold, the wind brisk, and as I walk to the yard from Freya's, I can already see the short but never-ending winter days on the horizon.

'Hey, ponies,' I call, walking across the grass, towards the post-and-rail paddock. There are four figures grazing in the field, and they all lift their heads at the sound of my voice. Cinder and Pheasant, Mackenzie and Jemima's elderly schoolmasters. They aren't the flashiest ponies in the world, but they're just lovely. Not only nicely-made and well-cared for, they both have hearts of gold, and more honest ponies could not be found.

I pick up a head collar from the grass before letting myself into the field, sliding it onto my shoulder. 'Jup. Ace. Which one of you's coming in first?'

The two ponies look up at me, ears forward and eyes alert. It's cold, the wind nipping at my cheeks, and the ground is muddy from the week of rain we've hand, water seeping into my old riding boots through the splits along the edges. It's Sunday evening, which means school tomorrow, and I'm halfway through a fantasy book I really want to finish tonight, not to mention all the homework I still have to do, but I don't hurry to catch one of the ponies. Instead I stop a few paces away, feet sinking deeper into the mud Newmarket's clay soil turns to whenever it rains, and wait, looking straight ahead.

And I smile.

Just a short while ago, I wasn't sure I'd have any pony to event. Jupiter and I had a bad fall during the first half of the season, thought to have been caused by a case of azoturia he suffered due to not being fit enough, and I was worried the rest of the year would be wrecked. But Rose and I worked him slowly, building up fitness and technique, with the intention of catching the tail end of the season. Except just as things were going right, just as Jupiter had started going to training shows again, I received what, at the time, seemed like the worst news possible: the family I loaned Jupiter from had hit hard times, and he was being put on the market.

I had some savings, enough to buy him in fact, but there was another spanner in the works. And that spanner was Ace. The little bay mare had been sent to Rose for schooling, and as Jupiter had been sidelined, Rose offered me the ride on Ace and allowed me to work with her. But the mare was tricky, to put it lightly, and I actually hated riding her for a while. But I kept at it, to even my surprise, and as the summer holidays drew to a close, I'd formed a bond with the pony, and had hoped to buy her with my savings.

Faced with choosing between the two, I realised I couldn't give up on Jupiter out of loyalty, as much as the thought of Ace going elsewhere, where she might be misunderstood, made me ill. But then, to my utter surprise, Rose cut a deal with Ace's owners by waiving all training and board costs for the time she'd been in the yard, and Ace stayed. It was a dream come true.

As the wind blows strongly again, making me shiver beneath my coat, Ace decides she's had quite enough of being outside. With a swish of her tail she starts walking forward, passing Jupiter with her ears back, and comes towards me, looking the picture of innocence.

'Hey, Maggot,' I say, using a well-earned nickname. Ace isn't mean, but she can still be nifty with her teeth and hind feet. Most of her problems come from lack of confidence, and she hasn't always been ridden well, but there's still an edge to her that she was born with. After all, when her previous owner tried to give her a life as a broodmare, Ace only ended up kicking her foal to death within minutes of it being born.

To be fair, I think, *you'd have to be delusional to look at Ace and think* maternal.

'You'd much rather be an event horse than a mum. Wouldn't you, Maggot?'

Ace snorts, showering me, and I close my eyes, wincing in disgust. I step back and shake my hands, laughing, and open my eyes again just in time to jump back farther, avoiding Ace's teeth.

'Cut it out,' I grumble. Most people respond derisively whenever I tell them this, but if there's one thing Ace hates, it's being laughed at. If she senses you're mocking her, or are apprehensive around her, she launches on principle. It's hard to find the balance between never letting her think you're afraid of her, and also being aware enough to avoid being her flavour of the day.

'You do want to be an event pony, Ace of Hearts,' I assure her, slipping her nose through the head collar. 'You love to jump, and you love being the centre of attention.' *And you're a cross country machine,* I add silently. I've only taken her cross country schooling a couple of times, but every fence I've jumped with Ace has felt different from any other on Jupiter. She comes alive on a cross country course, and jumps every obstacle like the universe depends on it. Though we still have yet to get around an event together, because on our first attempt recently, I flew head first into the first show jumping fence, much to my embarrassment. But Rose took Ace around an event last month and she was exceptional, and I know she's capable of even more.

And my hope, my pie in the sky wish, is that not only will Ace and I get around a ninety centimetre course, but that we'll eventually compete in Pony Trials and one-stars - the latter also confusingly sometimes called Pony two-stars. It's a long way off, but I think it's possible. I've never thought of working with horses in the long run, and there's no way I'm a good enough rider to go much higher than Novice anyway, but I've always wanted to get

Jupiter to that level, and now Ace, too.

Behind Ace, Jupiter starts coming towards us, clearly keen to cause trouble. He's already starting to lose his summer coat, which is leaving a woolly grey blanket in its place - and it's barely autumn. No wonder he needs clipping three times a year.

'You never know,' I say idly, leading Ace to the gate. Jupiter gets even nearer, and Ace pins her ears. I scratch her head in reassurance, white hairs of the heart-shaped star that is her namesake sticking to my fingers. 'You might even make it to Europeans.'

'Have you washed your competition things yet?' Mum greets me when I walk through the door. She's standing at the table, a pile of washing in front of her. A shirt is in her hands, and I watch her fold the linen and place it in the washing basket to her right.

I close the door and pause, eyes scanning the room. My younger brother, Gabe, is on the sofa, a thick paperback volume in his hands. He's looking down through the thick lenses of his glasses, and I wonder if he has even noticed me walk in. Beside him are our two rescue dogs, Frodo the Labrador taking up almost the whole sofa, his head in Gabe's lap, while Eleven the pit bull is curled in a ball at one end. *Some guard dogs,* I think. I could have robbed the place by now.

'Hello, Mum, nice to see you, too,' I say, voice full of sarcasm. 'Yes, I had a nice time at Freya's, thanks. And Ace and Jupi are fine, too.'

Mum runs a hand over the folded shirt in the basket, then looks up at me. Since she took on a job running a café in Newmarket at the beginning of the summer, part of the reason we moved here, her eyes have always been shadowed by dark circles. And she'd probably kill me if she heard me say this, but she looks older than her mid-thirties, too.

'Don't change the subject,' Mum says to me, face softening.

'I'm not changing the subject.'

'Have you, then?'

'Have I what?'

Mum crosses her arms across her chest. 'Have you washed your competition things yet?'

'I'm not eventing for a week,' I point out.

'That's still not an answer,' Mum says.

'I think it means no,' Gabe calls from the sofa, and I shoot daggers at him with my eyes. Clearly he's more aware of his surroundings than he looks.

Mum looks at me. 'Sybil.'

'Yes, I have, all right?' I snap.

'You have?' Mum repeats.

'Yes. I washed everything right away, just as you told me to. We do our own washing now,' I remind her. 'Remember?'

Mum has never been a helicopter parent, and Gabe and I have always had our fair share of chores and responsibilities, but since the divorce, since Mum started working again, our jobs have increased. Before, if we left a muddy sweatshirt or a used plate lying around, Mum would eventually clear and wash it, but that doesn't happen anymore. Gabe and I are in charge of all our own washing, and no pile of dirty laundry cluttering the house will change that. This is more irritating for me than it is for Gabe though, because my indoors-y brother is perfectly happy to wear the same geeky T-shirt for days at a time, and with the exception of walking the dogs he never ventures on grass, so his clothes stay clean for much longer than mine. Coming home from the yard generally comes with an eruption of hay and straw from boots, grass-stained tops, creosote stuck to coats, and that's only if Ace hasn't decided to throw me on the ground, because then I traipse sand all through the house, too.

Gabe and I are also in charge of cooking dinner two nights a week - Mondays and Thursdays - with Mum covering the other days, except Fridays which are reserved for takeout.

'Right,' Mum says. A smile tugs at the side of the face, and she shakes her head. 'Of course you have. Sorry.' She looks over at the sofas, at Gabe reading, then back at me. 'I'm going to go shower before I start cooking.' And with that she moves towards the stairs, which creak with every step, but in a way that is nothing but irritating, not quaint like the squeaky floorboards in Freya's house.

When I hear the bathroom door close above, I let out a sigh and move to the sitting area, collapsing onto the free sofa.

Gabe lowers his book to look at me, holding the paperback below his chin as he speaks. 'You haven't done your washing. Your jodhpurs and shirt are still in a pile in your room. I saw them this morning.'

'Shut up.'

Jupiter propels into the air with his knees tucked, and I lean forward to go with him, to follow the jump. My hands move up his neck, allowing the pony freedom, and I keep my weight in my heels as we fly over the fence.

'Super,' Rose says when we land, and I reach my hand forward to pat Jupiter's neck before bringing him back to a trot. 'Great, that'll do him.' She slides her hands into her coat pockets and leans back against the arena railings as I trot Jupiter over to her. 'Are you happy leaving him on that?'

I nod, face flushed. 'Yeah. He felt good.'

'You both were,' Rose says. 'You set him up really nicely, and you didn't interfere in front of the fence.' She nods decisively. 'Great, so he doesn't need to jump again before the weekend, does he? Or is there something else you want to work on?'

'No, I'm good. And if you think he's all right...'

'I do. Ride him like that and you'll have no problem at all.'

'Okay.'

Both ponies went clear round show jumping last week, and

I've evented Jupiter countless times before, but not since our last disastrous event, and I hadn't realised I was nervous until these past few days, now the competition is only a couple of sleeps away. He and Ace are entered in the BE90, a ninety-centimetre track I've been around before, and I know they're capable of it just as I am. I've never completed an event with Ace, so her rounds should be the ones I'm worried about, and yet it's Jupiter who's haunting me.

What happened before we fell earlier this year, while we were galloping around the course and I felt the pony beneath me lose all energy, was something I never want to experience again. Looking back, I should have pulled up, but I thought he was just tired, the way that is common towards the end of a cross country course. And coming into that fence, on a limp horse, and feeling Jupiter try to jump and not be able to... the thought makes me swallow back bile. It's a miracle neither of us was seriously hurt.

The logical part of my brain knows I can't compare the Jupiter I'm riding now to the one he was back then. I hadn't yet moved to Rose's yard, and Jupiter was only being ridden a couple of times a week, and not even for very long. He didn't hack, didn't do any proper fitness training, and knowing what I do now, I can't believe I was eventing him. But I *didn't* know any better then, and I can only learn from the mistakes.

Jupiter is fitter than he's ever been now. He works at least five times a week, does plenty of hacking and hill work, does timed canter sets, his flatwork has improved leaps and bounds, and all this has helped his jumping, which was already good to begin with.

'You're the best,' I tell the pony as I lead him to his stable. I lean forward to kiss his forehead, but Jupiter turns his head in disgust. He's affectionate and bombproof, but he's always hated having his head kissed. 'Silly muppet,' I mutter.

I've still got Ace to ride, and Rose waiting to teach me, so I untack Jupiter quickly. I throw his gear on the floor and sponge his saddle patch, frowning at his fluffy coat. I'll have to see if Rose can clip him after the weekend. And see if Mum or I can afford to pay her to do so. My family has never had a lot of cash to spare, but things have been even tighter since the divorce. Dad isn't one to skimp on child support payments, and he gives Gabe and me money every month, even though I'm not his biological daughter, and Mum makes sure that my share goes towards the ponies. But entry fees are expensive, as is general care, and there's very little - if anything - left over at the end of the month. Rose is nice enough about giving me free lessons, however much Mum tries to pay her, and counting on her generosity to clip the ponies free of charge is a step too far.

'You'll be fine for the weekend,' I say confidently, looking at Jupiter's coat. Objectively, it's a far cry from a wooly winter coat, but to my worried eyes he might as well be an angora rabbit. 'And the event will be fine, too,' I add, but I sound less sure than I did a moment ago.

There's no reason for what happened last time to happen again, I remind myself, but still. The worry doesn't go away. And neither does the memory of us both falling to the ground.

chapter 2

After all the bad weather we've had recently, I take the clear sky that rises on the morning of the event as a good omen. The horsebox lurches over the grass, bouncing me from side to side, and I grip the door handle as my stomach churns. *It'll be fine. Just another event.*

'Time check?' Rose asks.

'Almost half-seven,' I say, looking at my watch.

I was at the yard at six this morning, wearing tracksuit bottoms and a coat over my beige jodhpurs and white competition shirt (which I had to sneakily wash and dry when Mum wasn't around so that my white lie wasn't discovered). The ponies were plaited up last night, with Mum's help, who plaited Jupiter for me, because her standard for turnout is much higher than mine, and her braiding skills have not lessened since her Pony Club days. Ace's mane is much thinner than Jupi's, so I get the better end of the deal, though it was only last week that I discovered how much she hates having her mane pulled. The mare arrived at Rose's with a just-pulled mane only a few inches long, and this was the first time it had needed doing, hence the discovery of yet *another* thing the devil pony disagrees with. Thankfully plaiting is a different deal, and Ace is happy to pull at a haynet while I struggle to roll her mane for an hour.

'Okay,' Rose says, voice calm as always. 'We have an hour and a half until you need to get on Jupiter to warm up. Shall we leave them for now and go get the course walk out of the way? We can get numbers at the same time.'

I nod, swinging open the passenger door of the lorry as Rose climbs out her side. It might be sunny, but it's still cold, and I keep my coat on, checking the pockets to make sure I have money on me to pay Ace and Jupiter's starting fees.

The venue is still quiet this early. The 90 section I'm riding in is one of the first classes of the day, and I'm one of the first starters, so Rose and I are among the first arrivals. Mum is driving here later, arriving in time for Jupiter's dressage test, and I'm glad. She doesn't exactly do much of any use at an event, but I'm not sure I'd feel comfortable riding without knowing she's here should I need anything.

'The ground's good,' Rose says, kicking at the soil with the tip of her boot. She's riding Sunny, her six-year-old warmblood, in the Novice, and she also has a catch ride - a pony who's been taking advantage of an inexperienced rider and needs reminding who's boss - in the 100.

The BE90 track is no different from other BE90 tracks I've done. I've even competed at this venue before, and have jumped some of the jumps of the course. But they suddenly look bigger, more intimidating, impossible.

Get a grip, I tell myself. *It's a 90. You and your ponies have all been around a class higher no problem.*

'You're going to turn inside for this one,' Rose says, skimming an Intermediate fence to turn and face the palisade marked with the colour of my track. 'It's a tighter turn than going around it, but you'll be straight to the fence.'

I nod, looking at where Rose has walked. 'Okay.'

But Rose isn't satisfied, and she shakes her head as she motions me towards her. 'Walk it yourself. The exact line. Visualise it.'

I look back over my shoulder at the last fence we passed, then walk a curve to hug the huge Intermediate fence, until the palisade is directly in my line of vision. I try to imagine I'm on a horse, frame the fence with a pair of pricked ears, and feel slightly ill. 'Okay.'

Why do courses always look so much bigger when you're riding? When I watch other people jump these same fences, I think they look tiny, piece of cake, easy-peasy. Yet faced with them myself, it's a different ball game.

'Jupiter's last on the lorry, isn't he?' Rose says when we reach the finish. Even the last fence looks huge, and I swallow past the lump in my throat to reply.

'Yeah.'

'Do you want to start getting him ready on your own, and I'll just run my courses real quick.' Because of course Rose isn't riding around the same track as me, and this course walk was for my benefit and my benefit only.

'Sure,' I say.

'Sure?' she repeats. 'You can lower the ramp on your own, can't you?'

My limbs don't feel like they're up to anything right now, but Mackenzie is capable of lowering the ramp without assistance, so of course I reply to the affirmative.

On the way back to the lorry park, I pay Ace and Jupiter's entry fees in exchange for which the secretary hands me their numbers, check the start times to make sure there hasn't been a change, and glance at the show jumping course. At events, riders rarely actually walk the show jumping track, and you learn to memorise the course whenever you happen to be nearby.

There are more lorries in the park now, a few with the names of big riders - four-star riders; Olympic riders; European medal-winning riders - printed on them, and I glance enviously at the shiny horseboxes as I pass them. Open tack lockers reveal neatly-stacked saddles, every rider favouring only one make, each compartment revealing differently-branded saddle covers, and I know just from looking at them what make they are, recognise the brand colours. Some horses are being unloaded, and they're turned out to perfection, with plaits that make mine look like they were done by someone as amateurish as I really am, and matching fleeces.

I may not dream of being a professional rider, of going around huge tracks, but I still feel slightly jealous at the sight of equestrian luxury. It's such a normal thing on the British Eventing circuit that I don't often think about it, but when I do, I think how crazy it is to be rubbing shoulders with the best riders in the world every weekend when you're only competing as a hobby.

Before lowering the lorry ramp I drink a bottle of juice from the cab, hoping the sugar will give me some energy, and pull off my coat, now warm from walking the course.

One of the horses neighs in the back - Sunny, I think - and it kicks me into action. The ramp has springs and is easy to lower, and I jump up on it as soon as it hits the grass to see Jupiter looking back at me. His body is hidden behind the partition, but his head is turned to face me, a half-empty haynet behind it.

'Guts,' I mutter, glancing beneath his neck to see that both Ace and Sunny have double the amount of forage left in their respective nets. Ace's, which consists of haylage because she is such a fussy eater, is practically full.

Jupiter walks down the ramp calmly, though Ace lets out an irritated whinny behind me, annoyed at being left behind.

'He's going ten feet away,' I remind her, leading Jupiter to the side of the lorry, beside the tack locker.

The horsebox has a water tank, and I fill a bucket with water, which I offer to each of the horses in turn, before I start getting the grey pony ready.

Jupiter's been groomed, had his hooves polished, loose plaits retied, when I sense somebody walk up behind us, and I'm so relieved to see Mum when I spin around that I almost hug her.

'You okay?' she asks me, walking up to Jupi and laying a hand against his neck.

I try to reply, but my eyes well up, and I shake my head. 'I'm scared,' I croak.

Mum wraps her arms around me. 'Don't be. You'll be fine. You want to do this?' I nod. 'Then you'll be fine. It's normal to be nervous.'

'Freya doesn't get nervous,' I mutter, my voice more bitter than I intended.

'I'm sure she does get nervous,' Mum says sharply. 'Everyone does, and everyone shows it differently. But whether others are nervous is none of your concern.' She looses a breath and looks from me to Jupiter. 'You want me to help you tack up?'

I lean into the tack compartment and pull out a plastic box, thrusting it towards Mum. 'How about studs?'

Fifteen minutes later, I'm riding Jupiter to the dressage warm-up, Mum and Rose trailing behind. Neither me nor Jupiter has a dressage saddle, and I'm in the old general-purpose one Jupiter has always had, which is a wide fitting for his broad back, with the stirrups long. I've never sat in a dressage saddle before, so I have nothing to compare doing flatwork in a jumping one to, but they look more comfortable, and easier to sit in with their big knee rolls that lock your legs in the right place.

Jupiter is always spicier at a competition than he is at home, but this is my first time warming him up at an event since I started riding Ace, and while he's hot, he's also a much easier ride. I'd forgotten how reliable he is, how safe you feel on him, and coupled with the progress he's made since we've been having lessons with

Rose, I'm thrilled with how good he feels. For once I don't feel like an amateur next to everyone else, not embarrassed that I look like a beginner while riders around me look like professionals, but I feel like we're holding our own. Maybe I have been worried for nothing.

I shouldn't be focussed on anything but the horse beneath me, but I can't help glancing around the ring, searching the crowd of horse-and-rider combinations for one that is familiar, but I don't know anybody. Freya's riding today, as is India, a friend of hers I've only really spoken to a few times but who seems nice enough, except they're in the class above me, and not yet in the saddle. *The class you should be in,* a pessimistic voice in my mind says.

'How's he feeling?' Rose asks when I trot over to her. She's standing with Mum at the edge of the ring, on the other side of the white string that sections off the grass warm-up, and they each have a paper cup of coffee in their hand. 'He looks good,' she adds.

'He does,' Mum agrees.

'He's going better than he has before,' I say, which is true.

'Good.' Rose downs her last mouthful of coffee, then sets the empty paper cup down in the grass before climbing under the string and walking into the warm-up. 'Okay, I'll go ask how many there are ahead of you. Get him trotting again, and we'll work on some transitions. Which ring are you?'

'Two.'

Under Rose's watchful eye, Jupiter continues to work well, going in a nice outline, with just the right amount of contact, and is responsive to my aids. His back is soft beneath my seat, and I feel like I'm riding a dressage horse.

Then we go into our arena and Jupiter forgets everything he's ever learned about dressage.

'Cheeky bugger,' Rose says when we ride out of our test. I want to cry I'm so disappointed, but Rose looks amused. 'So typical. Whenever they work in well, they go into a test and act like loons. Don't beat yourself up about it, there wasn't much you could've done.'

As the disastrous test sinks in, and I relive the rigid trot, the way Jupiter chucked his head during every transition, how we cantered a stride when we were supposed to trot, my mood plummets.

'Stop that,' I snap when Jupiter tries to rub his head against my shoulder as soon as I dismount back at the horsebox. He's left a trail of foam along the arm of my tweed jacket, and I let out a curse as I try to wipe it clean. 'See what you've done now? I've still got to go into another dressage test, you know.'

'You all right?'

Mum is first back at the lorry, and her words make me wonder if she purposely hurried ahead because she knew what kind of mood I'd be in.

'He's just being a pain,' I grumble, temper rising again as Jupiter tries to duck his head to graze, and I yank the reins, pulling his mouth up, which he pretends to take great offence at.

'Don't take your anger out on him,' Mum says, sounding angry herself as she takes the reins from my hands.

'He's the one I'm angry at,' I say through gritted teeth.

'Well, then maybe we should just go home.' Mum runs a hand down Jupiter's neck, spoiling him as always, even when he's done nothing to deserve it, and swaps his bridle for his leather halter. 'Maybe you should go get yourself together before tacking up Ace.'

'I *am* together,' I say.

'All righty,' Mum says, sounding less patient than usual. 'Why don't you look after your pony, then?'

'You're the one who took the reins from me,' I point out. I walk up to Jupiter's body and run his stirrups up before undoing the girth and lifting the saddle and pad from his back.

'I really mean it, Sybil,' Mum says after a moment, as I'm

balancing Jupiter's tack on a saddle stand. 'You're allowed to be disappointed, but if you don't learn to control it, then we're going home, because I don't need to deal with this.'

'Go, then,' I snap.

'What did I just say? *This* is what I'm talking about. So you didn't do a great test, so what? I've warned you enough times that events will not be happening if you talk back and act like a spoiled brat any time something goes wrong. Stop turning every little mistake into a palaver. Now pull yourself together or not only will I be leaving, but I'll take you with me. Understood?'

I cross my arms across my chest. 'Whatever.'

Mum inhales loudly, then turns to the cab. I don't know what she wants from in there, because she came in her own car, but then she comes out with the plastic bag I got the ponies' numbers in, which often contains a catalogue or two, and pulls one out. It's the event schedule, printed with the names of every competitor, and I wonder what she could possibly be looking for - *now* of all times - but then she folds it over and passes it to me.

'Remember not so long ago when you were in tears because you didn't think you'd even have Jupiter?' she says steadily, eyebrows nearing her hairline. 'Well, maybe you need to remember that and get some perspective.'

I look at the catalogue, still unsure where Mum's going with this, then I see it's open at my section's page. Horses and riders are listed in a grid, along with each horse's age and breeding, and I lower my eyes to see Jupiter's name, Ardmore Galaxy, next to mine, Sybil Dawson. There's something exciting about seeing our names in print, even in just a small catalogue like this, but that can't be Mum's point, because she isn't exactly trying to reward me right now.

My eyes travel further, along the right of the page, and I see what Mum is trying to show me, the point she's trying to make. The last column is for owners' names, and I see the word printed

in Jupiter's, one I've never seen written down as *owner* before.
  Rider.

Jupiter's crappy test is still on my mind, but once I start tacking up Ace, I realise I can't think about it anymore, because I have too much else to focus on.

Like not being breakfast, for instance.

'Maggot,' I warn as the mare swipes her head around with pinned ears, threatening to take a chunk out of my arm as I try to girth her up. I'm getting her ready on my own, as Rose is warming up her catch ride for dressage, and Mum has left me alone because I was too stubborn to apologise for talking back and ask for help. I was hoping to get her to screw in Ace's studs, too, but I've just finished doing them myself, which isn't easy when you're desperately trying to keep your breeches dirt-free. 'You don't even mind me buckling your girth,' I tell Ace, which is true, because she will let you tighten the girth while on her without so much as flickering an ear. 'You're just being awkward for the sake of it.'

The mare gives in, pricking her ears, and I buckle the girth up another hole quickly before she can change her mind, and move on to the next job. I have my head in the tack locker, reaching for Ace's bridle, when I hear some commotion behind me - the unmistakeable sound of a horse spooking, and a loud voice I distinctly recognise.

'Get over yourself. It's a plastic bag. I know plastic bags are the root of all evil, but I *think* you'll survive. That's just a wild guess, mind.'

The deep female voice is wry and honest, while also sounding laced with sarcasm. I grab Ace's bridle by the headpiece and take a step back, dodging the open tack locker door above me. A few metres away from the lorry, a dapple grey is rooted to the spot, his front feet almost on top of each other as he looks straight ahead with pricked ears and wild eyes. He might be crazy, but he's gorgeous, with the sort of well-muscled frame I'd expect of an international eventer, perfect plaits, and a delicately curved head. His body is covered in silver dapples, accentuated by the black leather of his tack. I stare at the dressage saddle a moment, wondering how many thousands it cost and what it must be like to sit in, before raising my eyes to the rider, and my earlier suspicion is confirmed.

'Would you like me to move it?' I ask, eyeing up the stray plastic bag a few paces away.

Alexandra Evans shakes her head. 'Nah, you're all right. He can get over it. Thanks, though,' she adds, looking at me for the first time, and her expression changes. 'Hey, I know you.' She lifts her left hand from her horse's neck in recognition, and the action is just one more thing that spooks the grey, though Alex's posture doesn't change, even when her mount leaps sideways. 'Pack it in, Waffles,' she scolds the horse, and I try not to look taken aback by an event horse as beautiful and professional-looking as this one having a name like *Waffles*.

'Um,' I say, 'we were in the ambulance together at-'

Alex beats me to the event venue name, then laughs. 'Of course. With the incompetent paramedics.' She laughs again. 'Man, if I hadn't been running late for my next ride, that would've been hilarious.'

When I fell off Ace at our last event, Alex was already in the ambulance when I went for the compulsory checkup, and the paramedics were occupied for a while, leaving us both waiting for some minutes. I'm not sure she's even twenty-one yet, but Alex has already ridden to four-star level as of this spring, and has been on youth European teams too many times to count. The pony she took to Europeans, Lakota, is the same pony India rides.

We didn't discuss any of that, though. While waiting to be cleared to leave, Alex asked how I fell, and when I mentioned Ace being a mare, what ensued was a discussion about how they're both the best and worst.

'So is one of these the devil herself?'

'Sorry?' I ask.

'Your mare,' Alex says, not showing any annoyance at my inability to understand a sentence. 'The one who threw you into the first fence,' she goes on, and I'm surprised she remembers, then think the words are slightly unfair on Ace's part, seeing as I was the one stupid enough to fall, but I don't point it out, and instead run my eyes over Alex's tack as she speaks. When I met her, she was without a horse and spraying blood from her arm, so she didn't exactly look like the top event rider she is, but seeing her on a horse like this is slightly more intimidating. Expensive saddle and bridle polished, and a saddle cloth embroidered with sponsors' logos. Alex's jacket is navy blue with delicate trim, and the brand written on the top pocket is one I put in the category of *Never, Ever Affordable* and don't so much as browse their stock if they have a stand at a show because I know it would be pointless.

I make sense of what Alex is saying just in time to not look like a complete idiot, and I turn to the bay mare tied to the lorry. 'That's her,' I say lamely.

But Alex seems genuinely interested, and she makes Waffles step forward, nearer the scary bag in the bushes opposite, so she can see Ace from the side. 'She's really sweet,' she says, and she sounds like she means it. 'I mean, sweet-looking, obviously not sweet in character,' she jokes. Then in another breath, 'Isn't this Rose's lorry?'

I nod. 'Yeah. I train with Rose.'

'Oh, well Rose is great. You must know what you're doing then.'

That I know what I'm doing is not something I think I've ever been told in relation to eventing before, but I keep my mouth shut, not wanting to hold Alex up any more.

But she keeps going. 'She's a nice type. Are you going to do

Pony Trials on her?'

'I don't know. I mean, I'd *like* to, but we're nowhere near good enough yet.'

Alex shrugs. 'It doesn't take long to move up the levels once everything starts going right.' A breeze flutters the plastic bag, and Waffles leaps sideways, once again, which, once again, does little in the manor of unseating Alex. 'Stupid pony,' she mutters. 'Right, I'd better get going. Good luck.'

'Thanks.' Too late, I think to call, 'You, too,' but Alex has already ridden away, the grey gelding prancing as though the grass were hot coals, head tilted to the side as he watches the bag in the bushes flap with horror, his rider's laughter in the air until they're out of earshot.

Three down, three to go, I think.

'Our next starter will be number 87 Sybil Dawson riding Mrs Rose Holloway's Ace of Hearts. They come forward on a dressage score of 31.4.'

The start bell rings, and I touch Ace into a canter, forcing myself to let out a long breath, trying to calm my rush of a mind and my galloping heart.

Ace redeemed Jupiter by putting in a fantastic test. She stayed rideable throughout, never once anticipating the next movement, and I rode out of the ring knowing it was the best test I'd ever ridden, though admittedly that's not saying much.

Jupiter's show jumping was next, and I focussed on pushing his dressage test to the back of my mind as I tacked up and then rode him to the warm-up. Show jumping is the phase I get the least nervous about with Jupiter - if anything, I look forward to it - and I was calm while I worked him in, listening to Rose's odd instruction and popping him over the practice fences, and as I expected, he was on the top of his game in the ring, and we went clear.

And now I have three rounds left to get through - supposing Ace and I actually complete the show jumping this time - and they're the three hardest.

As soon as she hears the start bell, Ace lights up, but not in a good way. When Rose rode the mare some weeks ago, she made everything look effortless. Whenever Ace rushed, Rose was able to bring her back with only the lightest touch, and the mare was calm throughout the round.

I don't share that skill.

When Ace rushes, my first instinct is to pull, but I force myself not to. I try to sit still, to keep my seat quiet, my hands low, and my leg on. *You don't need to jump the jumps for her,* I hear Rose say in my mind. *Just keep her in a rhythm and steer.*

Ace hits the first fence on a good stride, and as we land over the oxer, I think that at least, no matter what happens next, we've done one better than last time by actually getting over a fence.

The first few fences pass, and I feel myself start to relax. We're doing it, we're going around a course, just like we did when we went clear round show jumping last week, except this time we're at a real event. Now we just need to make it to the end...

The combination is approached out of a right-hand turn, and Ace speeds up when she sees the two elements. My head knows I should just sit still and steady her with my seat, keeping my leg on, but my body doesn't get the message, and instinctively my hands come up, holding Ace off the fence. The mare pulls, pulling against the pressure, and I only release when it's too late, when I've interrupted the stride and we're in deep. For a moment, I think Ace is going to stop, but she chips in and pushes off her haunches, hitting the top rail of the upright and sending it flying. I lose my balance, but I stay on, and by the time I regain enough composure to look up and ride on, we're way off the one-stride distance, and I do the only thing I can think of and hold her, hold to add a stride. But there isn't room for two strides, and Ace knows it. She slams on the brakes, front feet skidding into the parallel, but she remains balanced in her body, and I'm able to stay on.

I shake my head as the bell rings, and volunteers rush to rebuild the two fences. Ace prances at the sound of the bell, and I run a hand down her neck, my eyes searching the edge of the ring for Rose. She's standing with Mum, near the start, and offers me a reassuring nod from the other side of the rope.

Ace jigs sideways, and I push her back into a trot as I wait for the bell to ring again, trying to stay calm. I just need to keep riding, and steer.

'Eight jumping faults and twelve time penalties for Sybil Dawson and Ace of Hearts.'

Ace lowers her head as we pass the finish line, and I slip her the reins as she tucks her nose to her chest. For what feels like the first time since we crashed through the double, I release a breath, chest aching from the stress of the last minute and a half.

'I'm so proud of you,' Mum says as Ace and I ride out of the ring, laying a hand on my leg, and I wish I could push it away.

'Well-recovered,' Rose says. 'Well done. Be proud of yourself.'

'I wouldn't have needed to recover from anything if I hadn't messed up in the first place,' I grumble bitterly.

 Rose lifts a shoulder, looking at me from beneath the navy blue silk covering her skull cap - she show jumped her catch ride not long before my round, and handed the reins back to the owner as soon as she rode out of the ring to focus on my and Ace's warm-up. 'Well, that would just be too easy, wouldn't it?'

'Are you going to ride her back and get Jupiter?' Mum asks, sliding her hands into her waistcoat pockets.

'Yeah,' Rose agrees, nodding. 'No point waiting around. They seem to just be taking numbers at the cross country, so you might as well. I've got to show jump Sunny at one, so I can warm you up before then.'

'I guess,' I say, but my stomach is flip-flopping at the thought of going cross country in a matter of minutes.

The blue sky that rose early this morning, promising a nice day, did not lie, and it almost feels like summer as I ride Ace back to the lorry. *Probably the last we'll see of it,* I think. We walk down the horse walk, and I'm just thinking about the cross country course, trying and failing to picture every fence, when my eyes focus on a chestnut pony coming this way, from the trailer park, and I think, *that looks like Leo,* and then realise, of course -

'Freya!'

My friend shoots me a reserved smile as she halts her pony beside me. 'Hey. What've you done?'

'Dressage and show jumping,' I say, and briefly sum up how the two phases went. 'You're on your way to dressage?'

'Yeah.' Freya drops her reins to run a gloved hand down Leo's ruby red neck, and I notice how perfect the chestnut's plaits are. Is that Freya's work? Or Nell's… 'How was the ground show jumping?'

'Good. I've got studs in, but they probably don't need them.' I glance behind Freya, looking down the grass alley that comes from the trailer and small horsebox park. 'Where's your mum?'

'She's coming. She was behind me, but we passed Catherine Humphries coming back from cross country, and they started talking. You know what they're like.'

I nod, but really I *don't* know what they're like. *Humphries* is India's last name, and I'm pretty sure I've heard *Catherine* said in conjunction with her horses' names by announcers, so I presume it's her mum. But even then I don't "know what they're like", because whenever I see Catherine Humphries, I'm terrified of her, struck by how intimidating she is, paralysed by the confidence she exudes as she helicopters around her hundreds of thousands pounds' worth of horsepower. She's someone I see and hear but never get close to, and I can't imagine actually speaking to her on friendly terms.

'Sophia and India's mum?' I clarify. 'What's she like?'

Freya lifts a shoulder. 'She's quite nice. Competitive. Loaded, but she seems kind enough.'

'Does all their money come from the Thoroughbred stud?'

'I don't think so,' Freya says, shaking her head slowly. 'I mean, I think the dad earns loads through horses, but Catherine's family has more money than he does. I think they founded one of the biscuit empires, I can't remember which - obviously not McVitie's or anything, but one of the big ones.' Her eyes lower to Leo's neck, and she shortens her reins. 'I'd better get going. I'll catch up with you later. You going cross country now?'

I nod, a lump forming in my throat. 'Untacking her and getting Jupiter.'

'Good luck.'

'Three, two, one, GO! Good luck!'

Jupiter powers out of the start box, and I try to stay calm. Normally I can set out onto a cross country course and leave all my worries behind, become aware of nothing but the horse beneath me and the fence straight ahead, but that isn't happening. My mind is still thinking of everything that could go wrong, and stressing about riding Ace around this same course in a short while.

But Jupiter knows his job, not one to ever refuse a fence, and he's ignorant of my worries, just happy to be jumping.

Until we reach a question that he can't work out for himself, one that requires me to think a little, too.

A curving line between two brush fences, which Rose made me walk exactly as I'd be riding it. She told me how to set up, how to turn so I'd be straight to the second element of the combination, but of course I don't remember any of this until it's too late.

I pull on my right rein, probably the first concrete demand I've given since leaving the start box, trying in vain to turn Jupiter and make the second brush, but it's a lost cause, and we fly right past it.

Jupiter isn't a stopper, and thinks nothing of clearing the fence when I turn him back to it on a correct line, and he carries on around the rest of the course with as much confidence as he set out with, even with me limply on his back, doing little in the way of helping him.

The only good thing is that Jupiter gallops through the finish full of running, pulling like a train as I stand in my stirrups and seesaw the reins to try to stop him, and I remember belatedly what I was worried about coming into today, about a repeat of what happened last time. *Sod's Law*, I think. My mind turned to such a maze of worry about other things that I forgot to even be concerned about the one thing that has been keeping me up at night. Though I guess it's probably just as well.

One thing's for sure: there is nothing wrong with Jupiter's fitness anymore. In fact, when I finally bring him back to a walk, he looks around as though expecting to go again, barely blowing.

Mum and Rose both utter words of praise, expressing delight at how well Jupiter looks, and saying that it was just an unlucky turn and whatnot, but I can't bring myself to focus on what they're saying. My day isn't over yet.

I feel like I'm going to be sick.

Ace powers forward, moving into a cross country gallop as we circle the warm-up ring, carrying herself in a round frame, the contact in the reins light.

'Jump the barrels once more and that'll do her,' Rose calls.

We've only jumped a few practice fences, since there's no need to jump twenty of them when we've already had show jumping as a warm-up, but luckily Ace has been looking after me and staying rideable into the obstacles. I remember the first time I cross country schooled her, how she felt different from any pony I'd ridden cross country before, like a little machine that could clear any jump, and wish I could switch off my nerves and just enjoy being on her back.

'Good. Go to the start,' Rose says when Ace lands clear of the barrels. The mare keeps her head up on landing, doesn't waste any time, and it makes it easy for me to keep my balance and not be jolted. *So why is my stomach in knots...*

The steward yells *Go*, and Ace doesn't need to be told twice. I've never ridden her out of a start box before, so I don't know what to expect, but she doesn't feel too different from Jupiter - eager, ready to run, ears forward as she searches for the first fence. I tell myself not to pull, not to make the same mistake as I did at the first show jumping fence some weeks ago, so I decide to go for the opposite.

Kick on.

I push Ace forward, hoping to see a flyer. But there's a difference between a flyer and taking out a stride you can't afford to take out.

Too late I realise that taking off where I'm asking the mare to is impossible, but I decide to commit to my decision and not backpedal and try to hold for another stride, so I keep going, closing my eyes because it really *is* a long one.

And before I know it I'm pitched forward as Ace slides to a halt, and I fly through the air.

'Go away.'

'Sybil,' Mum says levelly.

Rose had to hurry off with Sunny as soon as we came back from my cross country round, so luckily she isn't here to see the tears I'm fighting to keep from running down my face.

'I said go away,' I repeat, wringing out a sponge over Ace's back as I rub her sweat marks.

'You got back on and jumped the fence,' Mum says. 'That's

what matters.'

At BE90 level, a fall on the cross country course isn't eliminatory, meaning I had all rights to get back on and continue my round. Rose caught Ace as soon as I fell and brought her over to me, and suggested I only jump the fence I fell at and then retire, unless I was feeling up to the rest of the course. My body protector prevented me from being winded when I hit the ground, but I landed on my right side and my shoulder was aching, so I didn't fancy jumping more than one fence. We managed to make it over the stupidly easy and small first obstacle of the cross country course, and I then brought Ace back to a trot and raised my hand in forfeit.

'I should've kept going,' I say. Ace turns her head as I rub at her girth passage with more force than she considers acceptable, and I push her head away with little patience as she lifts a hind leg threateningly.

'Then you're going to have to learn to toughen up, aren't you?' Mum snaps, pulling a packet of Polos from her pocket and feeding two to Ace, as if apologising to the pony for her daughter's behaviour, and the action annoys me. On her other side, Jupiter sees the treats and stretches his nose out for his share, butting her arm.

'Well, what am I supposed to do?' I ask. 'She's not easy.'

'I never said she was, but you can't just blame her. You've got to suck it up.'

I scoff. 'It's not fair.'

'Oh, no.' Mum's voice is sharp, all sympathy gone. 'No more pity party, please, because I can't take it. Stop feeling sorry for yourself, or I'll give these horses to someone who really deserves them and then you'll have a reason to feel sorry.'

Voices drift nearer the lorry, and Mum and I shut our mouths. I look down, not wanting anyone to see my tear-stained cheeks, but luckily the passers-by don't seem to be looking at the lorry.

'Do you need your spurs, Mia?' a voice asks, and I recognise it right away as that of Catherine Humphries.

I look at the passing pony discreetly, and see the youngest Humphries daughter on a chunky dun gelding with thick plaits. He's wearing a grackle noseband, and a grey ear bonnet embellished with tiny crystals. His close-contact jumping saddle looks expensive, and I raise my eyes to see his rider immaculately turned out as she sits aboard the gelding in a relaxed manner. If I didn't know they were sisters, I'd never guess India and Mia were related. India has a rounder face, light blond hair that is all curls, and blue eyes, while Mia's hair is straight and brown, currently tied neatly beneath a Charles Owen hat, her eyes hazel, and her face angular.

'I don't think so,' Mia says, sounding as relaxed as she looks. She turns in her saddle and affectionately slaps the dun pony on the rump, and I recognise the gelding as one India used to ride at clinics, before she took over the rides on Lakota and Fendigo. 'I think Harvey's awake today.'

Catherine Humphries chuckles, and then another voice says, 'Harvey's always awake,' and I see India trot up on foot alongside the pony, wearing a fleece jacket over her white competition gear.

She jogs a few steps towards her sister and grabs hold of her - one hand seizing her leg, the other her arm - and pretends she's about to push her off the pony. Mia shrieks, sliding to the left, then laughs as India pulls her back to centre. The dun pony couldn't care less that he's being used as a climbing frame, but India still scratches his neck once her sister has regained her balance. 'Sorry, Harv.'

'Girls,' their mum says, and as she turns her head in fake despair, her gaze absently falls on us and she smiles self-indulgently, but luckily India doesn't notice me, now too preoccupied dodging Mia's whip as her sister gets her own back by trying to hit her with the crop.

'Race you to the show jumping warm-up,' India yells, and she breaks into a jog up the horse walk.

'Hey!' Mia shrieks, then kicks the pony into a trot, shortening the reins as she goes. I know she's twelve - or about to turn twelve - but she looks younger, her body slight, and I'm surprised to see her riding as polished as it is. She's only trotting, barely holding the reins, but her position is correct, balance perfect, and her lower leg is on.

'That was Indiana Humphries on foot,' I say to Mum once the Humphrieses are out of earshot. 'And her little sister. India has two FEI ponies that both went to Europeans.'

'Nice for India,' Mum says.

I look at the dun in the distance, the thick black tail that swishes from his golden body. How was that little girl so relaxed? I can't imagine being chilled enough to joke around like that at a competition. 'Some people have all the luck.'

'India still has to ride those ponies,' Mum points out, and I scoff. 'Didn't you tell me that they were her older sister's and she couldn't ride them and they were always getting eliminated?'

'Yes,' I concede. Of all the eventing stories I rattle on about, why did *that* have to be the one Mum listened to and committed to memory?

'Well, then she still has to work hard, doesn't she?'

I don't dignify that with a response, and focus on Ace, spongeing her saddle patch and then running a sweat scraper over her body. 'They're still schoolmasters,' I say after a while.

'And what do you think Jupiter is? He might not have competed at the same level, or be as polished, but he's still a schoolmaster. I don't remember you being the first to jump or compete him.'

I grit my teeth and bend to scrape water off Ace's girth passage. My body is aching, and I'm already looking forward to getting home and having a hot shower, should our boiler choose to cooperate. Tomorrow's Sunday, but it's not like I can stay in bed, because Ace and Jupiter still need feeding, turning out, and mucking out. I wonder, for a moment, what it would be like if I could. If I could sleep till ten like all teenagers do on weekends, if I could spend the day lounging in front of the TV, not even stepping foot outside.

'I bet India never has to get up early to look after her own horses, though,' I say, straightening up to look down the horse walk. I can just make out the Humphrieses in the distance, nearing the show jumping warm-up.

Mum frowns. She stands with her hands on her hips, and like me she's staring at the receding figure of a dun pony. 'Oh, I bet she does.'

chapter 3

I finish looking after the ponies and make it to the heart of the venue in time to catch the end of Mia's show jumping warm-up. India is in the middle of the ring, standing by the fences, her attention fully on the combination as they canter to the oxer and fly over it. He's only fourteen hands, but Harvey has some serious scope, and I brace myself for the jolt of landing when he clears the fence with half a metre to spare, as though I were the one in the saddle, but Mia isn't the least bit unbalanced, her small body barely moving as they land clear over the fence and canter on. I think of what Mum said earlier, about India having to work hard, and wonder if that goes for Mia, too. But still. She might have to ride her ponies, but it's easy if you only have to push all the right buttons.

'There's two until you,' India calls, raising a hand to her forehead to shade her eyes. She's taken off her fleece since running past me in the lorry park, and her jodhpurs are held up by a pink-and-grey polo belt around her slim waist. 'Do you want to leave him on that or jump one more?'

'One more,' Mia says, cantering past where I'm standing at the edge of the ring. 'I'm going to turn tight on the left,' she adds, and

I watch as she takes the dun to the middle of the ring, canters a ten-metre circle between the fences, then turns tightly to the upright.

Mia sits for her stride, and the dun pony rocks back on his hocks to propel himself into the air. Harvey tucks his knees up beneath his chin as he flies over the metre-high jump, his small rider's face full of determination, and India turns to walk towards the entrance to the ring before the combination has even landed, confident in the knowledge they will, where Mia's number is next on the board.

A small chestnut horse is on course, going around with his head in the air, and Mia halts Harvey by the gate steward, one hand on her knee and the other resting on her pony's neck. India walks up beside her and bends to readjust one of the gelding's tendon boots, and then her eyes fall on me as she straightens up, and she smiles.

'Hey.' She strolls away from her sister's pony to come up to me on the other side of the warm-up rope. 'You riding?'

'Just finished,' I say. 'You?'

India nods, and turns her head towards the ring at the sound of the chestnut hitting a rail. 'I rode Fendi,' she says. 'Just finished, too. And I've got Otto here tomorrow - can't someone put a martingale on that thing?' she mutters as the fifteen-two gelding goes around a turn with his head straight up in the air. 'And a flash while they're at it,' she adds as the gelding opens his mouth wide enough that I notice from here. 'God, he's so stiff. Poor thing. He's got no muscle, either.'

I watch the chestnut move around the course of jumps, trying to see what India sees. The horse carries himself with his nose out, his stride slow, and the rider isn't much more polished. I go a step further, looking at the lack of muscle along his top line, and I can see what India means about him being stiff - there's a rigidness to him, no bend, and he can't properly lift himself over a fence.

I *can* see it, but I'm not sure I *would* have if India hadn't pointed it out. As if I need reminding of just how little I know.

'How did she do?' I ask, changing the subject. 'Fendi.'

'Okay. We went double clear, but I wasn't going for time so I'm not sure if I picked up penalties or not. And they weren't the prettiest rounds, to be honest. You were riding your grey?'

'Yeah, Jupiter,' I say. 'It was his first event in a while, and he did okay. I turned too late for a combination, but that wasn't his fault.'

'Is Freya here?'

'Yeah, I passed her earlier, but I haven't seen her ride, so I don't know how she's doing.'

'Very well, I'm sure,' India says with a grin, and I know it's in no way a snide remark at Freya, but just her voicing how the rest of us feel when we watch Freya and Leo.

'Yeah,' I say, grinning back. 'I'm sure.'

The chestnut finishes his round, and India mutters another complaint about his tack as he passes close enough for us to see how loose his cheek pieces are, and Mia trots Harvey into the ring.

'Our next starter will be number 449 Mia Humphries, and she rides Mrs Catherine Humphries's Mendip Breeze. They come forward on a very competitive dressage score of 24.'

'Twenty-four!' I repeat, shocked. I can't even imagine what getting a twenty-four in a test would be like.

'Harvey's good on the flat,' India says with a shrug. Clearly dressage tests in the twenties are nothing out of the ordinary for her family.

'He was your pony, wasn't he?'

India nods, our eyes on Mia as she trots Harvey around, waiting for the start bell. 'Yeah. He's a great pony, really well schooled and everything, but he's not a ride for the faint-hearted, put it that way. I love him because he's insane. He's really hot, and he has this huge jump that can unseat you even over a crossbar. He cross countries in a Pelham, because he goes on the forehand and pulls like a train. But he's awesome. And he's dead easy on the ground, which is always a relief.'

'Surely all yours are?' I say, thinking too late that my words sound like a dig at India and her sisters and their perfect horses, but luckily if she's offended she doesn't show it.

'The eventers are, yeah, but we've got the stud, and so dealing with the mares and youngstock makes you appreciate a horse that will stand still to shoe, and that you can lead to a field without it trying to bolt or knock you over, put it that way.'

I think of Ace fidgeting and rearing when I hold her for the farrier, and also how I've always taken Jupiter's laid-back attitude for granted. 'I know what you mean.'

The dun gelding canters to the first fence, his head carriage round as he bounds along exuberantly. Normally I'd see a flashy schoolmaster like this, kitted out in expensive gear and with a tiny kid in the saddle, and stare in jealousy without taking in the details, but this time I really *look*. I watch how Mia sits in the saddle all through the turn, her reins short enough to keep Harvey on a contact, keeping him connected. I watch how her leg is on, beneath her seat, how she always looks like she's driving, doesn't look like a passenger. She's not seesawing the reins, or giving the pony sharp kicks in his sides or anything like that, but she always looks like she's doing *something*. Like she's having a conversation with him the whole way around the course, and not just barking out instructions when they reach a fence.

But despite Mia's good riding, she and Harvey get in slightly deep to the first fence, and he rattles the top rail, but it stays in its cups.

'Oh for goodness' sake, Mia,' comes Catherine Humphries's voice as she steps up beside India, watching her youngest daughter in the ring. Part of my impression of her has come from watching the competitiveness with which she supports her daughters, and

I've heard her give India an earful many a time for riding out of a ring with rails down, and I'm somewhat relieved to see my opinion of her be proven correct, if my prejudice about her daughters posing on schoolmasters is wrong. I've even seen India wipe away tears after a bad round before, which is hard to associate with the strong and confident person beside me.

One of the fences on course has a wooden filler painted to look like a brick wall, at the far end of the ring, and when Mia turns Harvey towards it, to my great surprise, the pony starts to baulk. But before he can even think of stopping, Mia brings her whip down behind her leg and growls at him, and she pushes him on to clear the fence, which he gives more air than any other on course.

'Little shit,' India says, and I wait for her mum to scold her choice of words, but she doesn't.

Catherine has India's fleece in her arms, and she uses it to cover her face, looking terrified. 'Bloody pony. I can't watch.'

Not long ago, if I'd heard the Humphrieses blaming a pony for a mistake, I'd have shaken my head and silently accused them of being in the wrong, but in this case I can't disagree. Mia didn't do anything wrong, and for all the years he's been competing, it's not like Harvey won't have seen every sort of filler in existence before now.

Mia sees a long stride to the last fence, and India laughs while Catherine winces loudly as her daughter hurries her pony to the oxer and yells, 'HOP!', hunching over his crested neck as they fly over the obstacle, all four of Harvey's feet tucked, his body stretching over the fence with inches to spare.

'Blooming heck,' Catherine mutters, pressing a hand against her chest as her daughter canters through the finish line.

India grins. 'Oh, Mia. She likes taking flyers,' she adds to me. And then realising her mum and I obviously don't know each other, she introduces us by pointing at us each in turn and saying,

'Sybil - Caddie - Caddie - Sybil' and I politely say hello as her mum smiles warmly.

'Very classy clear round for Mia Humphries and Mendip Breeze. Our next starter will be…'

India and her mum stroll towards Mia as she rides Harvey out of the ring, her face flushed and smiling. She pats the dun enthusiastically, and he looks bored as he comes to a walk, like the plod India said he is to handle.

Part of me wants to go up to them, to stroke that gorgeous pony and see what it's like to be part of an extravagant horsey family, but I barely know them, both feel and look like a complete amateur next to their well-turned out selves, so instead I turn around and head for the photographers' stand.

I found Mum and took her to see the photos after scrolling through them all myself, and she insisted on buying some - her treat, she said - and they're now in my hands, straight out of the printer. The pictures of Jupiter show just how much improvement he's made over the past months, and I can't stop staring at this one of him flying over a corner. All four of his feet are tucked, his ears are pricked forward, and he's giving the fence plenty of air. He looks so fit, so healthy, like he actually *could* be an FEI pony in the future. His muscles are well-balanced, and his expression alert. I can find faults in my own riding, the two-point seat nothing like the copybook position Freya has, but Jupiter makes up for it.

Because I fell off at the first fence last time, I didn't get any pictures of Ace, and even if today isn't really an event to remember, I'm glad to finally have proof of me riding her. None of the show jumping evenings we've been to has had a photographer, so this is the first time I've actually got to see what she looks like - how *we* look together - and it's almost enough to cancel out the disappointment of the day.

Jupiter looks good, but the bay mare is in a whole other league.

Unlike my Connemara pony, who has to work hard to gain fitness and keep off weight, Ace is a born athlete. She's fit, with muscles that ripple beneath her shiny coat, and everything comes easy to her. The photograph is taken head-on, because the few profile ones of us were ruined by my riding, but this fence I seemed to do okay over. Ace is inches over the top rail, looking straight ahead, plaited forelock revealing the heart-shaped star on her head.

I try hard to remind myself that this pony, this beautiful pony with FEI potential, is mine to ride, no matter how badly the day went, and that that's something to celebrate in itself.

'I need to put that up in the kitchen,' Mum says, pointing at the picture of Ace. 'We haven't got any pictures of Maggot in the house yet.'

I'd been planning on putting the picture in my room, so I could look at it before falling asleep, but I like that Mum wants pictures of Ace up, that she considers her part of the family. 'Okay.'

Back at the lorry, Rose has changed into jeans, having finished riding for the day. Mum and I watched her cross country round on Sunny, and as always, Rose gave him a perfect ride.

Rose sees the envelope in my hands and asks to look at the pictures straight away, and I glow with pride at her praise when she sees how good the ponies look.

'They look fantastic,' she says again, then her eyes lift to Mum. 'So have you told her the plan yet?'

'What plan?' I ask. I know Mum and Rose stayed together a while after my and Ace's cross country, but I figured they were just commiserating over what I did wrong.

'We think maybe having to ride both ponies was too much for you,' Rose says, and if Mum had said the same thing I'd have spat something back quickly, but to Rose I don't. 'Until they're both established again,' she clarifies. 'And because we have two events left you want to go to' - she names them, and I nod. There are more events than those two before the end of the season, but we're staying local - 'we've decided it would be best if you only took one pony to each. Start with Jupiter finish with Ace.'

Rose rattles on more details about withdrawing Ace from the next event, which she's already entered for, and how I can still get the entry fee money back, but I feel deflated.

'But what if I mess up with Ace?' I say. 'It's the last event, so if it goes wrong I won't have another chance to ride her.'

Rose smiles. 'I guess you'll just have to not mess up, then.'

* * *

'It's just not the same without Dippy.'

We're standing in Hintze Hall, the entrance to London's Natural History Museum, with our heads tilted back as we stare at the suspended skeleton above us. I'm sandwiched between Dad and Gabe, and the three of us in turn squashed between however many hundred tourists and visitors. From the ceiling of the grand building hangs a whale skeleton, high enough that we can walk beneath it. The windows in the ceiling shine light through the bones, and I lower my head, neck aching.

'It's not the same without Dippy,' Dad agrees, his hands in his chino pockets.

Gabe and I have always loved the Natural History Museum, touring the many floors one of the few days out we both enjoy. This is the first time we've been in a while, though, due partly to our parents, and also me being busier with the ponies - especially now that there are two of them - than before. But we got so bored the last weekend we were at Dad's, sitting around his flat reading and playing card games, that we planned a day out for our next visit in advance.

Last time we were at the Natural History Museum, the skeleton in the entrance was that of a diplodocus - known as

Dippy to his friends. Dippy's been in Hintze Hall since long before I was born, and it never occurred to me he would ever be replaced.

Yet here we are, standing beneath a whale.

'Even though it's not Dippy,' Dad goes on, walking in a slow circle while still staring up at the ceiling, 'you've got to admit it's pretty cool. I mean, *kids'* - he wraps an arm around each of our shoulders, and I groan as I close my eyes in embarrassment - 'we're standing *under* a whale!'

'Maybe if it were a real whale,' I say.

'It *is* a real whale, dumbo,' Gabe points out.

'Just the bones,' I say. 'If it was the whole thing, then it would be more interesting.'

'Are there any taxidermy whales in Britain?' Dad asks. 'That could be our next trip!'

I groan again, and Dad laughs a quiet and triumphant laugh. He takes great pleasure in playing the lame dad role, and goes to great lengths to embarrass me and Gabe, but only ever at his own expense.

'Can you even stuff a whale?' I say.

Gabe pulls his phone from his pocket. 'I'll Google it.'

Dad holds his arms out to the side, which earns us a funny look from a group of tourists conversing in a tongue I don't recognise. 'God bless the Internet. You know, we used to not be able to look something up at any given moment. We'd have to wait and make time to go to a library.'

'Poor you,' I mutter. 'Rough life.'

'It *was* rough,' Dad says too loudly. 'You know, I remember this one time we - Mum and I,' he corrects quickly, no longer a *we,* 'saw a whale at your grandparents' in Norfolk.'

Gabe lowers his phone. 'Really?'

Dad nods, and we start walking through the hall, trying to find a path amongst the sea of people. 'It had washed up on the beach - you've never heard this story?' Gabe and I shake our heads, and

Dad goes on. 'So, it had washed up on the beach-'

'You already said that,' I point out.

'-and some other people had already found it. Anyway, it was almost dead, lying there on the sand.'

'And it died?'

'No.' Dad smiles at the memory. 'Marine rescuers came out, the village pitched in, and we got it back out to sea. It wasn't the biggest whale, mind.'

'When was that?' Gabe asks.

Some shrieking children dart in front of us, parents running after them in despair, and I wonder which party to root for.

Dad thinks about the question a moment. 'You weren't born,' he says to Gabe, 'and I don't think Sybil was talking yet, and - quite some time ago.' He looks like he was going to say something else, that he *stopped* himself from saying something else, but he looks unfazed, so I wonder if I imagined it.

'I can't even imagine just finding a whale on the beach,' I say.

'Yeah.' Dad smiles, but this one is sadder than the last. 'It was a special day. Anyway.' He claps his hands together and looks at us, and I see so much of Gabe in his face - the same blue eyes, the same scattering of freckles, the same way of getting excited about the smallest things.

Out of nowhere, I'm struck by a queasy feeling, something nagging at the back of my mind. *What is it?* It's funny how memories come out of nowhere, pushing past whatever it is you're doing, and take over your mind. *You can't play boardgames with three people.* Freya said something like that a few weeks ago, and while it went over my head at the time, it didn't go far. Settling in a corner, waiting to strike. *There will only be three of us,* I realise. This is our first Christmas without Dad, which I *had* obviously realised, but you only notice the big things when you notice the little things. I knew I wouldn't be spending this coming Christmas with both of my parents, but understanding that I won't be playing charades with them is a far greater hit.

'What're we going to see first?' Dad says, and I shake my head, my mouth dry, and blink to stop tears from escaping my eyes. I look up, suddenly very interested in the whale skeleton.

'The moving tyrannosaurus rex,' Gabe says straight away. The dinosaur model is an animated model, and definitely top of my list, too, even if I've seen it countless times before.

'All right.' Dad grabs on to each of our arms. 'Come on, team, we have a dinosaur to find.'

'So how are the ponies?'

I swallow my mouthful of shortbread, wiping crumbs off my jeans. 'They're okay.'

Three hours after arriving at the museum, we're sitting in the food hall, which, like the rest of the museum, is overly crowded. Dad and I are balanced on chairs around a small, round table, with cups of tea and biscuits.

'Just okay?' Dad says. He glances behind me, checking Gabe is still in the queue, then looks back at me. My brother may be skinny, but he sure can eat, and the packet of biscuits he ordered did little in the way of filling him up, and he's waiting for seconds.

'They're good,' I say with more enthusiasm. *But coming here for the weekend means being away from them and losing precious riding and training time,* I add silently.

'I still haven't met the famous devil-pony. What is it again, Midgey?'

'Maggot,' I correct. 'But I don't exactly think you're going to get along.'

Dad pulls a face. 'Why not? I'm great.'

I try not to laugh at his rubbish joke. 'But you don't know anything about horses, and Ace hates everyone on the best of days.'

'Ah, but that's only because she hasn't met *me* yet.'

Over the years, Dad has been to maybe two competitions, and his contributions have never been anything more than carrying sandwiches from food stands to the trailer and saying exactly the wrong thing just before I'm about to ride.

Gabe is still queuing, and I glance over my shoulder at the table behind us, where two men are having a very loud discussion. One is old enough to be the other's father, and I wonder if the dad and grandfather have been made to take the kids out for the day as I look at the four small children sitting opposite them. The kids are busy on their tablets, but I can't help but hear their elders' conversation as they make no attempt to be quiet. Every other words is *Brexit*, and they're both speaking with loud self-assurance, as though saying said word loud enough makes them sound like they know what they're talking about.

Dad is looking that way, too, when I turn back around, and I roll my eyes at him. 'Can nobody have a conversation anymore that doesn't contain the word *Brexit?*'

'Politics are important,' Dad says levelly.

'Maybe, but they're only talking about it because they think it makes them sound clever.'

As if to prove my point, the two men raise their voices further, using plenty of big words that don't actually say a thing.

Dad raises his eyebrows at me. 'I reckon you're right there.'

We sit in silence for a minute, and I glance at Gabe still waiting in the queue, my mind drifting to Ace and Jupiter, hoping Mum has remembered my instructions and that Rose is checking everything's done right. Mum looked after Jupiter most days I was at school before taking on the café, so it isn't like she doesn't know what she's doing, but I've got used to being in charge of everything myself over the summer, and can't help worrying. Leaving the ponies is the worst thing about spending weekends in London.

I'm still listening absently to the conversation behind me, which has now turned to the topic of the royal family, when Dad says, 'I still want to meet her, you know.'

'What? Meet who? The Queen?'

He splutters. 'What? What are you talking about the Queen for?'

I point over my shoulder, and he nods. 'That's what they just said. I don't know what you're talking about.'

'Maggot,' Dad says. 'I still want to meet her.'

Whenever Dad picks me and Gabe up, or drops us off, it's usually evening time, after the horses have been fed, and he's never made it to the yard to see the ponies. He's met Jupiter before, of course, though I doubt he could pick the pony from a line-up. I bet he couldn't even tell Ace and Jupiter apart, even though one's grey and the other's bay.

I shrug. 'If you want.'

'Maybe I'll come watch one of your events,' he pushes. 'When's the next one?'

'Um, couple of weeks,' I say noncommittally, though the truth is next weekend. The last thing I need is the added pressure of Dad watching when I'm good enough at screwing up as it is. 'But it's the end of the season, so you might be better off waiting until next year.'

Then again, according to the two people seated behind me, the world is ending soon, so there might not be a next year at all.

chapter 4

'Next in the ring we have Sybil Dawson, riding her own Ardmore Galaxy.'

The bell rings, and I push Jupiter into a canter. It's been raining all morning, even during our dressage test, and while it was only a drizzle, it was enough to leave us both soaked to the skin. It was only ten minutes ago that the sky cleared, but I'm still wet and cold now, as I'm sure Jup is, too. I'm even more grateful that Rose not only found time to clip him for me this week, lessening his chances of catching a chill, but also taught me how to clip myself, patiently giving me instructions, so that when Jupiter will need clipping again in a few weeks, as he's bound to because his coat grows like a Shetland pony's, I'll be able to do it myself.

Our dressage was nothing to brag about, but not a disaster, either. I hadn't imagined just how bad our last test was, because when I looked at the results before leaving, I found out it was enough to be dead last after the first phase, which only increased my disappointment, but Ace was in the top fifteen, which made me more confident that I *am* capable of riding a semi-decent test if I set my mind to it.

The first fence is a red-and-white oxer, and I sit in the saddle, keeping my eyes on the jump. *We can do this.*

'And that is a lovely clear for Sybil Dawson and Ardmore Galaxy to send them forward to the cross country phase on their dressage score of 35.4.'

'Good boy,' I say to Jupiter, patting his neck as I circle him after the finish line.

'Well ridden,' Rose says when she reaches us outside of the ring, her dark hair tied back at her neck. 'Just ride him like that cross country.'

At least I don't have any qualms about Jupiter's fitness anymore. He's jigging all around the start box, tugging at the reins, desperate to run. I try to keep my own nerves in check, to hold them back the way I'm holding back Jupiter, but they're more difficult to restrain than a near half-ton pony.

'Keep his head with you the whole way,' Rose says as I walk Jupiter around the start box. 'Think of the whole course as a conversation, and not just each fence as an order. You'll be fine, just keep riding. You're both doing great.'

The steward looks up at me and nods, counting down. 'Three, two, one, GO! Good luck!'

The exuberance with which Jupiter launches out of the start box throws me backwards in the saddle, and it takes me a couple of strides to regain my balance. I changed after show jumping, but I'm still cold from getting wet earlier, and Jupiter's mane, curly from the plaits I took out, is damp.

Jupiter takes us over the first fence, galloping on to the second with determination, and I stand in my stirrups, going with him.

Over the second, third, fourth, fifth... Jupiter doesn't know how to refuse a cross country fence, how to slam on the brakes and point-blank refuse to jump. It's not in his make-up. If he could speak, I'm sure he'd say *Um, Mum, it's a cross country fence, why would I choose not to jump it?* He loves his cross country, has never been taught not to, and that in turn has always given me confidence. Before Jupiter, I'd only ridden stubborn, thuggish, sour loan ponies at Pony Club events that did absolutely nothing to help you out, bored out of their brains from years of teaching beginners. And then I got on Jupiter, and I couldn't believe that I was riding a pony who actually did what you asked of him. I'd never got to experience that before, and it was the best feeling. Even if he wasn't the flashiest mover, not the best dressage horse, and still had his little quirks, he aimed to please. I got to ride a pony that *wanted* to jump, and didn't try to refuse every one for the sake of it. A horse that didn't nap and buck any chance he got, a horse that actually did what I asked him to. And most importantly I experienced the feeling of gaining confidence in riding a pony cross country that would always jump. Everyone needs to sit on a schoolmaster, even just once, to experience that.

Jupiter gallops through the water, and I sit up, steering him towards the log on the other side of the complex. We canter up the bank, out of the water, and fly over the jump, Jupiter's ears already seeking out the next fence.

I'm not wearing a stopwatch, but I feel like we're up on the clock, know we haven't lost a second anywhere, as we head for home. The last fence isn't difficult, but bigger than some of the others on course, and I push Jupiter on. The grey pony takes off when I ask him to, and we fly over the obstacle to land clear, and I push him on all the way to the finish line, before dropping my right hand from the reins to pat him.

Double clear. We did it.

Jupiter and I were one of the first combinations to go in our section, so I have a while yet until I know whether we'll be getting a placing. Mum drove Jupiter in the trailer, as Rose only has a catch ride today, so we're free to stay as long as we want, and also leave as early as we like. But I really want to know the results first, and also catch my friends' rounds if I can.

I pick the chestnut pony out of the warm-up right away. He stands out, even surrounded by other high-calibre horses and ponies. His red coat shines, despite this dull weather, and his plaits are perfect. As I get nearer, my eyes rise to Freya, cantering Leo around the ring in a two-point seat, and my gaze lingers on her navy blue jacket, and beautifully cut and fitted at the waist, and I think sadly of my own scruffy tweed jacket on the back seat of Mum's car.

Nell is in the middle of the ring, by the jump stands, ready to adjust fences if her daughter needs her to. Her tied-up hair is wet, baggy raincoat smeared with dirt, and she doesn't carry herself with the same confidence as the other parents acting as grooms around her. An outsider would never guess that Nell owned what I'm certain is the most expensive horse in the ring.

Freya turns Leo to the crossbar, and the pony's stride never changes as he canters to the fence, staying in the same collected rhythm as when he was schooling on a circle, and he pops over it with ease. And when his rider turns him back to the fence, they clear it again on the same perfect stride. *How does she do that?* It's only a little fence, but it doesn't matter because little or not, Freya sees perfect strides to everything. It's like she never even *looks* for strides, just hits the right one every time. I wish I could do that.

I watch as Freya brings Leo back to a trot on the far side of the ring as horse and rider combinations start crowding the fences. It's not the biggest warm-up ring in the world, and it's suddenly doubled in numbers. One glance at the whiteboard tells me that Freya has five horses to go until she's up, and I realise she must be waiting for a couple of them to go through before continuing with her own warm-up, waiting for the fences to clear.

Spectators crowd the edge of the ring, and I look around me as I wait for Freya to start jumping again, my eyes falling on a couple of girls farther along. The taller one has her back to me as she speaks to her friend, who looks familiar. Her thick blond hair is tied back at the nape of her neck, and she has an anorak on over her white competition clothes. I'm sure I know her…

The other girl turns around, and it clicks. Alex, speaking to Leo's former rider Leni. And as the latter's eyes are on the same chestnut pony I was watching a moment ago, I think I can guess just what she's doing watching a BE100 warm-up. I don't know her, but she was beside me at an event not long ago, talking to Alex while I was waiting to be checked out by a medic, and she seemed nice enough. Alex must be about to jump on a horse, or has just jumped off one - or both - because she's not only dressed to go in a ring, but she's wearing a hat, and has a short whip in her hands.

'Come on,' I hear her say to her friend, tapping Leni on the arm, 'let's get closer.'

The two girls start moving towards me, towards Leo, and I wonder whether I should say hello, if Alex will even remember or recognise me, but she quickly clears that up.

'Oh, hey, it's my ambulance friend!' she greets me. 'Look, Leni, it's my ambulance friend.'

'Hello,' Leni says warmly to me, before shooting Alex a wary glance. 'Your ambulance friend?' she repeats.

'Yeah, when Anchor threw me off.'

'When you *fell* off,' Leni corrects.

'Anyway, we're friends now,' Alex says, but the way she says *friends* makes me feel about six years old. 'We both have annoying mares.' She looks at me. 'I'm like your - what's the word?' She snaps her fingers, looking around as though hoping the word will spell itself out in the air. 'You know, like a guide.'

'If you don't know the word,' Leni says, 'then maybe you're not qualified to be one. You're like a walking advertisement for why people should stay in school.'

'Leni,' Alex whines. 'Come on, you're clever, you know what I'm talking about. It begins with an M.'

Leni keeps her mouth shut, as though the word would fly out if she didn't grit her teeth, but caves. 'Mentor.'

'Yeah, that's the one!' she says triumphantly. 'I'm your mentor. Right?'

'Uh, okay,' I say.

'Blink twice if you need help,' Leni whispers to me, and I laugh.

Alex taps her whip against her leg in a continuous rhythm. 'You're so mean,' she says to her friend. 'So are you going to see that pony of yours or what?' she goes on, and I feel weirdly anxious when I realise she's referring to Leo.

Leni shakes her head. 'I'm not going to disturb her warm-up. I'll see her afterwards.'

I don't say anything, just watch silently as Freya eases Leo back into a canter and turns him to the upright. As always, the two see a perfect stride, and fly over the obstacle. Freya pushes her hand forward to touch the pony on the neck, then moves him onto a fifteen-metre circle, sitting in the saddle as she works him as though she were about to go into a dressage test, then stands in her stirrups again to push him on down the long side.

'She's good,' Alex says with approval, and I instantly feel relief on my friend's behalf, but also hear a green-eyed monster climb into my head to remind me that no one would say the same about me. Freya turns Leo to the fence again, with more pace, and the pony clears it with even more air to spare, and Alex adds, 'She rides like you, Leni. No wonder he goes well for her.'

I glance at Leni, whose eyes are on Leo, and while she hasn't said anything yet, she looks happy. 'He looks really good,' she says finally, no resentment or sadness in her voice as I excepted there to be. 'Doesn't he?'

'Better than he went for you,' Alex deadpans, and Leni lunges for Alex's whip, which she tries to turn on her, and the two of them laugh, interrupted only by the disapproving snicker of a parent walking beside their child's part-cob, the piebald pricking his ears and spooking at Alex and Leni's antics.

'Geez, lighten up,' Alex mutters, lifting a hand to shade her eyes as a grey cloud shifts to bask us in sunlight.

'To be fair, you'd say much worse if someone spooked one of your horses,' Leni says to her, then turns to me. 'You know her stupid grey, Waffles?' Alex jumps to her horse's defence, rambling on about how he is far from stupid and more talented than most of the half-witted nags (her words) on the eventing circuit, but I nod in affirmation. 'We were riding to a warm-up side by side the other day, and some kid was shaking a branch near the horse walk, which freaked Waffles out because, hello, he's nuts, and Alex went ballistic.'

Alex scoffs. 'The kid was a brat.'

Leni raises her eyebrows. 'Yeah, I think he got the message when you referred to him as *Oi, Bratty Kid being a nuisance!* You made him cry, for god's sake!'

'Not my fault he's a wimp.'

'Waffles is looking really good, though,' Leni says, nodding to herself.

Alex sighs wistfully. 'I know. Man this girl's good,' she adds, her eyes still on Leo. 'What's her name again?'

'Freya,' I answer before anyone else can. 'Freya Fitzgerald.'

Leni looks at me. 'You know her?'

I nod. 'She's my best friend.'

'No way? Small world. She really does ride well,' Leni goes on. 'I'm glad Olivia sold Leo to her. They seem to be doing great. Oh, do you ride with Rose Holloway? My friend Georgia told me she'd met someone who knew the person Leo had gone to. Sybil, right?'

'Yeah,' I say, impressed by Leni's memory. 'That's me.'

'Your name's Sybil?' Alex says, and while I'm not sure she's saying this to comment on my name, I once again wish I had one that didn't make me sound like a ninety-nine-year-old.

'I thought you said you were friends!' Leni says, pretending to be outraged. 'How can you not know her name?'

Alex shrugs. 'Never came up.'

'Yeah, probably because you never shut your mouth long enough to let anyone else speak.'

'Geesh, Helena, what did you have for breakfast?' Alex snickers. 'I think I prefer you when you're annoyingly nice. Actually, maybe you're *not* nice, maybe we all think you're nice because you just look nice next to me.'

'Stalin would look nice next to you,' Leni retorts.

'Oh, ouch.' Alex touches her heart, pretending to have been struck. 'Seriously, what *has* got into you?' Freya turns Leo to the oxer, sitting in the saddle through the turn, and they fly over it in the same style as the other fences, the sunlight catching the chestnut pony's coat when he lands and making him glimmer as they turn left. Alex lifts her right arm and holds her palm out flat toward Freya in the warm-up, still looking at Leni. 'Is it because she rides your pony better than you do?'

'He's not my pony,' Leni says, voicing my thoughts as her eyes dart cautiously to me. 'And nothing could make me happier than him going as well for some else as he did for me.'

Alex frowns. 'I actually said *better-*'

'Or better,' Leni says, and she looks like she means it.

'He's a really nice pony,' I say to her after a while, for the sake of saying *something,* and it's true. 'He's gorgeous.'

Leni smiles kindly. 'He's the best. My mum owns a riding school in Devon, and we were always buying and selling ponies to help make ends meet, and Leo hadn't done anything when we got him, and we didn't know what he'd be like, and now...' Her voice trails off, and she looks back towards the ring with glassy eyes, and I follow her gaze to watch Freya turn to the oxer once more. 'I'm so happy to see him doing so well,' Leni goes on, clearing her throat. 'I never would have sold him if I hadn't had to financially, but seeing him go well for somebody else is the best feeling.'

'Have you not seen Freya ride him before?' I ask, and Leni shakes her head.

'I hadn't caught them yet. I've either been at different events or our times have clashed, and I've never noticed him in the lorry park.'

'She'd be in the trailer park,' I say. 'She has one of those little one-horse lorries.'

'That's why, then.'

'Three-four-nine,' the gate steward calls. Freya's number.

Freya trots Leo to the ring without noticing me or his previous rider watching, her attention solely on the track ahead of her. Even as the pair is waiting for the start bell, Freya trotting Leo around the ring, they look amazing. The chestnut pony in on the bridle, his neck round as he bends his hocks and steps under himself with his hind end, with an even top line and healthy dapples shining through his coat, Freya's hands and legs perfectly still as she rises his trot.

'She rides like you, Leni,' Alex says again, watching the combination as she speaks. 'She's got a quiet seat, too.'

'Our next starter is number 349 Freya Fitzgerald, riding her own Battersea, and they come forward on that very good dressage score of 25.'

The start bell rings, and Freya touches Leo into a canter. The first fence is jumped from the right, coming down the long side, and Freya takes Leo to the far end of the ring before turning to the fence, her eyes on the obstacle. They see a perfect, bold stride. The pony clears the fence with his knees around his chin, ears pricked, a copybook jump, and they continue on to the next.

Freya rides the course perfectly. She sits in the saddle through every turn, keeps her hands low and quiet on the approach to the fences, her leg on, face determined, and manages to both look like she's not doing anything and yet always look like she's doing *something,* always connected to her pony.

'And that's a lovely clear round for Freya Fitzgerald and Battersea…'

'Yeah,' Alex says, clapping briefly as she speaks, 'she's good.' She nods as she says the last word, stating a fact, and I wonder if she'd have been just as frank if the opposite were true. Probably.

Leni looks at the pony coming out of the ring, then back at us. 'I'm going to go introduce myself,' she says, then hurries towards the chestnut gelding. Considering the record she had with Leo, I'm sure no introduction is necessary.

'While we're on the topic of super ponies,' Alex says, leaning closer to me as she points at something behind me, 'that's mine.'

I turn around to see Otto and India riding to the warm-up, Catherine and another woman I don't recognise trailing behind.

'Get him trotting right away,' the woman calls, and I realise she must be India's trainer. 'Trot and canter, then bring him back to walk for a breather afterwards. Get him concentrating.'

'I know India,' I say to Alex once India and her entourage are out of earshot. And then I add, 'She rides well.'

Alex frowns. 'Do you know everyone I know?' she says, but she doesn't seem to be expecting an answer. 'She's doing okay with him,' she goes on, which I'm pretty sure is praise coming from Alex. 'Better than that useless sister, anyway.'

'He's a nice pony,' I say, watching the bay walk into the warm-up. He's no Leo, not a horse that stands out, but he *is* nice, and with the results he had with Alex, I certainly wouldn't turn my nose up at riding him.

'He's the best,' Alex says simply. 'Leni will say that Leo is better, but it's not true. Otto is a *pony,* you know? Not like Leo.'

Uh, no, I don't know, because they're both fourteen-twos, ergo both ponies. 'I don't understand…'

'Leo is like a little horse,' Alex says. 'And he rides bigger than he is. I sat on him a couple of times when he was still Leni's, and it was no different from riding a Thoroughbred or an Irish Sport Horse. He rides like a horse, you know?'

I think of Ace. 'Yeah, I know what you mean.'

'Well, Otto is a pony through and through. He's *such* a pony. He's cheeky, and playful, and he has a real pony stride. He's so much fun.'

Now I think of Jupiter. He rides like a pony, compact and straightforward. Acts like one, too. I understand what Alex is saying, and I try to think which I prefer, but can't decide. Like comparing chocolate to crisps - both equally good, depending on what you're in the mood for.

Farther away, Freya has halted Leo, and Leni stands beside the chestnut pony, chatting with both her and Nell. Leni's face is open, friendly, and Nell seems to be returning the feeling, a smile on her face as she speaks. Freya has a hat on and the visor slightly hides her expression, but even from here I can see she looks reserved, not as comfortable as her two companions, but it's hardly surprising. She's shy anyway, and I can't imagine being relaxed myself if faced with the person who won a European medal on the pony I'm riding. I try to imagine myself in the same situation, try to imagine Ace having had a successful career with somebody else, and that same somebody coming to talk to me at an event. And they'd see what a bad job I'm doing...

Maybe there are perks to having an unproven horse after all, because if you fail on a good horse, you have nowhere to hide.

I smooth the last of the gel onto Jupiter's legs before straightening up and flexing my fingers. The liniment makes my hands feel how toothpaste tastes, and I wiggle my fingers again. Sometimes the tingling last for hours.

Jupiter's rug is folded over the stable door, and I pull it off and throw it over his back. The grey pony keeps eating hay, unperturbed as I fasten the rug. Then again, all the other horses in the yard could sprout wings and fly into the air and Jupiter still wouldn't stop eating. I'm not sure which he loves more - food or cross country.

I bend to fasten the surcingles, pull Jupiter's tail free from the filet string, then step backwards to watch the chunky pony pull at his hay with zeal.

Food it is.

'You did good,' I say to him, rubbing his clipped neck, but my words are hollow. I should be thrilled, should be ecstatic that not only is Jupiter fit and well, but he ended the season on a double clear. But I *so* wanted to place, so wanted a top ten finish and a rosette to remember the day by, and we just missed out. By one placing. I don't think any placing is worse than eleventh.

The few rays of sun that were present this afternoon are long gone, and the day is cold and dreary once more. It's getting dark earlier, and at six o'clock I can already see that night-time isn't too far away.

I shiver beneath my big coat, but the sight of Jupiter wrapped up in his quilted rug, standing on a thick bed of straw, makes me feel slightly warmer. I think back to his stable at Eva's, at the thin layer of shavings on concrete, and wonder how I ever thought that was nice for him to sleep on.

'I'll be right back,' I tell Jup, sliding out of his stable.

Ace is also eating, but with less passion than Jupiter. She's a fussy eater, and the only forage we can count on her clearing up is haylage.

'You all right, Maggot?'

Ace lifts her head at the sound of my voice, grinding the haylage thoughtfully, and decides she can't be bothered to humour me, and I step back as she pins her ears and shoots me a dirty look before returning to her forage.

'You're so kind,' I mutter.

I let myself into the stable, which the mare pretends to be

irritated by, but I know it's an act. It's like she thinks she has to show distaste at everything and anything, and not to do so would be a waste of her time.

The rug over Ace's door is one of Rose's, navy blue with a grey checkered pattern. Ace hasn't needed clipping yet, her coat so much thinner than Jupiter's, but she gets cold, unlike Jupiter who has a hot body even clipped, and she's been rugged for a couple of weeks. And by rugging her now, hopefully her winter coat won't grow too thick, and she'll be able to go longer without being clipped. As she hates everything that involves human contact, like being shod and having her mane pulled, I can't imagine the mare is going to be the easiest to clip, though I'd still like to get her done before her last event.

'There,' I say, tucking the straps into their keepers. 'You're next, Maggot,' I add after a beat.

Jupiter's season is finished, and even though I'm a bit disappointed today, I know it's gone well, too, even if it's different from what I'd planned at the beginning of the year. Now he can have a small holiday, then show jump all winter, ready to start the next event season in the spring.

'Now you and I have just got to get around an event,' I say. I run a hand down Ace's neck, and she pins her ears. I pull a packet of Polos from my coat pocket, which immediately piques the bay mare's interest, and she pricks her ears and does her best to look sweet, nothing like the flesh-loving devil she is most of the time.

'You don't deserve it.' But I feed her mints anyway, because when Ace is like this, when she's friendly and trusting, it cancels out all the bad times.

I think of Leo and of Otto, the perfect ponies with loving personalities. What I would give to sit on one of them, to ride an FEI pony…

But I look at Ace, who in turn is looking at me with what could almost be described as affection. Would I trade her for a pony like that given the choice? I don't think so. I don't *think*. Not that I'll ever be faced with the decision, but I can't help but wonder.

'We've got two weeks, Maggot,' I say, sliding the packet of Polos back into my pocket. 'Two weeks to be event-ready. What do you think, will we get round?'

I hold out a hand to the bay mare, but Ace only wanted the mints, and now that I've stopped feeding them to her, she just pins her ears.

chapter 5

With Jupiter now enjoying a holiday, Ace becomes my sole focus. The week after Jupiter's event, I take her cross country schooling and clear round show jumping, both of which go well. But between schooling outings, I take Ace hacking, because we've found that lots of hacking is what she thrives on. If she works in the school a few days running, the mare gets sour, and when she doesn't want to work, she lets you know. Rose's horses are on holiday now, their season over, so I either hack Ace alone, which she is happy to do, or with Mackenzie and Cinder, and occasionally Freya and Leo.

'Shall we trot down here?' Freya calls from in front of me, turning in the saddle.

'Sure,' I say, shortening my reins. I squeeze my legs against Ace's sides, and the little mare lifts into an expressive trot, moving forward into the bridle.

After a week of an icy wind so strong that riding wasn't deemed possible some days, the gale so violent the horses were like tornadoes themselves just to lead around the yard, let alone work, today's blue sky is a relief. It's still chilly, but the periwinkle overhead, the bright light that illuminates the tracks and the general feeling of vibrancy and life, is like stepping out of a cave after days underground. Sometimes you don't realise just how much weather affects your mood until a run of bad days is broken. Ace is happier, too, much more relaxed in the sunshine than she is when it's raining.

Earlier this week, Rose's yard began a small renovation. A large barn stores hay and straw, and Rose had been looking into putting stables up in part of it, and hanging an overhang off the building to make up for the loss of space. Apparently she's been thinking about expanding for a while, due to many in Newmarket looking for spaces to send racehorses for holidays and rehabilitation, somewhere they can simply be fed and turned out for double the price of a competition livery, and finally took the plunge. Only four extra stables, and a walker which is more costly, but Rose said the money she'll earn in a few months for even two Thoroughbreds on holiday alone will cover all the costs.

The expansion is great, but it also comes with some noise, which shouldn't be a problem for most horses, but Ace isn't most, and when I tried schooling her she only spooked and bolted every time a worker hammered a nail or dropped a plank, so hacking is the safer option. Labourers go home by four o'clock, and never work weekends, so I've taken to sticking to using the school only during those times.

The bridleway widens, and I steer Ace to the right, trotting her up alongside Leo. I'm bundled up in my fleece-lined waterproof coat even though the day is clear, but Freya is only wearing a thin long-sleeved top beneath a waistcoat, and every time I ask her if she's warm enough, she replies to the affirmative, though I'm not convinced. We've been riding for an hour now, though most of that was at a walk. We took the ponies along a bridleway that runs through one of the large studs, gawking at the huge post-and-rail fields and the luxurious stable barns. Thoroughbred mares trotted up to the fence to see us, ears forward and tails in the air, which

Leo and Ace weren't the least bit bothered by, to my relief. The ponies merely continued to walk along the sand-covered path, while Freya twisted in her saddle to try to read the names on the mares' leather head collars, keen to spot a famous winner.

After coming back out onto the road, we passed *The Compasses*, this huge 16th-century listed house we've always admired from afar only to see a *FOR SALE* sign by the gate, and proceeded to spend ten minutes listing what we'd each do if we won the lottery and could afford to buy it - our plans including luxurious American barns, heated indoor arenas, and space to rescue as many animals as we please. We both know neither of our plans will ever happen, but it's fun to imagine, and I wonder what sort of people *will* actually be moving there.

'I wish the weekend would just get here already,' I say, keeping Ace at Leo's side. The two ponies are parallel, their strides equal, making Freya and me post the trot to the same rhythm. 'Not because I'm excited,' I go on, sick at the thought of competing Ace, 'but just to *know*. What about you?'

Freya tilts her head, shrugging without moving her body. On a hack, especially without Rose in the saddle alongside me, I often ignore my position, don't really think about my riding too much, but either the same can't be said for Freya or she doesn't have to because it all comes naturally. Her heels are beneath her seat, hands and legs still, back straight and shoulders square as the chestnut pony flows beneath her.

'I dunno,' she says. 'Same, I guess. I want the season to be over, not because I don't want to compete, but because I want to know how it ends.'

'You're going to be fine, though,' I say. Freya is riding on the Saturday, the day before me, in the BE100 Ou18. 'It's not like you both haven't been around the tracks before.'

'Yeah, we'll see.'

A robin flies past us, its small body darting across the bridleway, but neither pony reacts, both focussed on their trot. I smile, then laugh internally at Ace *not* spooking, because she rarely does when she's on a hack. I remember when she first arrived, when Rose started taking the mare out, and said something along the lines of her having not been taught to fear hacking the way she does schooling, as though the bridleways are a safe place for her and the school isn't, and think there's a lot of truth to that. I could never pick a favourite between Jupiter and Ace, even if I did sort of choose Jupiter when I had to out of loyalty, but I feel like a better rider on Ace. She's built much more like Leo than Jupiter is, a natural athlete, and while Rose says there's no reason Jupiter shouldn't be able to contest Pony Trials in the near future, I think I have a much better shot with Ace. To the point that right now, trotting alongside a pony who has been to Europeans, I feel comfortable, and not like a beginner desperately trying to keep up, as I so often have before.

'They're so good together,' I say aloud, nodding at the two ponies when Freya turns her head to look at me, the trot uninterrupted.

She smiles. 'They are. They're like the same model but in different colours.'

I laugh, and butterflies flutter in my stomach at the thought of somebody else acknowledging that Ace looks like the most gorgeous FEI event pony I've ever seen.

'Oh, hey.' Freya's words cut off as we dodge a rain-made hole, which was a puddle last time we came down here. 'Remember that article in *Horse & Hound* a while back?' she continues seamlessly. 'About how more and more old horses are being sent to slaughter?' She meets my eyes, a disgusted expression on her face. 'Well yesterday my dad had to take one to the kennels' - as a horse transporter in Newmarket, Craig mainly works with Thoroughbreds, but still hauls all sorts of horses - 'and get this.'

She pauses again, but this time for emphasis. 'It was a metre-thirty *show jumper*, and he competed just last weekend, but he was getting on and the people were told they needed to retire him, and they shipped him off just like that.'

I frown. 'Couldn't they have just sold him for lower levels or something? He didn't have to do one-thirties.'

'I don't know the details,' Freya says. 'I think they might've already dropped him down in height or something, but that's not the point. Like, he's no use as a ridden horse anymore, and so they just ditch him like that. Even after he's done so much for them. He's competed for years, and the second he can't any more, they make him dogs' dinner.' She scoffs bitterly. 'Makes me sick. If you can't afford a retired horse, you can't afford a horse.'

I open my mouth to say something, but Freya goes on.

'It's just so ridiculous!' Her voice rises slightly, and I know she's clearly passionate about this. 'A horse does everything for you, competes for years, looks after you, and then the second he's of no use to you you put a bullet through his head? It's not right. I told Dad next time to bring it home if he ever gets hired to take another one to the kennels.'

'You can't just collect retired horses.'

'Why the heck not?'

'Uh, because it's not up to you? I mean, they're not your responsibility. Their owners are the ones who should be looking after them.'

'Yeah, but they're not, so someone has to.'

I shrug, and Ace shakes her head as a fly lands in her ear, snorting in disgust - the noise is the same one Freya just made, which makes me smile.

'Shall we trot all the way to the corner then canter up the hill?' I say, glancing at the chestnut pony.

Freya nods in response, her eyes never leaving the track ahead of us, but I don't think she's thinking about the ride. And sure enough, she confirms my suspicions by speaking again.

'You know why Dad did it?'

'Huh?'

'You know why Dad picked up the horse? I mean, these people compete every weekend, they have transport. But they didn't want to face having to take the horse to the kennels themselves.'

I frown as I continue posting to Ace's rhythm. 'They actually said that?'

'Well,' Freya says, which I think means *no,* 'it's obvious.'

I still don't know if what Freya's saying is a fact or just a conclusion she's come to herself, but I figure there's no getting through to her regardless. For somebody so shy and seemingly passive where most things are concerned, she is narrow-minded when she wants to be, and not even a tornado could divert her train of thought.

'It's sad,' I say.

Freya shakes her head, jaw clenched. Leo continues to trot in a flowing rhythm, his short mane as red as his rider's ponytail. 'It doesn't make me sad, it makes me *angry*. This is something *people* are *willingly* doing. It's not a natural disaster, or something else we have no control over. And-'

Freya doesn't get to finish her sentence.

Dried-up puddles have left ruts in the ground, and Leo's right fore lands directly in one filled with stones, sending him forward. It isn't an extravagant stumble so much as it's awkward, and it completely catches Freya off guard. Leo can't get his feet out of the way in time, and his head ducks as he falls forward. I tug at Ace's reins, keeping her trajectory away from the chestnut pony, and hear myself gasp a gasp I'm not conscious of emitting.

Under usual circumstances Freya would never be unseated by a stumble, but the suddenness of the action, coupled with the fact that she was talking to me when it happened, turned in the saddle, unbalances her. Leo's left fore hits the ground as his right foot catches on a big stone, though he recovers in time to prevent himself from falling further, though the same can't be said for his rider. Freya flies forward, causing Ace to spook as her body collides with the ground with a thump. I pull my mare to a standstill as quickly as my body can process the command from my brain, and Freya jumps to her feet with almost as much speed, seizing Leo's reins.

'Are you all right?' I ask. My elevated heart rate makes my voice come out more panicked than I intend, but I'm not sure Freya's even listening to me.

'Is he okay? Is he okay?' she cries, crouching in front of her pony, pressing a hand against the knee that took the impact.

'I…' Leo is standing still, his flaring nostrils and some scratches on his brushing boots the only indicator of the fall. His limbs look clean, no cuts that I can see. 'I think so. He looks fine.' Though my words don't reassure Freya.

'I'm so sorry,' she mutters to the chestnut pony, still focussed on his legs. She pulls Leo forward a step, and a tad of colour returns to her face when the gelding walks perfectly sound. 'Good boy. I'm so sorry…'

'He looks okay, Freya,' I say, but there's hesitation in my voice. Not because I doubt the words, but because I doubt that somebody *else* is. 'Freya,' I say again, 'he looks okay.'

It's like what I'm saying finally reaches her, finally pushes its way through the wariness and panic, and Freya looks up from Leo's legs, tears running down her even-paler-than-usual face, and as quickly as she switched into *Action* mode, she switches off. Ace snatches at the reins to rub a fly off her face, and I let them slide through my fingers as Freya lets out a small cry and rocks back on her heels until she's sitting on the ground, still holding on to Leo.

For a few seconds, I don't move, just stay perched in the saddle, words eluding me as the bay mare continues to rub her head against the inside of her left fore. *Will I be able to get back on*

Ace if I dismount, I wonder, then tell myself not to be so selfish, that Freya would have already jumped off her ride if our roles were reversed. I also remember that I've already had to get on Ace halfway through a hack before, when Rose and I swapped ponies, but I like to think I decide to get off before being reassured of the fact.

'Freya,' I say. I've pulled Ace's reins over her head, and hold them tightly in my fist.

Freya is hugging her knees to her face, arms wrapped around her legs, her shaking shoulders giving her away as crying. If I saw a rider making a scene like this at a competition, I'd assume they were sulking after a bad ride, throwing a temper tantrum because their horse hadn't done what they wanted, but this is *Freya.* She doesn't sulk or throw tantrums - she's the person my mum brings up whenever I do something the tiniest bit bratty, usually by knotting her eyebrows and muttering a sentence along the lines of, 'I bet Freya never behaves like this.' I'm not sure I've ever even seen Freya *cry* before, and if I'm being honest, it kind of freaks me out.

'Freya,' I try again. I dart my eyes to Ace, and the little mare steps forward enough for me to get nearer my friend, and I sit down next to her. Tiny stones and specks of dust cover Freya's thin top, along the arm she landed on, and I start dusting them off with my hand, except I then wonder if it's her arm that's *making* her cry, whether she landed on it funny and is now in agony, so I stop. 'Does your arm hurt?'

Freya shrugs without looking up. 'It's fine,' she says, voice muffled.

'Okay.'

I don't know what to say or do now, so I don't say or do anything, my gaze fixed on the two ponies standing in front of us, probably wondering why on earth their riders are sitting on the ground and not in the saddle. A cold gust of wind blows towards us, and like mirror images Ace and Leo sidestep, clamping their tails and angling their quarters towards the bad weather. Freya looks up at the movement, at the tug of reins, only to bury her head in her limbs again once she sees that Leo is all right.

'He could've injured himself,' she says finally.

'But he didn't.'

'Not *yet.*' Her voice is strained, like she's fighting to speak past tears. 'His knee could still be swollen tomorrow.'

'I'm sure it won't be,' I say. 'It's nothing.'

'Or he could go lame. And it's all my fault. I should've been paying attention and not ridden him straight into the empty puddle.' Freya lifts her head to look at Leo, then shivers as another breeze whistles past us.

'It was just an accident.'

'But it was still *my* fault.' Fresh tears fall down Freya's cheeks, and she shakes her head as she wipes them away. 'I can't take it anymore.'

I frown. 'Can't take what?'

'This.' Freya jerks the hand holding on to Leo's reins, which makes the pony jump, and Leo's spook in turn sets Freya off again, and she jumps to her feet, crying further, and wraps her arms around his neck, muttering apologies to him between scolding herself. 'I'm so sorry, I'm so sorry, I'm so stupid…' I wonder how long this is going to go on for, but she turns back to me sooner than I expect. 'I can't take it, Sybil,' Freya cries.

'Can't take *what?*' I say again.

'*This!* The pressure.' At the word *pressure*, Freya collapses back into a sitting position, the feet of her riding boots scraping across the hard ground, and if I had my phone on me I'd call Nell to tell her that her daughter appears to be having a panic attack of sorts, but it's tucked away in Ace's grooming box back at the yard, and I know Freya never rides with hers. It's just the two - or four - of us.

'What pressure, Freya?' I ask, as softly as I can. I've never been good in these situations. If there were a crisis, and the only people available to help were me and a hamster, I'd put my money on the rodent being the one to save the day. 'Talk to me.'

She blows out a breath, and I take one myself. 'I can't take the pressure of riding a pony this valuable,' Freya says slowly, her voice calmer than it was a moment ago.

'No one's putting pressure on you,' I say carefully. 'Your parents don't care if you win or not, they're not like that.'

'*They*'re not putting pressure on me, and it's not about pressure to win, it's just… it's so much *money. He* is worth so much money. I mean, I know he's insured, but one wrong step and - I can't take it,' she says again. 'It's too stressful.'

'But that whole "one wrong step" thing goes for all horses,' I point out.

'It's not the same. I…' Freya lets out a strangled sound, her eyes fixing on the chestnut pony. 'I can't enjoy it knowing how valuable he is. I'm so terrified of messing him up. And I feel like such a hypocrite because I've always hated how people buy rides, buy themselves a place in a team, spend tens of thousands - even *hundreds* of thousands - on a horse, and now I'm no better. And then I hate myself even *more* for feeling like that, because I should be grateful, and I feel so guilty. I can't win, anyway, it's a lose-lose situation, because if we do well, people will say it's only because of the pony, and if we do badly, then it's all my fault because the pony has the results and I'm the one who's wrecked him.'

'Okay,' I say. 'First off, you're not going to ruin him. Not only are you amazing, but you can't just mess up a pony by making a mistake. Second, even an FEI pony isn't going to get round if it's not well ridden' - this contradicts what I just said, but I hope Freya is too hysterical to notice - 'I mean, look at Sophia Humphries. That proves you can't just buy a ride, you still have to *ride* yourself, if that makes sense. And third, the fact that you're even conscious of how lucky you are and feel guilty just shows that you're nothing like the people who *do* buy rides. And didn't Leni say you're riding him really well?' I add. Freya was both brief and modest in relaying her conversation with Leo's past owner to me, but Nell was more encouraging, saying Leni was full of praise, which I witnessed firsthand myself, too.

'We couldn't afford him,' Freya says, still staring straight ahead and not looking at me, as though Leo's stumble has knocked over her bottled-up feelings and they are now pouring out all over the place. 'When Mum and Dad first brought it up, when we discussed it with Lydia, it seemed like something that would happen when pigs fly, and then it all, just, *did,* and I didn't want to let anyone down…'

'You didn't,' I say. 'You're *not.'*

She shakes her head and squeezes her eyes shut. 'It just never occurred to me I'd feel so stressed.' *Stressed* is a word I'm used to hearing my mum use, relating to her business or paying the bills, not one I'd expect to come out the mouth of somebody my age. 'We all worked more,' Freya goes on, 'took out loans, borrowed money from family, sold *Diamond* to make up the rest… And when Olivia handed me Leo's lead rope, all I could think of was every penny that had gone into him, and this weight settled over me that not only had all this money, including what came from Diamond's sale, gone into a pony, for me, but that I was now responsible for this pony, and I was terrified. Part of me resented him, which sounds awful, but it's true. And you know I've never *cared* about things like money, and now I just couldn't - *can't* - stop thinking about it. Eventing is so expensive, and it's not like I competed Diamond every week, but now I can't exactly have a pony like Leo and *not* take him out, so we're always scraping together money for entry fees… That's why I'm always helping out at Parsonage.' Parsonage stables is a DIY livery yard a few minutes away, which unlike Rose's doesn't boast a school and is mainly used by happy hackers. Freya's always been brief about looking after "friends' horses", helping out down the lane on weekends and when said friends are away, but I realise, as she says this, that there's money, albeit a small amount, involved that she feels pressured to earn. Between entry and starting fees, a single affiliated event is kicking one hundred pounds at the lower levels, and that's without everything else that goes into it. Every ten pounds earned adds up quickly, which I'm sure she's only too conscious of. 'I know my parents tell me not to worry about all that, but how can I not? And it's all just not fair on *him*' - Freya nods at the gelding standing obediently in the bridleway, ignoring the evil eyes Ace keeps shooting him.

Part of me wants to fire all sorts of questions, and the other doesn't know what to say, so I stay silent a moment, considering my next words carefully. The wind has quietened down, and a seagull squawks as it flies overhead, which makes Ace snort with disapproval.

'Do you like Leo?'

Freya scoffs, but I go on.

'I mean it. Forget everything else, just answer that question. Do you *like* him? I know you love him and care about him and all that, but that's different from actually liking him.'

Freya stands up to approach the pony, running her hands down his clipped neck. Leo lowers his head at the attention, leaning into Freya's waist.

'Of course I like him,' Freya says finally, and I'm a little surprised, which makes me realise that I actually expected her to reply negatively. 'Who wouldn't? He's easy to handle but still a hot-enough ride to be interesting, forgives just about anything, never refuses a fence, and riding dressage on him is magic.' She smiles to herself, remembering something else. 'In the mornings, he neighs as soon as I turn the mudroom light on. He watches for it from his field, because he knows it means *breakfast*. Every *single* morning, without fail. And then when I open the door, he's always there, watching, like he waits for me to come out.'

'Then that's all that matters,' I say. 'He's just a horse, he doesn't know what he cost, so you can't treat him differently because of it.' I stand up and stomp my feet a few times to warm up, which Ace takes great offence at. 'C'mon, let's get back on. We'll just walk,' I assure Freya, though I doubt Leo's injured himself in any way. 'I'm cold.'

The ponies stand still as we remount, and settling into the saddle, on Ace's back, feels like coming home. Freya lets her reins slip as she leans forward to kiss Leo's chestnut mane, neither of us speaking.

We ride on, the four of us, no words in the air, and I don't try to start a conversation, because I feel like there's no need right now. Sometimes being there for your friend means just that.

chapter 6

'Steady her with your outside rein through the turn - sit up! Outside leg guards the outside shoulder. Good.'

The bad weather hasn't let up these past few days, and I scrunch my face against the wind, tucking my chin into the collar of my coat. Ace feels the cold, too, and any breeze slightly stronger or chillier than the already-crap climate we're facing sends her shooting away from my leg and seat.

'Keep her together,' Rose reminds me from her spot at the edge of the sand school, all four of her limbs crossed as she holds a mug in her right hand. 'Don't let her run away. There's no point getting the turn right to just let her fall apart coming out of it. Come round again, and incorporate ten-metre circles if you feel her start to get bored.'

I know I let Ace lose her rhythm coming out of the turn, and even as my aids slackened, as I lost concentration, I knew that Rose would only make me repeat the movement again, and yet...

'Better. Bring her back to walk before you lose it. And make the transition a good one.'

That last sentence is unnecessary, a lesson I've long since learned, and I keep Ace in an impulsive trot right up until she moves forward into a walk stride, and slip her the reins. So many things weigh on my mind today that it's hard to tell which is sinking in its claws with the most intensity, and while I know it's ridiculous - a lame, pathetic, spoilt excuse - I can't help but prematurely blame every one for tomorrow's failure - *if* we fail, that is.

'What else is there left to practise for tomorrow?' Rose takes a swig from her mug of coffee, and the wind whips her brown ponytail over one shoulder. 'Long rein walk. Have you done that yet?' I shake my head. 'There you go. Do that until she stops anticipating, and then I think you can call it a day.' She glances over her shoulder, looking towards the stable yard. 'I'm going to go tack up, but I'll still be watching.'

I'm sure, I think, but not meanly. I don't know if it's because of having horse or having kids - probably both - but Rose is a black belt where the whole eyes-in-the-back-of-your-head thing is concerned.

A Saturday morning jogger runs past on the distant country lane, and Ace comes to a standstill and spins around, ears pricked and eyes fixed on the colourful Lycra form, visible through the bushes.

'You're fine,' I say, squeezing my legs against the mare's sides. *Rose isn't the only one with eyes in the back of her head,* I think bitterly. If Rose is a black belt, then Ace is the karate kid himself. 'Come on, Maggot.'

On a diagonal across the school, I let out my reins and encourage Ace to stretch her nose to the sand, squeezing my lower legs in rhythm with her strides. When we reach the long side of the arena and I shorten my reins to a correct contact, Ace jigs in anticipation of the next movement, but I carry on at a walk.

'This is what Rose is talking about, you know,' I say, but in truth I know it's my fault. I've run through the test too many times in the past weeks, always making a trot and canter transition after the long rein walk, and the mare knows it.

'You should never really run through a whole test,' Rose has told me countless times since, 'because you don't want the horse to learn it. You want to keep her guessing.' That's why we've been picking the routine apart, practising each movement individually and never in the order we would between the white boards at an event.

I repeat the exercise, walking Ace on a long contact and then shortening my reins when we reach the track, without going into an upward transition, and as I run through the movement again and again, knowing the session isn't over until Ace lets me gather my reins without changing her rhythm, my mind drifts to all of the thoughts fighting for prime attention. Worries are usually muddled to the point of no longer being sure what it is exactly that's weighing on your subconscious, but right now I could easily sort each concern into a clearly-labeled box. The only problem is that I can't get the lids shut.

Freya. That's the first, and probably the least concerning. It's been a few days since our ride, and in spite of the state she was in that afternoon, my friend has seemed happier and more relaxed than usual every time I've seen her since. Maybe what I said really helped, I don't know, but I'm still worried about her. It had never occurred to me that she was suffering in silence as she was, and I can't help but feel bad at not having been there for her earlier, especially when I'd been judging her in my head for so long.

The second label bears Gabe's name, and brings a fresh pang to my chest every time I think about it. Mum and I both suspected he wasn't terribly happy at school, though he said little about it. We were both new at the beginning of term, but unlike me, who had the comfort of being in the same establishment as my best friend, Gabe knew no one in his year. He didn't have many friends in Cambridge, either, so that wasn't so much of a change, but we noticed he was even quieter than usual when the topic of school was broached by Mum while watching TV in the evenings, or enquired about by Dad as a conversation starter across a restaurant table. Then yesterday Gabe came home with bent glasses and a paperback book in shreds, and neither silence nor a muttered excuse could hide the truth. Our paths rarely cross, but we go to school in the same building, and if yesterday hadn't also marked the start of half term, there would be no stopping me from tailing Gabe to class Monday morning and slamming a ten-year-old boy's head into a blackboard.

'Can't you think of something that won't get you suspended, Sybil?' Mum muttered when I voiced my plan. 'Though I don't rule out the idea quite yet.'

The bay mare marches beneath me, her nose lowering to the ground as though the diagonal across the sand were dotted with Polo mints - the only treat she prefers to human flesh - and I release a breath through my mouth, worries spinning in my stomach like a tornado itching to cause carnage.

Third worry? Tomorrow. Though technically, I don't think I can label an event as something distracting me from said event. My mind jumps back to the Humphrieses, no stepping stones between the thought of tomorrow's competition and the memory of how relaxed India and her sister Mia had been when I saw them last, how they were laughing and enjoying themselves. India had finished riding for the day, I remind myself, and everything had already gone well for her so she had reason to be relaxed. But Mia hadn't, and I'm sure India had been just as chilled between her own rides, too. Why can't I be like that?

A robin lands on the top railing of the school fencing as we reach the track, and I smile at its little red-and-brown body, which reminds me of my next packaged concern. Christmas. I should be looking forward to it, should be counting down the days and dusting off boxes of decorations, trying to convince Mum that there's nothing wrong with putting up a tree in October, and then bargaining for a while before meeting halfway in November, but none of that's happening. Instead Christmas is a taboo topic, one I'm desperately trying to ignore and never address, because it'll be our first without Dad, and the whole situation is awkward. Gabe brought up Christmas the last time we saw our dad, speaking excitedly and wanting to make plans, and my brother might be clever in some aspects, but he certainly didn't cotton on to how uncomfortable Dad and I were. I didn't want to ask Dad what he was doing for Christmas, don't want to live in a world where the holidays are something you have to plan around two houses and two families, so I'm ignoring it. The only problem with that is I have no idea what we'll be doing during the festive period.

Ace barely jigs when I collect my reins and walk on towards the corner, and I carry on down the long side to turn her back down the diagonal. Her mane touches my fingers as I lower my hands to her neck, and I feel my limbs ache at the thought of having to plait this afternoon.

Walter Morrigan. The final issue on my mind. A week ago, the name would have rung a bell, but not much more. Since moving to Bluebell Cottage, which is adjacent to one house and a stone's throw from another, I've only got to know one of the two neighbours, and that is Liam. When we first settled in, it became clear that both our neighbours were loners who rarely left the house. Of course, Liam's reasoning was soon discovered, but the tenant of the semi-detached cottage next to ours was no more than a stranger. Mum mentioned that our landlord said he was a retired widower, but that was it. I knew his name was Walter Morrigan from the odd letter that was posted through our door by mistake, but it never particularly stuck in my mind. To the point that when I found myself confronted with him yesterday, it took me a moment to remember it. I was coming home from the yard last night, with Ace's bridle over my shoulder. It needed cleaning before Sunday, and I wanted to do it a day early for once, and also in the warm comfort of our kitchen, now that autumn weather was well and truly here.

The sun was just beginning to set, and Walter Morrigan was in his front garden, reading a paper. My first thought was that he really had to be off his rocker to be reading outside in such weather, especially since I wasn't sure I'd seen him set foot in the garden all summer. My second thought was that, despite his age and frail appearance, he was a psychopath about to leap off his chair and throw me in a ditch somewhere. I walked faster, towards the stone path that led to our front door, and scolded myself. *Don't be stupid, he's an old, lonely man. Be nice.* Mum always says it's better to say hello first than be the person who doesn't say hello back, and with that in mind I offered Walter Morrigan a small smile and mumbled a greeting. I wasn't sure I'd actually spoken to him at all in the months we'd been neighbours, so I wasn't expecting much of a reply, but he met my smile with a bigger one, and for a moment I wondered if my earlier concern about him being a murderous villain was correct. Except the corners of his smile reached his eyes and made them crinkle in a way that looked too genuine to be the expression of a madman.

'Good evening,' he said with a northern accent.

I thought that would be it, that he'd return to his paper and I'd keep walking to the front door, but he pushed a blanket from his knees and stood up. I'd never realised before how short he is, and felt reassured by the fact. His limbs thin, head bald, figure clad in tatty clothes.

Was I supposed to say something now? Walter had stood up, which meant I stopped in my tracks, because I couldn't just walk away if he was trying to talk to me.

I shoved my hands into my pockets, pushing the bridle up against my side. 'It's cold,' I said for lack of any other ideas.

Walter shrugged. 'It is. I don't mind.' Definitely a Yorkshire accent. 'Well, don't let me keep you out here in the cold.'

I nodded slowly, unsure why, exactly, we were having this conversation in the first place. He seemed to have just noticed how frozen I was, my nose pink and my teeth almost chattering, and was embarrassed to have held me up. But why speak to me in the first place?

As much as I wanted to walk away, I couldn't. I knew Walter was widowed and lived alone, but I hadn't given it much thought before. And right now he seemed so lonely…

'I'm competing this weekend,' I said before I knew what I was saying, 'and I'm cleaning my tack.' And then I held up the bridle as proof. There. I could still walk away and go on with my evening, but I'd also offered Walter a few words in return, thus clearing my conscience. I didn't expect him to really understand the meaning of what I said, but he stepped forward slowly and gave me a knowing nod.

'I loved tack cleaning. I still have a pot of Neatsfoot oil on my windowsill because I love the smell of it.'

Okay, so maybe he wasn't completely sane, but his words were slightly sad, and I smiled again.

'You have that little bay mare?' he said.

I wasn't sure whether to be unnerved or impressed. One thing I did know was that he obviously knew more about horses than I was giving him credit for. 'Yes.' *How do you know?* The next words on my tongue, but Walter beat me to it.

'I've seen you riding past through the window,' he explained, and it didn't sound at all creepy. 'With a chestnut pony. That's a lovely little mare you've got there.'

'Yeah,' I said. 'Not quite as nice as the chestnut, though,' I added.

He shrugged. 'I dunno. The chestnut's nice, but I prefer the bay. Lovely looking pony,' he said again. 'She got Thoroughbred in her?' I nodded. He chuckled. 'You can tell.' Walter looked down at his hands, as though suddenly remembering where he was, and cleared his throat. 'Right, well, I won't keep you. Good luck this weekend. An event?'

'Yeah,' I said.

'All right. Have fun tack cleaning.'

'Yeah,' I said again, and then to prove I knew other words I said, 'I need to get this bit clean.' I held up the snaffle between my fingers, the silver rings covered in grease from the old bridle. It's one of Rose's, which she's never asked to have back since I started riding Ace, luckily for me because I only have one of my own, Jupiter's, and I'd hate to be swapping bits every day.

'Vinegar.'

'Pardon?' I said.

'Vinegar,' Walter repeated, almost shyly. 'Try polishing the bit with vinegar. That'll do the trick.'

When I went inside that evening, I asked Mum what she knew about Walter Morrigan, and the response was not much. He was widowed and rarely left the house. And now I couldn't shake the image of him all alone, living out his days inside when he used to be involved with horses in some way. Surely he was a jockey or an exercise rider, at his height? You can almost guarantee that any guy shorter than average in Newmarket has worked as one of the two at some point in his life, and I was sure Walter was no exception.

'You could ask Rose,' Mum said. 'She's lived here a while. I'm sure she knows most people in the village.'

My thoughts of yesterday evening, both of Walter and of Gabe, are interrupted by Ace, who hears the front door of Rose's farmhouse slam and takes great offence, leaping sideways into the air. Not long ago, a spook like that would have unnerved me if not unseated me, but now I think nothing of Ace's random freak-outs.

'No running, Jemima,' Rose shouts from the yard as her youngest daughter makes her way to the stables, and I scratch Ace's neck before continuing across the diagonal.

'There'll be plenty of kids running around events, Maggot,' I say. But she doesn't actually mind that, funnily enough. It's random noises that make her jump, and despite my attempts to desensitise the mare, she can still be a loose cannon. 'Quirky,' I say, carefully enunciating each syllable. 'That's the word we use.'

'It looked like she was walking well by the end,' Rose says to me when I ride Ace into the yard. My coach has a big hunter tied up outside his stable, an old saddle on his back. The horse belongs to an elderly gentleman in the area who's sent the gelding to Rose to be brought back into work and got fit for the hunting season, something he can't be bothered to do himself. I try to imagine only having to show up at events and never riding in between…

'Yeah, she was,' I say. 'She got scared of a jogger at first, but she settled, and she wasn't anticipating at all by the end.'

'I know, I saw.' *Of course you did.* 'You did well.'

'Thanks.' I swing off the mare's back and scratch her neck, which makes her pin her ears.

'Most stubborn creature alive,' Rose says with a smile, noticing Ace's disapproval.

I run up the stirrups and grin. 'I'm just going with *quirky* at the moment.'

Rose laughs. 'Yep, you're right. Quirky all the way.' She looks over her shoulder at the sound of footsteps, and I see Jemima walking circles with a book in her hands, reading as she moves. Rose shakes her head. 'She is Ben all over.'

'Is Mackenzie you, then?' I ask.

'Spitting image, unfortunately. Not that I tell her that, I'll never hear the end of it. What are you reading, Mima?' Rose calls

Unlike her sister, Jemima is a child of few words, and she holds up the book to show us the cover rather than responding, and I chirp up excitedly.

'I've read that!' I say, and my excitement is shadowed by surprise at someone Jemima's age being capable of reading such a tome. Then again, Gabe would have at that age, too. 'The author, W.J. Heathcote, lives next door to us!'

Jemima looks up from the book for the first time, and Rose's eyes go wide as she says, 'You're kidding!'

I shake my head. 'Nope.'

'In that red brick hall?'

'Yeah, that's him. Liam. My brother and I thought he was a bit weird at first, but he's actually really nice.'

'How amazing!' Rose says. 'Isn't that amazing, Jemima?'

Jemima looks at me, then at her mother, then down at her book, before turning on her heel and walking back towards the house.

'Did I say something wrong?' I ask.

Rose frowns. 'No, she's just like that. So rude,' she adds, and she calls after her daughter, but her voice goes ignored. 'Sorry about that.'

'It's fine,' I say, running my fingers down Ace's forehead. 'Speaking of neighbours, actually, I meant to ask you something.' Though I'm less optimistic now, seeing as Rose obviously hasn't crossed paths with Liam before, and probably doesn't know Walter, either.

She tightens the bored-looking hunter's girth. 'Yeah?'

'Yeah, do you know the person who lives next door to us? Walter Morrigan?'

Rose's face lights up. 'Of course I know Walter! One of the nicest people you'll ever meet.'

'I was chatting to him last night, and he seemed to know quite a bit about horses…'

'Should jolly well think so. He was a jockey way back when, though he didn't win anything big, but he's best known for pinhooking.'

'Pinhooking?' I repeat.

'It's when you buy a Thoroughbred at the sales for a small

amount - or, less than you think they're worth, anyway - and hold it until the next sale and sell it for a huge profit.'

'How does that work?'

'Well, sometimes you get lucky because maybe there's not that many people at the sale and you pick up a good horse for a ridiculous price. Or you buy a foal whose breeding isn't fashionable but you predict will be by the yearling sales next year. Make sense?'

'Uh, sort of,' I say. 'And Walter did that?'

Rose nods enthusiastically. 'He's done it for decades, but I best remember this one filly some five years ago. She was a chestnut filly foal from Ireland - bit of a late foal by an average stallion, scrawny little thing. Walter bid the minimum bit of eight-hundred guineas, chucked her in a field for ten months, then sold her as a yearling for two-hundred grand.'

'Two-hundred grand?' I repeat. 'How?'

'So the filly's dam had only had one runner by the time of the foal sales - this black filly - and she'd come third.'

'Okay…'

'…Which wasn't particularly impressive as results go. But, anyway, Walter had seen this black filly run her maiden race at the Rowley Mile, and he was convinced she was a future Group horse' - I don't know what a Group horse is, which is probably a criminal offence for somebody living in Newmarket, but I nod along - 'and so when he saw another foal out of the same dam, he jumped on it.'

'All right,' I say, thinking I understand this whole concept. 'And, so, he sold her as a yearling?'

'The black filly - Branedina, she's called - ran four times between him buying the chestnut filly and sending her to the yearling sales, and she won every start. Of course, that made any foal out of the same dam worth a small fortune.'

'Wow,' I say. I struggle to get interested in racing, even if I do live in a town that is famous for it, but there's something special about hearing horsey success stories. 'Does he still do that? Walter? Pinhooking.'

Rose frowns, then shakes her head. 'I don't think so. His wife died a couple of years ago, and I think he just lies low now. He's getting on a bit, I guess. Why do you ask?'

'Just curious, I guess.' I shrug. 'He'd seen me ride past on Ace before, and wanted to talk about horses... Just curious.'

'Well, he's lovely. I feel sorry for him, on his own, and I remember sending him flowers when Eileen passed, but I don't really know him enough to call by...' Her voice drifts off as we hear the farmhouse door slam again - which makes *Ace* jump again - and I follow the sound with my eyes to see Jemima running out of the house, a stack of hardback books in her arms. She mustn't do much running, because she's out of breath when she reaches us, but she looks giddy with excitement, and Rose must see this, too, because she doesn't even make a comment about the running, something she's usually very firm about.

'Can you ask Mr Heathcote to sign these, please,' Jemima says, possibly the most words she's ever said to me at once, as she holds out the first three books in *The Quest of Byron* series towards me.

'Uh, okay,' I say, as Ace snorts at the hardbacks, unsure of the shiny foil lettering on the covers.

'Why don't you put them in the tack room, Jem,' Rose says. 'Sybil can't hold them right now. If she doesn't mind, that is,' she adds.

'No, not at all. And Liam won't mind, either,' I say.

'I'll put them in the tack room, then,' Jemima says, staring at me intently. 'You won't forget?'

I shake my head. 'I won't forget.'

'And you'll ask him to address them to Jemima Leigh Victoria Holloway?'

'Don't go too far, Jemima,' Rose warns.

'I'll tell him,' I assure Jemima. 'Maybe you could just write that down so he gets it right?'

Jemima looks at her mum. 'Where can I find some pen and paper?'

'Check my bag in the tack room,' Rose says.

As quickly as she appeared, Jemima hurries off again, running to look for writing material.

'You don't have to do this for her,' Rose says once her daughter's out of earshot.

'Honestly, I don't mind and neither will Liam.'

'I can't believe that.' Rose shakes her head. 'She's obsessed with those books lately.'

'So's my brother,' I say, and I have a light-bulb moment. A girl a few years younger than him isn't exactly the friend I had in mind for Gabe, but maybe I have a solution to one of the issues on my mind…

'I can't find a pen,' Jemima calls, running back towards us with Rose's handbag in her hands. '

'There's one in there somewhere,' Rose says.

Jemima shakes her head, rummaging through the bag, and before Rose can take over, the bag has slipped from Jemima's hands and fallen to the ground, sending the contents flying. Ace jumps as a wallet skids towards her across the concrete, and Rose grumbles as Jemima lets out a small cry.

'Sorry, sorry,' Jemima shrieks, falling to her knees to put the items - including a blue biro, which has rolled a few paces away - back in the back.

Rose looks like she was about to snap, but the apology calms her. 'No, it's fine,' she says, holding up a hand with a sigh. 'It was an accident.'

I bend to retrieve the open wallet at my feet, and words escape me before I can help it. 'Was this your horse?'

The worn suede wallet had fallen open, its catch long broken, and in one of the card holders, protected by a piece of plastic, is a photograph of a grey horse. And as soon as the words escape my lips, I wish I could take them back, because I know, without being told, that this must be Rose's horse of a lifetime she parted with for a life-changing sum of money. Mackenzie told me about him, but Rose has never discussed the horse, and I'd never bring it up.

'Yeah.' Rose smiles sadly as I hand her back the wallet, our eyes lingering on the small photo of the grey horse and her flying over a trakehner. 'You know, we used to get sent proof photos through the post like this, before they were printed at events like they are now.'

I nod, still wishing I'd just handed the wallet back without saying anything. 'He's nice.'

'He is,' Rose says.

'Is he still alive?' I say, and immediately wish I hadn't spoken again, but Rose *did* say *is*...

'As far as I know. Last I heard, after he retired from top-level competition he moved to his owner's estate to be ridden out by her children, but I don't know. How old would he be?' She thinks a moment. 'Twenty-two, twenty-three? Something like that.'

My eyes dart to Jemima, oblivious of the tension as she scrawls her full name on a piece of paper, a receipt pressed against the ground as she writes on the back of it.

'He looks pretty special,' I say.

Rose smiles again, this one not quite as sad as the last, flushing with what I'm sure is pride as she looks down at the photograph. 'Yeah, he's pretty special.'

Wind whistles around us, and when Ace lifts her head to look out over the half door, it blows strands of haylage right from her mouth.

'You take too much in one go,' I say to her. She's a fussy eater, but she's also gluttonous when she likes what's on the menu.

Ignoring me - or as though she understands me and chooses to retaliate - the bay mare snatches another large mouthful from the pile of forage, and the wind once again whips away the strands that hang from the corner of her mouth.

'Told you.'

I stand to the side, staring at the plaits that run along Ace's mane. Plaiting still isn't my strong suit, but I think I'm somewhat improving. I'd already started Ace's mane when I realised I'd grabbed the wrong elastics from the grooming box, Jupiter's white ones and not the mare's black ones, but then decided I actually liked the white on black effect, and have done her whole mane with the different coloured elastics.

Ace lowers her head again, and I step around her chest to pull her rug forward. I bought the heavyweight cover for Jupiter the first winter I had him, but he's always been hot-bodied, and even clipped has never been able to take it. Ace is rarely hot, always a rug or two up from the other horses, and this one fits her perfectly. Rose was going to clip Ace for me a few days ago, the two of us fully prepared for a herculean task, but it turned out clipping is one thing Ace doesn't mind, and she patiently stood tied up as Rose worked the clippers over her body before handing them over to me. My lines aren't great, patchwork-like where I stopped at the top of her legs, but I still managed. Ace wasn't keen when the clippers got near her head, though, and even with the small ones we didn't risk going past her ears.

I slide my hand beneath the rug, satisfied Ace is warm enough. It's still only October, but a freeze has been predicted for tonight, and I'm already dreading being out here in the dark tomorrow morning.

Tomorrow. This time tomorrow, the event will be over. Ace and I will be home, either ecstatic and relieved, or devastated. Sink or swim.

'Which will it be, Maggot?' I ask.

She still pins her ears and threatens to bite for no particular reason many a time, but Ace is a lot more tolerant of me now than she is of most people. The odd moments she lets her guard down and shows affection still take me by surprise and make my heart swell.

'You're pretty special,' I say, smiling. 'I'm not sure why, but you are.'

And emotion bubbles in my chest as the mare turns her head, lowers her nose to my hands, and rests her weight against my chest, the two of us warm and safe as the wind rages on.

chapter 7

I wrap my hands around the thermos of milky tea and stare at the windscreen. A thin layer of frost covers the glass, and the noise of hot air blasting from the dashboard fills the car. It's still dark out, and the headlights eerily illuminate the steam on the inside of the windscreen.

'Iced over in October!' Mum keeps saying for no apparent reason.

We'd already locked the front door and trudged to the car when we saw the frosted glass, and decided to wait it out with the heating rather than go back inside for boiling water.

'You could use a CD case,' Gabe had said, and I'd snapped at him to climb out the car and do it, then, to which he responded that we were all out here because of *me*, which made it my job, and Mum told us both to be quiet, and we've been doing just that in the sixty seconds since. Well, except Frodo, whose panting is so loud I swear Ace can probably hear it all the way down the lane in her stable. Eleven went straight to the middle seat of the car, curled up in a ball, lowered her head, and fell asleep as though she'd never been woken in the first place.

Mum has insisted that Gabe come to my event today, which

neither of us is particularly pleased about. We're maybe eight minutes into the day and I hope she's already regretting her decision.

'It's dark so late now,' Mum says, voice light as though we weren't all in the freezing cold at the crack of dawn. 'Remember when daylight was at four?'

'Uh-huh,' Gabe and I mutter.

It's going to be a long day.

'Hey, Maggot,' I whisper as I slide the top bolt of the door across and kick the one at the bottom, holding both handles of her feed bucket in my right hand.

Being evil is hard when you're caught unaware, and even in this dusk Ace looks as innocent as a lamb as she steps towards the door. I put down the bucket in the straw and the mare lowers her nose to the feed, taking a mouthful before raising her head and threatening me with pinned ears. So much for my earlier thought.

'Sybil! Good luck today! Are you excited? I bet you're going to win. Good luck! Sorry, did I scare you?'

'No,' I lie, leaning forward to recover from the breaths that escaped me. My hand instinctively flew to my chest, and I lower it to my side. *Of course you didn't scare me. Who wouldn't start a hundred-word-per-minute conversation at five in the morning? In the dark, no less.*

'You sure?' Mackenzie says, her voice the loudest thing in Newmarket right now.

'Uh-huh. You're up early,' I say, my voice not nearly as awake as hers.

'I'm always up early.'

'Right.'

'Do you need a hand with anything?' Mackenzie chirps, following me to the car park. Mum is reversing her car towards the trailer, lining up the tow bar, and I unlock the tack locker to retrieve Ace's travel boots. Rose used them when she was competing the mare herself, and told me I could keep them indefinitely as they were too small for any of her horses, anyway.

'I think I'm all right,' I say. 'Thanks, though.'

'Oh. Okay.' Mackenzie goes silent, but it doesn't last long. 'How about Jupiter?' She claps her hands together. 'Shall I look after him for you? I'll muck him out for you.'

'You don't have to -'

'And I can groom him! Shall I groom him for you?'

Jupiter is on his mini winter holiday, and I haven't really been brushing mud off him, just letting it stay caked to his face and legs while swapping an outdoor rug for an indoor rug and vice versa, only casting my eyes over his feet and limbs for anything amiss. I'd tell Mackenzie this, that she needn't go to the hassle, but from the look on her face, *not* grooming the muddy grey would be a far greater hindrance than free rein to scrub away.

'Sure,' I say. 'If you like.'

She squeals as though I'm the one doing *her* a favour, and starts rattling on about something else until another voice interrupts.

'It's too early for this much chattiness, Kenzie,' Rose says, striding towards us from the house. 'Morning voices, morning voices.' She's riding today, but later on and a catch ride she's meeting at the event, and therefore will be driving along in her car a little later.

'I'm going to look after Jupiter!' Mackenzie tells her excitedly.

'You do that.' Rose stifles a yawn as Mum continues lining up her tow bar, and nudges my shoulder. 'Give her a hand, would you?'

I should've thought of that already, but I hurry to the trailer and help Mum manoeuvre the car until its tow bar is in line with the trailer, and watch through the car window as she lifts the handbrake, shuts off the ignition, and opens the door.

'Morning, all,' she says,

'Morning.' Rose covers her mouth with her hand as she stifles another yawn, then shakes her head as though trying to shake away sleep itself. 'Right, who else needs a coffee?'

The first person I see at the event is India. We only arrived a few minutes ago, and Mum sent me straight to collect my numbers and pay the starting fee before unloading Ace, while she promised to climb through the trailer side door with a bucket of water.

Only one person stands ahead of me, sliding a twenty pound note across the counter, and there's no denying it's India Humphries. Ariat waterproof coat, blond plait down her bag, jeans and walking boots. The secretary hands her a five pound note as change, and India politely thanks her before turning around, and her face morphs into a smile.

'Hey.'

'Hey,' I say back, stepping up to the secretary's desk. 'Two-nine-six,' I tell her, then look back at India. 'You're riding?' It might be a stupid question, considering she's just collected numbers and paid a starting fee, but it's not like she doesn't have sisters who ride, too, and could have sent her on a task.

'Sybil Dawson, Ace of Hearts?' the secretary confirms. I nod, and she runs a highlighter over my name on her entry sheets, then turns to find my number.

'Yeah,' India says, nodding as she replies to my question. 'I'm only riding my sister's pony, though. We don't usually compete past the beginning of October, but a few weeks ago Mia fell off Harvey in the 100 - he over-jumped this brush fence, taking all the brush as a fence, and she just couldn't stick it. Anyway, our trainer Merritt suggested she drop him back down to a 90 to finish the season, so we entered him here, but then last week Mia only goes and breaks her arm.'

'Oh no. How, riding?'

'Yeah, but it was her own stupid fault.' India scoffs. 'Well, actually, it was kind of mine, too. We were talking about puissances, and, like, I dunno, somehow we got into a debate over which one of us would win, and we ended up building up an upright in our school. I *told* Mia not to be so stupid as to try the one-forty on Harv, but did she listen?'

'Two-nine-six,' the secretary says, sliding a plastic bag over the desk. 'That'll be fifteen pounds.'

I hand the woman two tens, then return to India, wanting to know more. 'So, he refused the one-forty?'

'Oh, no, he jumped it all right. You've seen him jump, he's hard enough to stay on at the best of times. Mia had no hope.'

'Was someone else around with you?' I ask.

'Yeah, yeah, our mum was there,' India assures me. 'It was perfectly safe and all. Anyway, that's why.'

'Is she okay? Mia? Not scared or anything?'

'Mia?' India laughs. 'God, no. She doesn't really get scared. It would take a lot more than a broken arm. This is the third time she's broken something. No - fourth! All falling off.'

'Right.'

'Five pounds,' the secretary says, giving me my change, and I thank her.

'So now you're riding Harvey in the 90?' I clarify, as India and I turn away from the secretary's desk and make our way out of the tent.

'Yep. Mia was already entered, so we did a rider sub. Are you in the 90, too? Is Freya here?'

'Yeah,' I say, feeling less bad about this knowing that India is riding in the same class. 'Freya won the U18BE100 yesterday,' I say, remembering the excited message I got from my friend last night. She deserves it. 'Are you nervous?' I blurt. India speaks of falls and metre-forty fences and broken bones as though they were nothing, yet all of those things would terrify me. I always think she, and others in the same situation, succeed because they have the means, all the tools in the box and a foolproof instruction manual. I try to imagine myself in the same situation, with top unstoppable ponies and facilities and endless funds, and even then, if my life were like that, I can't imagine not still getting nervous or being afraid of galloping into an enormous jump. Money can't buy everything.

'Nervous?' India repeats. 'You mean because Mia fell off?' She shakes her head. 'No, that doesn't bother me. It's not like Harvey did anything wrong, and, besides, it's not like I haven't ridden him before. You get used to his huge leaps after a while.'

'No, I don't mean that,' I say as we step farther out of the tent and come face to face with the show jumping track. The fences are all under ninety centimetres. Tiny, really, but because I know I have to jump them, that shortly I'll be cantering Ace towards the coloured poles, they seem massive. 'I mean in general. Do you feel sick the day before? Can you not eat anything till it's over? Do you walk a course and get terrified by the size of the jumps?'

'I guess.' India frowns, as though the question had never occurred to her before now, then goes on. 'I used to. Not on Doris and Harvey so much, but when I started riding Otto and Fendi. I used to be terrified. I don't think I was scared of falling off so much as I was afraid of messing up. And I messed up a lot. Well, you know that whole situation with the ponies.' I nod, knowing the two FEI ponies had already been competing with India's sister Sophia, with whom they started refusing until they were consistently eliminated. 'So it's not like I had anything to lose. I mean, the ponies were already going badly, so it wasn't like it could get any worse.' I think of Freya, whose pony has an impeccable record, and belatedly realise, for the first time, how much more pressure she must be under than India. 'But I really *wanted* to succeed. I wanted to ride them well, and I wanted to compete, and I wanted to prove I could do it. And' - India laughs quietly, as though only just remembering what she's about to say - 'I used to cry *all* the time. Seriously. I can't believe it when I think about it now, but it's true. Every time something went wrong I just couldn't stop myself, and I kept going and everything, but I just couldn't stop myself from getting upset. And what I eventually realised was that *wanting* to do well didn't mean a thing. *Sophia* wanted to do well. We *all* want that. But there's a difference between wanting something and actually getting up and working for it. It's fine to cry and be upset, but it doesn't solve anything. Once I realised that, everything got better. When things went wrong, I didn't get upset, I just stopped and asked myself how to fix it. So I *do* still get nervous - I mean, if you're not nervous galloping into some massive trakehner, then there's something seriously wrong with you. I dunno.' India looks away, like she's just realised everything she's said. 'With mares and foals, things go wrong all the time, and you get used to it. Worrying doesn't solve anything. The only thing that makes a difference is *doing* something, and I guess I think of riding like that. Sure, sometimes I get upset and nervous, and I also want to do well, but none of those things means anything at the end of the day. It doesn't matter how much you *want* to get around a course, you're not going to if you just sit in the saddle and don't do anything. I'm sorry, I think I went off topic there.' She laughs. 'What was the question again?'

I shake my head and smile, swallowing past a lump in my throat. 'No, you answered it. You've done really well, by the way. With the ponies,' I clarify. Otto and Fendi look better every time I see them, and they don't always give India the smoothest of rides. No matter her situation, that her rides have been on European teams and she has everything she needs to succeed at her fingertips, she's worked for her results.

India smiles back at me, a close-lipped smile that reaches her eyes and looks equally pleased and shocked. 'Thanks. I don't think I've seen your new one yet. What time are you riding?'

I give India my ride times, the words *new one* whirling in my mind. That's something competitive riders would say to one another, when they have so many horses they have one they can refer to as *new*. I only have two, and Ace doesn't even belong to me, but the words make me feel a sense of belonging, like I'm part of a club.

'I'll try to get a look at her,' India says.

I scoff. 'There's not much to look at. I mean, she's great, I'm the one making her look bad.'

'No you're not!'

'I am, just you wait.' I laugh, and it feels good to laugh. Laughing, at an event. Even though I'm terrified. And laughing about my own lack of riding skills at that.

'Have you learned the show jumping course yet?' India asks, nodding at the ring.

'No. You?'

She shakes her head. 'Wanna walk it now?'

We jog around the course of jumps, walking every line exactly as we would ride it. I concentrate on the track, committing each fence to memory and picturing how I'll ride it with Ace, but I also chat with India and laugh and let myself think about other things. We'll be discussing the hell Mia gave the doctors when they told her she couldn't ride for weeks, India halfway through an impression of her sister as she paces the strides between two fences, only to break off and ask if it's a long five or a short six, and we'll debate it before moving on to the next fence and seamlessly continuing the earlier conversation.

'I'd better go check on Ace,' I say once we finish walking the course. I push up my coat sleeve to see my watch reads a quarter to eight. It's Sunday, most of the world still in bed, and we've already been up hours.

'Yeah, same. Hey, have you already walked the cross country?'

I shake my head. I'm supposed to walk it soon, once Rose arrives.

'I'm walking it with Alex in fifteen minutes. Evans,' she adds, as though there could be any question as to which Alex she's referring. 'Do you want to walk it with us?'

'Alex wouldn't mind?' I say.

'Course not. I'm only walking it with her because she says she needs company to walk around an Intro track without falling asleep.'

That sounds like Alex.

'Okay, sure,' I say. 'I'll have to check with my mum and Rose, though,' I add, remembering Rose has come to walk the course with me.

'All right. If you want to, meet us at the start in fifteen.'

chapter 8

I needn't have worried about going off to walk the course with Alex.

'What a brilliant idea!' Rose says when I reach the trailer and tell her the idea. She's hasn't been here long, and leans against the trailer to drink a cup of coffee from one of the many flasks Mum prepared this morning.

'Should I just memorise the course and walk it again with you?' I ask.

Rose shrugs. 'If you like, but I doubt you need me. Alex has been around Badminton and I haven't - if she offers you advice, I'd take it. She knows what she's doing.'

Alex isn't anywhere in sight when I reach the cross country start box, but India is. Her phone is pressed to her ear, and she's looking down at her boots as she speaks, moving from one foot to the other, stepping from side to side.

'Yep. I'm just walking cross country now. Okay.' She looks up and spots me, smiling before rolling her eyes. 'Yeah, look, I've got to go. I'm walking the course with Sybil and she's just arrived. Yeah, okay, see you later.' She hangs up and sighs. 'My mum.'

'She's not here?' I say.

'Not yet. She's coming with Mia later. Bree drove the lorry.' I presume Bree is a groom, but I don't ask. 'And Alex's timekeeping sucks.'

I nod slowly, then grin as a thought occurs to me. 'Would you still be walking the course with Alex now if your mum were here?'

India grins back and laughs quietly, answering my question. 'I know, right? I mean, in my mum's defence, Alex *has* been pretty rude to her and Sophia.'

'Take everything she says with a pinch of salt,' I recite.

India laughs again. 'Right?'

'Speaking of,' I say, nodding at a figure behind her shoulder.

'I have had the most disappointing morning you could ever imagine and it's barely even started yet,' Alex announces as she walks up to us.

'Is it Waffles's fault?' India asks, and I smile, because I was thinking the same thing.

'No, it's not, for once. Alert the bloody pope, because that's a miracle.' I feel silly for so much as thinking I might be intruding by joining this course walk, because Alex takes my presence for granted, speaking to India and me like old friends. 'Anyway, is anyone listening to my story?'

'Yes, you're having the worst morning humanly possible,' India says, spinning her hand in a clockwise direction as she speaks.

'Yeah, okay, so get this. I bit into what was supposed to be a peanut butter Kit Kat Chunky, and it turned out it was just a regular Kit Kat Chunky.' Alex pauses to let her words sink in.

'First world problem of all first world problems,' India says.

'*Yes,* thank you!'

'That wasn't a compliment.'

'I live in the first world, so your words confirm that it *is* the problem of all problems.' Alex frowns sadly. 'That's my whole day ruined.'

'Maybe you shouldn't be eating Kit Kats for breakfast,' India says.

'Well I haven't now, have I?' Alex cries. 'I was too disappointed to go on.'

I listen to them bicker back and forth, happy to witness the banter while also wishing I could contribute witty replies so easily. Alex and India are both extremes of the eventing scale - Alex isn't rich, but she comes from riding royalty, while India has holiday houses and staff. I have no idea where I fit in.

'Don't you like regular Kit Kats?' I ask.

'Oh, no, I do,' Alex says, zipping up her waistcoat as she speaks. 'I mean, how can you not? But I *don't* like them when I think I'm biting into a peanut butter one. Make sense?'

'Yes,' I say, at the same time as India says, 'No.'

'At least *someone* has my back.' Alex crosses her arms and looks from left to right. 'So are we walking this thing or what?'

The air is crisp and the sun is shining. Dew covers most of the grass we walk across, and frost the areas that are in the shade. I was worried about walking a course without Rose, that I'm not capable of assessing the jumps for myself, because I hardly expect Alex to give me instructions when she has no idea how I ride or how my horse goes, but she voices her own thoughts, anyway. And even though she spends most of the time we're walking talking about things that have nothing to do with the course, she still looks at each jump and walks every line with professionalism.

'Two strides if you go straight on the angle, three on the curving line,' Alex says, pacing out the distance between the first combination. 'I prefer the curving line, but if you have any doubts about turning, go straight.'

I stare at the two jumps, trying to decide which option is best for Ace. I've never had a problem turning her cross country schooling, and tackling the second element on an angle looks daring, so it makes sense to jump it on a curving line.

Alex's phone starts ringing, and as she fumbles to answer it, I turn to India.

'Which one are you doing?'

'Straight,' India says without hesitation. 'Harvey's dead straight, and it'll be easier than trying to turn him.'

'Hello?' Alex says into the phone. 'Oh, yes, hi.' Her voice sounds older than it does when she speaks normally, and I get the feeling the phone call is business-related as we start walking to the next fence. 'Yes, I know, I'm sorry, I was competing all day yesterday, and then I left for another event early this morning and I'm just walking a course now. Right, yes, well I've been thinking about it, and I'm afraid my offer is still the same. Eleven hundred cash, but I can't go a penny more.'

We pass a pheasant feeder, our next numbered fence, and Alex barely glances at it as she continues her phone call.

'Look, you know as well as I do that his back's not right, and I'm going to have to pay a few hundred quid in osteo sessions right off the bat, which is going to come to more than your asking price, so from my perspective, I really can't go any higher. I shouldn't be going for him *at all*, if I'm completely honest, but I trust you, and I do like him.' A pause. 'I know, he's a nice-looking horse. Look, at the end of the day, I've shown you my hand, my cards are on the table. I know you want a good home, and you know that with us he's going to get the help he needs.' Another pause, and Alex stops walking to look at India and me, her eyebrows raised and a slightly smug expression on her face that turns to a smile. 'Great, that's super. All right, thank you. Look, I've got to go, but I'll text you later with a time. Tomorrow's still okay to pick him up, yeah? Great, thank you. Okay, see you tomorrow. Bye.' Alex hangs up the phone and smiles triumphantly. 'And *that* is how you buy a horse.'

'What kind of horse?' I ask.

'An ex-racer straight outta training. I saw it online, and I don't normally get them right out of racing yards, only because I don't have the time or money, but I *really* liked it.'

'What's wrong with its back?' says India.

'Huh? Oh, not much. Bad fitting tack, tiny bit stiff, nothing one osteo session and working correctly won't fix.'

'You should be in business or something,' India says, shaking her head.

'Too boring,' Alex says. 'But horse buying? That's my element. Oh,' she adds with a big smile, 'I'm excited now!'

'Does this make up for the Kit Kat?' India says jokingly.

'Not quite, but it helps.'

'What's he like?' I ask. When I think of how hard it was for me to acquire Jupiter and Ace, the struggle to obtain a horse, it's hard to get my head around somebody buying one so casually. And referring to said horse as an *it*.

'Five-year-old gelding, dark brown - almost black. I need a name for him now.'

'What's his racing name?' says India.

'Something stupid I can't pronounce,' Alex mutters as her eyes lock on a figure in the distance. 'Oh, hey, look, it's Leni. LENI!' she shouts.

Leni turns her head at the sound of Alex's voice, veering from her trajectory towards the last fence, and starts walking over. Her dressage must be any minute, because she's in her jodhpurs and jacket, newly-polished black boots reaching her knees, and even has her hat on with the strap undone.

'What is it?' Leni says, then to me and India she adds, 'Hello,' with her usual warm smile.

'What do you mean *what is it?*' says Alex. 'I was just calling you over to say hi.'

'You've already said hi to me today. In the lorry park, you moaned to me about your Kit Kat.'

'She's still upset about that,' India chimes in.

'Don't tell me you bored them with the Kit Kat story too?'

'I never *bore* anyone.'

'Uh-huh.' Leni smiles, then her expression turns more serious. 'Did you actually want to ask me something, because I need to get to the dressage warm-up in ten.'

'Nah, just saying hi.'

Leni rolls her eyes. 'You're impossible.' She looks at me and India and grins. 'Good luck.' And I know she isn't referring to the event.

'Nice to see you, too,' Alex shouts behind her as Leni jogs off to finish her course walk. 'Oh, wait, I did have something to tell you. I just bought a horse!'

'You buy horses all the time!' Leni yells back as her figure jogs towards the last fence.

'Right.' Alex turns back to India and me. 'Where we were?'

'Heading to eleven,' India says, pointing at an upcoming coffin fence.

'What about number ten?' I say quickly, looking back at the fence we passed while Alex was on the phone.

Alex follows my gaze. 'What about it?'

I've listened to Alex's comments for every fence up to now, and feel worried about not getting her input for even a single one. Will I ever feel capable of walking a course on my own? I can't imagine ever being that confident in my own ability. 'What should we do?' I ask lamely.

Alex keeps her eyes on the distant fence for a few seconds before turning her focus back to me. 'Jump it.'

India snorts, and a bubble of laughter escapes me.

'Does that help?' Alex says.

'Is it that easy?' I say.

'A let-up fence like that?' Alex looks over her shoulder again. 'Yeah, it is.'

'It's huge.'

Alex shakes her head. 'That doesn't mean anything. Don't look at size when you walk a course like this. Think of it as though there's a shield over your mind stopping you from taking in the size. At least, that's what I do. When I walk up to a fence, I stop myself from really taking in the size. But seriously,' she goes on, 'that fence is straightforward. A horse could trot over that. A *pony* could trot over that. Heck, I'm pretty sure *I* could jump it if I had a run-up. Okay?'

'Okay,' I repeat.

'Hey,' India says, 'speaking of ponies, did either of you see that video of that Shetland that's been going around? Show jumping?'

'Yes!' I say, sure I know which one she means. 'The jump-off round?'

'Yeah, that's it!'

'Wait, what video's this?' Alex says.

'I'll show you,' India says, pulling her phone from her pocket as we walk towards the next fence, which is still a way away. 'So it's this video of some tiny kid on a even tinier pony in a jump-off, and it's insane.'

We all stop as India passes her phone to Alex, and watch as a little pony comes onto the screen, its ant-sized rider posting in the saddle, a look of determination on her face. The start bell rings, and the two zoom off at a full out gallop towards the first fence. The obstacles aren't exactly huge, but big enough for a pony that size. The rider's arms and legs flap between every fence, and she turns the pony on a sixpence, taking the shortest of lines.

'Oh my god,' Alex says. 'I want one. The pony, that is, not the kid. Though saying that, the kid could exercise the horses for me. Huh. Tempting. Do you think it would sleep in a stable?'

'I hope you never have kids, for their sake,' India says as she slides her phone back into her pocket.

'I don't plan on it,' Alex says happily. 'And if I did, I plan on keeping them away from horses at all costs.'

'Or you could train them and have your own personal team of riders to keep your horses fit,' India jokes.

'Hey, I never thought of that.' Alex looks much too thoughtful as she takes in the idea. 'Actually, that's a good idea. That video's good, anyway. Almost as good as the baby monkey backwards on a pig, but, I mean, nothing's better than that. Right, so which one are we again?' she says as we come up to the next fence.

'On the right,' I say, nodding at the smallest jump in a line of three numbered *11s*, each labeled in a different colour.

'Right,' Alex says, looking disappointed. 'The tiny boring one.'

'Let me guess,' India says. 'Jump it?'

Alex nods. 'Jump it.'

I lift the saddle onto Ace's back and pull up the saddle cloth beneath the pommel so it doesn't rub her withers. The bay mare is being quite agreeable - at least, she is for her - and I hold on to the idea, trying to use it to calm my nerves. No pinned ears and lunging open-mouthed, or kicking out with a back leg. What more could I ask of her?

'You're the best, really,' I tell Ace.

Mum and Rose went to get hot coffees, already through Mum's flasks, and the promise of a bacon-and-egg muffin was enough to get Gabe out of the car, taking the dogs with him.

When I reach for the girth and straighten up, I'm met with a sharp nip to my side, but when I yelp and turn to look at Ace, she's looking the other way, the picture of innocence.

'Little Maggot,' I say. So much for my earlier thought.

'Hey, feeling prepared?'

I spin around from buckling Ace's girth to see Alex standing with her hands wrapped around a paper cup. She's changed clothes since our course walk, now in her off-white breeches and navy jacket. Her first dressage start time is almost the same as mine, so no doubt she's about to jump on a horse. I wonder if she even has to tack up, or whether a groom does it all for her. Probably the latter.

I shrug. 'I guess.'

Alex waves. 'Nah, you'll be fine.' She takes a step closer to Ace and me, only to stop short. 'Can I redo your plaits? Wait, what's the time?' She pulls her phone from her pocket and nods. 'Yeah, I have a few minutes.'

I don't have time to register Alex's insult of my plaiting skills as she shoves her hot chocolate into my hand and pulls a comb and a bag of black elastic bands from my grooming box. Ace turns a threatening head towards this new person, ears pinned back, but Alex ignores her, not the least bit fazed by the mare's behaviour, and Ace responds by dropping the act. I gape at the pony, now standing perfectly still for Alex and even turning her nose towards her with affection, as though I've just been betrayed by an ally. *Who feeds you?* I think. *Who's the one taking care of you? Me!*

'She likes you,' I say.

Alex inclines her head towards the mare, fingers still undoing my plaits, and smiles at her. 'She's sweet.'

Sweet. Ace. I love her, but those aren't two words I'd ever put together.

'Your plaits aren't terrible,' Alex says after undoing a couple of them, reminding me what she's doing. She speaks casually, like there's no reason for me to take offence at her being so horrified by my handiwork that she felt compelled to take matters into her own hands. 'But white elastics on a black mane should be a criminal offence. It's tacky. And you'd be better off not doing so many. There's nothing worse than seeing a horse with, like, twenty plaits in a dressage test. No.' She shakes her head. 'Nine to fourteen including forelock, no more. That's my rule. Loads of plaits is even worse than white bands on a black or chestnut mane.'

'Okay. Are you sure you have enough time?' I ask.

'Oh, yeah. It'll take me five minutes tops.'

It definitely didn't take me five minutes to plait Ace's mane last night, but Alex has it looking amazing in that little time, and I'm immediately grateful. Seeing the difference, the even plaits more widely spaced apart, accentuating the bay mare's top line, makes me realise just how awful mine were.

'Thank you so much,' I say, still staring at Ace, at how good she looks.

Alex shrugs. 'It would've driven me crazy if I hadn't. I hate looking at badly plaited manes. My god, the other day I saw someone in a dressage warm-up with a talon plait. Talon plait,' she repeats for emphasis. 'This is British Eventing, not a circus or a Pony Club rally. Ugh.' She shudders at the thought. 'Anyway, good luck, I need to go tack up. See you. Break a leg. Or, you know, don't.'

I'm fastening my hat when another voice speaks behind me, but this one is much more unexpected than Alex's.

'There's my favourite rider!'

Sticking out like a painfully sore thumb, Dad stands by the trailer, a smile on his face. Hay would stick to the jumper he wears like glue, and I'd be surprised if his feet weren't already soaked through his loafers.

'What are you doing here?' I say as he walks up to me and squeezes my shoulders to plant a kiss on my hat.

'What does it look like? Watching my daughter ride! And meeting the famous Maggot.' He nods at Ace. 'Is this the devil pony itself?'

'Yeah,' I mutter. 'She'll try to bite you,' I add quickly as Dad strides up to her, but I'm not quick enough because Dad has already stretched out a hand to touch the mare's face. I expect a sudden lurch - first from Ace as she tries to sink her teeth into my dad, and then Dad himself as he jumps backwards to escape said teeth - but Ace's ears remain pricked as she allows Dad to stroke her, and she even tries to step closer to him.

Thanks a lot, Maggot.

'She seems all right to me,' Dad says.

'Fluke,' I say.

He grins. 'Or maybe she likes me?'

I can't think of a reply to that, so I turn to my attention back to the tack locker to search for my gloves. 'Does Mum know you're here?' I say finally.

'What?' At first I wonder whether Dad didn't hear me, but then he lets out a single chuckle, and it's not because he thinks something's funny. 'Of course she knows, Sybil. I wouldn't show up without checking first - and I wouldn't know where you were riding, either, would I?'

'O-kay,' I say, wishing he'd just go away. How am I supposed to focus on today with him here? 'Why did you come, then?'

'Because I want to see you ride,' he says.

I shrug. 'You could watch me at Rose's.'

'I wanted to see you compete…' Dad's voice tails off, and he shakes his head. 'What's wrong, you don't want me here?'

'I just didn't know you were coming,' I say. 'And Mum's here-'

'Your mother and I are perfectly capable of being around one another,' Dad says. 'We're still friends, and we still want to do things with you and Gabe together.'

'Could've fooled me,' I mutter under my breath, and before either of us can go on, we're interrupted by another voice.

'Dad!'

'Hey, bud,' Dad says as Gabe hurries over to him, the dogs at his heels.

'What are you doing here?'

'Cheering on your sister,' he says.

Behind Gabe, Mum and Rose are walking with paper cups, both of them with windswept ponytails and muddy boots.

'Did you know Dad was coming?' Gabe asks Mum.

She nods. 'Why do you think I made you come?'

'Why didn't you say anything?' I ask, but my voice has much

more of a bitter edge to it than Gabe's did a moment ago.

'It was a surprise,' Mum says.

'I'm the one who asked Mum to keep it a secret,' Dad says, and I know the explanation is more for my benefit than Gabe's.

'Can I show you this new book I got on quantum physics?' Gabe says. 'I brought it with me.'

'Can we do that later? Sybil looks like she's about to ride.'

'It's fine,' I say, 'I don't mind.'

'Don't be silly, I've come all this way to see you ride.'

'Well, nobody asked you to,' I snap.

There's an awkward silence, and from the corner of my eye I register Mum's gritted teeth and angry expression. Behind her, Rose coughs and steps forward with an outstretched hand.

'I'm Rose,' she introduces herself. 'It's so nice to finally meet you.'

'Lewis. Likewise.' Dad shakes Rose's hand, the two of them trying to shake away the awkward moment with the greeting. 'Sybil talks about you non-stop, it's great to finally put a face to a name.'

'Same to you. Do you need a hand with anything, Sybil?' Rose asks me, and I shake my head.

'I'm ready.'

'On you get, then,' Mum says, and I can't tell from her tone whether she's still angry, or just as keen to get past this uncomfortable moment as the rest of us.

'Here, I'll leg you up,' Rose says, putting her coffee down on one of the trailer wheel fenders.

I remove Ace's head collar, which is over her bridle, and turn her away from the car. The grass is already marked with tyre tracks, and I try to avoid the worst of the mud for the sake of my newly-polished boots.

Ace halts a safe distance away from the trailer, and I pull down my stirrups before shortening my reins.

'Hey,' Rose says quietly, coming up beside me. I wonder for a moment whether I'm about to get a lecture, the sort I'd expect from Mum, but Rose's face is kind. Mum and Dad are engaged in a conversation by the car, with Gabe, and I doubt they can hear what Rose is saying. 'Just focus on Maggot, okay? Ride for you two, not anybody else.'

I swallow past a lump in my throat, and nod.

'I used to hate my family coming to watch me ride,' Rose goes on, 'because I'd think I had to do well to impress them. Know what I mean?'

I nod again.

'But you know what's good to remember? Non-horsey family members can barely tell one end of a horse from the other, let alone the difference between a medium and an extended trot…'

The warm-up is busy when I ride Ace past a steward holding a clipboard, but it's less intimidating than others I've been in. Being the end of the season, a lot of the professionals have already turned their horses out for their holidays, having completed a larger event at the beginning of the month or the end of last. The World Young Horse Championships are this weekend, and Blenheim and Burghley have passed, all of which will have been top riders' goals. You get used to warming up a pony in the same ring as an Olympic rider on a young horse, and it's different to ride amongst competitors in the same boat as myself. There will still be a few good riders here, like Alex and Rose, with inexperienced horses, but the venue is noticeably in want of them, and I feel more comfortable than usual.

Rose is trailing behind with Gabe and our parents, and I ride Ace to the farthest end of the warm-up after checking my ring number with a steward, where I can forget about Dad watching. I try to forget that he's here altogether, but the thought keeps creeping through, along with annoyance. Why did he have to show up now? Why couldn't he or Mum have at least asked me first? I have enough to worry about without the added pressure of him coming all the way here just to watch me. And he'll probably be watching me fail, if my and Ace's track record is anything to go by.

While Ace walks on a long rein, I look around at the other horses, which relaxes me slightly. If there are twenty of us in the warm-up, I feel confident that Ace and I look better than at least half of them.

But definitely not that combination, I think sadly as India trots past me on her sister's pony Harvey. The dun looks every bit the dream event pony as he moves effortlessly around the warm-up, his rider more than up to the challenge. India wears white breeches and a navy blue jacket so smart that I look down at my own tweed one with a critical eye. Catherine and Sophia Humphries are standing by a steward, near the three individual rings, as is Mia with a cast poking out from beneath her coat, her good hand holding the lead of a cocker spaniel.

'Four-three-four you're up in three minutes,' the steward calls, and I glance at India's number bib to see that she is the rider in question.

India nods to show she heard, and touches Harvey into a canter with such ease that I don't even notice her aids. The dun has a short, bouncy stride, each one rounder and slower than the last, and India steers him onto a twenty-metre circle before coming back to trot and turning down an imaginary centre line. She's in her own world, focussed only on the pony beneath and not the people around, and doesn't notice me even as I'm straight ahead of her. Harvey comes to a square halt, India sitting tall in the saddle, and I can't help the pang I feel in my chest at how good they both look, how professional. India gives the pony a quick pat on the neck, and he lowers his head, mouthing the bit. He's clearly just been clipped, which accentuates his well-muscled frame and makes his white blaze look that much whiter before it reaches the pink of his nose. I wish Ace would have let Rose and me clip her head, but she flat-out refused, and Rose decided it was safer to not attempt it than start and be left unable to finish and with a random line down the front of the mare's head.

Mia hurries over to the dun pony to remove his brushing boots while he's halted, and she says something to India I don't hear, but it makes them both laugh.

'Four-three-four,' the steward calls again.

India pushes Harvey back into an impulsive trot as Mia jumps out of the way, yells the word, 'Coming!' and turns towards the ring. Although we're in the same class, India and I are not in the same section, probably due to her and her pony being far more qualified than Ace and me, and I'm very glad of it. I probably don't stand a chance at placing as it is, but in a section of Indias and Harveys, there'd be no point even trying.

There are mumbles of good luck from India's family as she rides towards her ring, dropping her schooling whip to the ground on the way, which Mia hurries forward to collect, but they don't look too worried. I watch them, huddled together to watch, Sophia lifting a camera to her face, and wonder what it would be like to have your whole family involved in horses. India's dad isn't often at events, but he is occasionally, and as he runs a Thoroughbred breeding stud, he obviously knows a fair bit about horses, to say the least.

No matter how many times I tell myself that India is a good rider and that she works to be good, that she gets out of bed every day just like the rest of us, it's impossible not to linger on her expensive tack, and her quality ponies, and her support system.

'Suck it up,' I mutter to myself, watching Harvey trot perfectly down the centre line, head straight and hocks engaged. That's all I can do: suck it up, focus on Ace, and keep practising.

For the next half hour, I work Ace in, practising individual movements of the test, working on getting her between my hand and leg and listening to my aids. When Alex rides into the warm-up on a stunning grey Connemara, I barely glance up, too focussed on my own pony. When something goes wrong, I don't doubt myself, or get upset or angry. I do the movement again, remembering the aids, focussed on what I'm doing. Ace is rideable, and my being calm only helps her remain so, too.

'Two-nine-six, you're next,' the steward calls.

'You both look fantastic,' Rose says to me before I go to the ring. 'Keep riding like that.'

The horse finishing his test in our ring now is a bay with plaits almost as bad as the ones Ace was sporting before Alex showed up. His quarters are angular, neck absent of any top line, and I feel proud of my pony in a way I never usually think to. We might mess up and not have as much experience or funds as other people here, but I *am* confident in Ace's condition, and that's something to be proud of. I think of how fussy she is, how Rose immediately set about sourcing haylage and a high-quality fattening feed when the mare first arrived, how her coat shines with good health and feeding, how she's lean and strong but not ribby and skinny like the horse in the ring now. Riding badly and making mistakes is one thing, but riding an underfed and unfit horse is another. If I can't be confident in my own riding, I can at least be confident in Ace's condition, and that puts me at ease.

As the bay horse leaves the ring, the judge presses the car horn, and I push Ace into a trot, taking her near the white boards so that she gets a good look at them now before going in the ring.

Relax and keep riding.

The mare is soft in the mouth, her neck arching into my hand, her back supple beneath me, hocks bending to step under herself and overtrack. Before we turn into the ring, I push my right hand forward, touching her neck in front of the withers, a silent reassurance. Ace flickers an ear, listening to me, and I feel like we're truly working as a team.

We turn down the centre line, towards C, and put in our best test to date.

chapter 9

'Ready?'

I straighten up from fastening Ace's tendon boot, and nod.

'Okay. Need a leg-up?' Rose says, grabbing Ace's reins with one hand and holding out the other to help hoist me into the saddle. Ace sidesteps, but not before I find my balance in the seat, and I assure Rose I'm fine as she releases her hold on the reins.

'Good girl,' I say to Ace, patting her neck.

'We'll meet you down there,' Rose says, taking a step backwards, towards my parents, and I nod again to let her know I heard.

The horse walk to the show jumping ring takes me right past Alex's lorry, and I admire the horses tied to the Iveco's side as Ace strolls past it. They may just be Connemara ponies, not the flashy international eventers that usually grace the lorry with their presence, but they're every bit as smart. Both ponies are grey, one lighter than the other, and stand at fourteen-two. The lighter one has a cooler over its back as it pulls at a haynet, while the darker one is tacked up, a groom shortening his noseband on this side, and it isn't until she moves out of the way that I spot Alex on the other, tucking a strap into its keepers.

'Hey,' she calls to me. 'How did it go?'

'Really good,' I beam. 'The judge smiled at me at the end, so I think they liked her.'

'Great. You heading to show jumping?'

I squeeze Ace to a halt. 'Yeah.'

'Can you wait for me one sec?'

I nod. 'Sure.'

Alex turns the dark grey pony away from the lorry and pulls down his stirrups. 'Can you give me a leg-up, Poll?' she asks of the girl helping her, and I can't refrain from making a comment.

'Couldn't you hop on him from the ground?' I say. I need a leg-up to get on Ace, but Alex has got to be only inches from six-foot tall.

'I *could*,' Alex says once she's in the saddle, 'but I've had these jodhpurs since I was fourteen and they're one wrong step away from ripping.'

'Why are you wearing them?' I ask as she bends down to tighten her girth. She's riding in a close-contact saddle, and has to bend so far down she could probably touch the ground if she wanted to.

'Because I went through four pairs competing this week and didn't get any washing done last night. I mean, these are a bit tight but they're fine so long as I don't bend, and I always keep them in the lorry in case I need them. Anyway.' Alex straightens up, girth tightened a hole, and shortens her reins. The grey ducks his head immediately, mouthing the bit, and Alex sits as straight as though she were about to ride down the centre line at Badminton. Even though she's too tall for the pony, she doesn't actually look *wrong* on him. For one thing, the Connemara could easily take close to double Alex's weight, because she doesn't exactly have any to spare. I wouldn't ever think to call her skinny because she's so muscly that one look at her would probably stop even a boxer from picking a fight, but she's certainly lean. And the pony has a sloping shoulder and wide chest that take Alex's height easily.

'He's cute,' I say, nodding at the dark grey.

Alex snorts. 'Nappy shit is what he is. Why do you think I asked you to wait? I couldn't get him to leave the lorry earlier until someone else rode past and I followed them to the dressage warm-up. He's fine once he's in a ring or on course, it's just *getting* him there.'

I look at the grey pony, his ears pricked forward, expression innocent as though he weren't capable of misbehaving, and lift a shoulder. 'At least he looks nice.'

'I know.' Alex squeezes her legs against the grey's sides, but he's rooted to the spot, and it isn't until I push Ace forward that he walks a step. 'You know, I think I'm going to start picking the ugly ones. I mean, surely a horse can't be ugly *and* difficult?' She clicks her tongue at the pony as he slows again at the realisation that he's leaving the lorry. 'Roger, c'mon.'

I can't help the laugh that escapes me. 'Roger?'

'See, I have a rule when it comes to naming horses. The more badly-behaved they are, the stupider the name I give them. That went for Waffles, too, in case you were wondering.' She touches Roger's neck. 'This one got off lightly - the one back at the truck is called Edwin.'

I smile. 'Well,' I say, nodding down at Ace, 'her nicknames's Maggot, so I can't say anything.'

'Maggot?' Alex repeats. 'Oh, that's a good one. I'll have to use that for the next one.'

When we reach the muddy warm-up, India is already cantering Harvey around the perimeter, standing in a two-point position. The dun has swapped his dressage saddle for an equally expensive jumping one, and a blingy numnah. There are only a few other horses in the warm-up, but the stewards standing by the whiteboard don't look overly concerned by the lack of combinations, and there isn't even a horse in the ring.

'Indiana, do you want to go next?' a steward calls.

'I need two minutes,' India calls back, cantering Harvey down the long side and sitting in the saddle before the turn. She eyes up the shabby red-and-white oxer in the middle of the ring, Harvey's ears locking on to it, and canters towards it on a stride that is both increasing and collected. I feel slightly ill at the leap Harvey makes over the fence, adding half a metre to the ninety-centimetre jump for good measure, and I even hear Alex make a vomiting sound.

'I bet you need guts to ride that,' she says.

I glance at her. 'You wouldn't?'

'You kidding? It looks awesome' - the way she says it, Harvey is the *it* - 'but I like horses that are nuts. What's the fun in a sane one?'

I beg to differ, I think as Ace shies at a toddler in a yellow raincoat on the outside of the warm-up.

India turns Harvey back to the same fence, turning on a tighter line so that he only has two strides to reach the fence, and he clears it with his usual exuberance. The gelding tucks his nose to his chest, the muscles in his neck bulging, and as India pushes a hand forward to pat him, she looks across the ring at the gate steward and nods decisively.

'Four-three-four,' the steward says aloud as she wipes India's number off the whiteboard.

Catherine, Sophia, and Mia stand near the gate as India trots Harvey past them without so much as a backward glance, and once in the ring she halts the dun pony, nods at the commentators' box, and pushes him into a balanced canter, keeping the gelding on a ten-metre circle.

'Now in the ring we have number 434 Indiana Humphries riding Mrs Catherine Humphries's Mendip Breeze.'

The start bell rings, and I halt Ace by the rope to watch India's round, to remind myself of the course.

'Have you walked the course?' Alex asks, riding up beside me on Roger.

'Yeah.'

'I haven't.'

The first fence is a blue-and-white oxer jumped from the left rein. India circles Harvey in the right half of the ring, gathering him, before turning to the obstacle. She sits in the saddle down the long side, hugging the rails before making a curving line to the fence. Harvey rocks back on his hindquarters and launches into the air with his usual dramatics, but India is at ease, following his movement and staying balanced in the saddle. They continue on the left lead to make the turn to the second fence, another parallel, and India sits up on landing without wasting a beat, driving Harvey with her legs. It's the line we discussed while walking the course, the long five or short six between fences two and three, and it's clear that India is committed to five. She pushes the pony on, all while maintaining a stride that is bouncy and full of impulsion, and they make the five strides look effortlessly.

'Yeah,' Alex says, 'I really love this pony.'

'He's pretty cool,' I say. 'Not sure I'd ride him, though.'

I glance over at Alex, but her eyes are only on the dun pony cantering around the ring. There's a mischievous, longing smile on her face. 'I would.'

India is approaching the combination now, having jumped the fourth fence, and Harvey is fighting her. He's pulling against the bit, revving to go, and even with a Pelham India is struggling to hold him. Something I've learned over the past months with Rose is that there's a big difference between pulling and holding, between interfering with a horse's stride and collecting it. The same way there's a difference between galloping flat-out into a fence and increasing a stride to get there. Harvey is taking off, ignoring his rider's instructions, wanting to drag them in to the fence, and India is trying to hold him together, to contain his stride.

And India doesn't back down.

Three strides from the fence she gives Harvey a strong check with one rein, a quick command, and releases again, making sure he can still move to the fence. She did the right thing - at least, it looks like she did to me - but the damage was already done, and Harvey gets careless as he takes off too close to the base of the jump. I've seen enough of his talent to know that he's more than capable of clearing the fence without rattling a rail, but he chooses not to, instead hitting the top pole with his forelegs and sending it falling to the ground.

'Oh for-'

I glance over my right shoulder, as Catherine Humphries loudly shows her discontent, then back at India in time to see her gather Harvey for the one-stride distance and clear the second upright with ease.

'Bloody woman,' Alex says of India's mother.

India isn't going to make the same mistake twice, and she keeps Harvey collected for the remainder of the course, never letting him take off or get away, gathering impulsion to clear the fences with plenty of height to spare.

'Just the four faults for Indiana Humphries and Mendip Breeze to add to their dressage score going into today's cross country.'

'Unlucky,' I say to Alex as India lets her reins out and pats the pony's neck.

'Yeah,' Alex agrees. 'Not the easiest ride. I'd still get on him in a heartbeat, though. Well, I would if I weren't five-ten.'

Harvey can't be more than an inch or two smaller than the grey Alex sits astride, and I frown at the comment, but she's oblivious.

Mia Humphries hands the dog lead to Sophia and hurries over to India, pulling a packet of Polos from her pocket for Harvey, and I notice Catherine cross her arms near the gate beside me, a sour expression on her face.

'Since when does Harvey have rails?' she huffs. 'You should've steadied him sooner.'

'Well, I didn't,' India snaps.

I wait for her mum to say something back, the way my mum would to me, but no scolding comes, and as I glance at Catherine's face again, I wonder if she's too disappointed herself to care. What is with these event mums? I know I wish my own parents were more involved sometimes, or that Mum had more time to spend with the horses, but if the reality of that were a competitive parent who cared about winning more than I did, than I think I'd stick with what I have.

'Right, I'd better start warming up,' Alex says to me. 'Besides,' she goes on quietly, nodding at Catherine, 'that woman can't stand me, and I'm bound to say something to get myself in trouble if I'm around her.' And with that she clicks her tongue and pushes Roger off into a trot. A perfect, collected, impulsive trot, I daresay.

Ace snorts as a spirited puppy scurries past her, on the other side of the rope, dragging with it a hopeless-looking kid, and I lay a hand on her neck in reassurance.

'Come on, then,' I say. 'Let's start warming up.'

I turn her away from the rope, just as India starts riding towards me, back towards the horse walk that leads to the lorry park.

'Well done,' I say. 'That rail was really unlucky.'

She shrugs. 'Yeah, I probably could've prevented it, but woulda coulda shoulda.'

Mia walks up beside her sister, leading the same cocker spaniel she was earlier, and I glance behind her to see Catherine and Sophia engaged in a conversation with a couple of other people whose faces I recognise but couldn't name.

'Five strides, though,' I say to India, aware of how intently Mia watches me as I speak. I look down at her quickly, the way you do when you sense somebody watching you, expecting her to look away just as quickly, but she just flashes me a big, warm smile, so I smile back.

Ace pulls the reins from my hands, lowering her nose to the cocker spaniel, and before India can reply to my earlier remark, Mia says, 'No, Troi, come here,' to the dog, pulling the lead back towards her. 'She won't bite or anything,' she assures me, bending down to hold on to the roan spaniel's collar.

'That's all right,' I say. If only I could say the same about my horse. I look back at India. 'Yeah, the five strides looked good.'

India grins. 'Five strides all the way.'

'Our next starter is Miss Sybil Dawson, and she rides Mrs Rose Holloway's Ace of Hearts.'

I trot Ace in circles, waiting for the start bell to ring. I don't run through the whole course, don't try to think past the first fence, because if I do, I know I won't be able to visualise it, and I'll panic. But once I'm over the first fence, once I've cleared that oxer, I know the course will come to me.

The start bell rings, and I touch Ace into a canter, standing in my stirrups. I sit to guide her onto a twenty-metre circle, around the third fence, and when I feel the mare come up and over her withers, balanced on her hocks and responsive to my aids, I widen my circle and head down the long side, turning left towards the first fence. Ace eyes up the blue-and-white parallel eagerly, ears forward. I stay upright in the saddle, careful not to throw my weight onto her shoulders, my hands quiet and my leg on. I don't interfere but I don't just sit limp in the saddle, expecting Ace to do everything. We work as a team.

We clear the first jump, and I turn her towards the second oxer, which we hit on an easy stride, and too late after landing I remember this is the line, the one India and I discussed. India made the five strides look easy, but I forgot to think about the distance when I jumped in, and now I've already gone two small strides and don't see how I can hurry the next three without making a mistake. So I override my initial plan and sit steady, keeping Ace collected and my eyes on the upright. The six strides are easy, and Ace makes a copybook jump over the vertical, and then we're turning right towards fence four. Another parallel, another copybook jump, and I sit up on landing, my eyes already on the next obstacle. It's the one-stride combination, the one Harvey dragged India into, and I focus on keeping my stride steady and impulsive, pushing India's trouble to the back of my mind, along with the memory of how our last combination at an event went. I just keep riding, working with Ace, and before I know it, we're over both elements and turning to the sixth fence, which we clear, and towards the next. I ride this jump the same way, keeping Ace's rhythm bouncy and impulsive, not interfering with the stride. We hit it right, and then we're turning towards the oxer numbered eight. It's a bigger distance to this fence than we've had yet, and I stand in my stirrups, allowing Ace to move, but sit back in the saddle in time to make a good turn, gathering impulsion. Ace jumps cleanly over the parallel, and I sit up for the next fence, an upright, which she clears just as carefully. *One fence to go. Don't take it for granted.* Ten is an oxer at the far end of the ring, and I keep my eyes on the jump and my lower leg glued to Ace's sides. I don't think about the fact that this fence is all that stands between me and a clear round, or of the people watching, or of a placing later. I think of nothing but the jump coming at me, of this one fence and giving Ace every opportunity to clear it.

And she does.

'Lovely clear round for Sybil Dawson and Ace of Hearts sends them to the cross country on their dressage score. Our next starter...'

We did it. A clear round, we actually did it. I can't believe it.

I lengthen my reins, and Ace remains in the same round rhythm, same collected canter, as I pat her neck, a grin tugging at the corners of my mouth. *Clear round, clear round, clear round...*

'Now *that* is how you ride a show jumping round,' Rose says to me as I bring Ace to a halt outside the ring, and the words - and knowing they're true - mean more than a clear round.

'That was super,' Mum says.

Dad grins and pats my knee. 'You've improved a bit since I last saw you.'

I smile back. 'Wouldn't be hard.'

'You looked amazing,' he says in earnest, and I'm struck with appreciation that he was here to see my round.

'Super round,' Rose says again. 'You did everything right, I can't think of a single thing that wasn't.'

'I didn't get the third in five strides,' I start to say, but Rose shakes her head.

'No, you were absolutely right to go for six. You didn't land far enough out for five, and even if you had it would've been a bit long for her. I would've aimed for six, anyway. Five would've been long for her.' She leans forward and pats Ace's neck, looking at the mare with adoration. 'You're the best, aren't you?'

'She is,' I say, leaning forward to wrap my arms around Ace's neck.

Ace, who has given me all sorts of wounds, not all visible, who has made me doubt my ability and left me in tears more times than I can remember. Who has taught me to get over my fears, to leave my worries on the ground and work hard to achieve my goals. Who has taught me more than any schoolmaster ever could.

The bay mare turns her head to my boot, her forelock plaited to reveal the heart-shaped star on her forehead, and I lean foreword to scratch the spot between her eyes.

'You are,' I say. 'You're the best, Maggot.'

'You're sure you know the course?' Rose says to me.

I nod slowly, thinking back over all the jumps. The show jumping high wears off quickly with cross country to focus on, but

I don't feel as nervous as I have done in the past. Whether we triumph or fail is up to me, so there's no point worrying about an outcome I'm in control of.

'Tell me,' Rose says. 'Tell me the course.'

We're at the trailer, and I'm pulling out Ace's plaits, my fingers moving of their own accord, the movements embedded in my brain to the point of not needing to focus. Mum, Dad, and Gabe are getting another round of hot drinks, which is probably the only thing stopping them from hiding in the car. I'm warm from riding, and Rose seems equally okay in the cold climate. It's just starting to warm up, and maybe this afternoon will be bearable, but there's still an icy wind stinging our eyes and turning our toes numb.

'The first fence is a roll top…'

I list off each jump, having to pause and remember some of them for a few seconds, but I get there, naming every fence.

'There's a combination I'm not sure about,' I say when I reach it in my mind. 'Alex says you can either go straight or jump it on a curving line, and India says she's definitely going straight, but…' But Harvey did five strides where Ace did six in the show jumping, where I'd have struggled to do five, and I'm now doubting whether what works for her pony will work for mine.

'Which do you think?' Rose asks.

I drop an elastic band to the ground and loose a breath. 'I *thought* the curving line, which is what Alex is doing, but she's Alex and won't exactly have any trouble turning, and India's sure she's going to go straight…'

'Well, do you want to run down and look at it now before warming up?'

The mere suggestion calms me. 'Yeah?'

'Sure. Once your mum gets back she can keep an eye on Ace, and we'll run down together to have a look.'

I could so easily have chosen a line. Could have gone with what Alex, a four-star rider, said, or even listened to India and just kicked on to go straight, but instead I choose to be indecisive and go look at the combination with Rose. If I'd just made a decision myself, trusted my own judgement, the outcome would have been different, for better or worse. But I choose to go back down to the course, choose to go watch some horses go through the combination…

'So it's the palisade, and then the roll top with the brush behind it,' I say, stepping to the side of the first element. 'Alex said it's three strides on the curving line, or two straight if you jump the second fence on an angle.'

I glance over my shoulder to check no horses are coming, then step up to the second jump. To India and Alex, it probably looks tiny. A little roll top with a brush behind it, nothing much. But to me it's terrifying. The roll top is a metre wide, and the brush that in height, too…

'You're not going to like what I'm going to say,' Rose says, wincing, 'but I really don't think either is better than the other. I can see why Alex is saying three, to give you an easy stride, but I don't think you'll find turning any easier than just going straight on the angle. You can always decide when you jump and see what you've got, but I think you'll be better off just picking one and sticking to it.'

'What would you do?'

'If I were on Ace?' Rose puffs out her cheeks and stares at the two fences. 'I'd aim for the straight two, and just think quickly if I had a bad jump over the first. You know, I know you'd get a twenty, but there's nothing stopping you from making a circle if you're really in trouble.'

'Yeah,' I say, but my voice isn't convincing, and I'm sure Rose knows it.

'Why don't we watch a few go through? See what everyone else is doing.'

The first horse jumps straight on two strides and makes it look easy. The second does the curving line on three and makes it look even easier.

'Well, that's not very helpful,' Rose jokes as the combination gallops on to the next fence. 'See what the next one does and go with that?'

I nod. Clearly both options are viable, so I have no reason to worry...

'Oh, I recognise that horse,' I say as the next horse-and-rider combination jumps the fence before. *Why do I recognise that horse? Oh, I know.* 'India and I watched him show jump a few weeks ago,' I say, even though none of this will mean much to Rose. He was in the 100 then, and unsurprisingly it must have gone badly cross country for him to have dropped back down a class 'None of his tack fits and his back's really stiff.'

'Poor bugger,' Rose says quietly.

As the chestnut horse gets closer, I see he hasn't improved in the weeks since I saw him - if anything, he looks worse. He's lost more muscle, his sides are heaving, and the rider in the saddle is flapping about obliviously.

'Let's keep out the way,' Rose says, holding a hand out towards me as we step backwards, giving the combination more room than we have others.

If India were here, she'd be muttering complaints about the horse's tack again. The snaffle hangs too low in his mouth, and his noseband flaps, so when the rider makes any attempt to use her reins, the horse just pokes his nose and carries on. Neither he nor the rider looks fit to be on a cross country course, and the lack of decent equipment certainly isn't helping.

'I don't like this,' Rose whispers. 'They should be pulled up.'

The rider turns the horse to the combination with no balance, reins flapping and the horse turning with his head bent to the outside. Already I have a sense of foreboding, that there's no way this can go well. I'm surprised they've even made it this far.

Even with the lack of collection and control, the rider would probably get away with galloping gung-ho into the fences, because they're small enough that they're still forgiving. But she approaches the first with no impulsion or rhythm, and then pulls. Somehow the horse clears it, but he drops his nose on landing, which the rider lets him do because her reins are too long, and then carries on to go straight, to jump the second fence on the two strides, except she turns at the last minute and hooks, trying to add another. The horse obeys, even though it's impossible - impossible for him, at least.

The chestnut chips in a stride, and I don't know whether it's the lack of condition and fitness, his stiff back, the terrible tack, the terrible riding, lack of experience, or a combination of everything, but he can't lift his forelegs, and hits the solid base beneath the brush. The sound is one of the worst things I've ever heard, and I lift my shoulders as though they could cover my ears, helplessly watching as the horse dives forward and hits the ground. I'm reminded of myself and Jupiter doing something very similar some months ago, before moving to Rose's, and wonder if it looked the same. Did it look as scary as this? It felt terrifying, but I somehow always thought it didn't *look* bad. But it probably did. Probably looked this awful.

I used to think that it didn't matter if I was a good rider of if my pony was super fit because I was only competing as a hobby, but I now know that changes nothing. It's still a dangerous sport, still two lives at stake, and no horse should be made to do something unless he's capable of it, unless he's been given every possible chance. Riding for fun is no excuse for a horse to be underfed and not fit enough to do the job he's being asked to.

The horse falls, the rider falls. The horse gets up, the rider lies there and cries enough to know she's fine. A fence steward hurries towards her, and Rose sprints for the horse, who is standing nearby and looking the picture of terrified. His sides and nostrils are heaving even more than they were when he was galloping, and Rose wastes not a second in getting him moving, making him walk. He's stiff, but it slowly wears off as he moves, and a member of his support team arrives before the rider has stopped wailing enough to stand up.

'Thank you,' she says briefly to Rose as she takes the reins, and even though I know this person is worried and possibly traumatised, there's something about her tone I don't like. 'You all right?' she asks the rider on the ground as another woman, presumably her mum, hurries up to her.

'She can move everything,' the steward says as an ambulance drives up to us, but the girl still continues to wail.

Rose and I remain nearby, too caught up in the action to walk away, and after the paramedics fuss over her for a minute, the girl stands up and dusts herself off, every limb intact. Whatever she was wailing about can't have been that bad if she's fine now.

'You're okay?' the woman walking the horse asks, and I notice the name of a Pony Club branch embroidered on her coat. 'That was your fault,' she quickly goes on. 'You should've just shortened your reins you'd have been fine.'

Beside me, I feel Rose stiffen, and I know what she's thinking: there was a lot more wrong with the combination than just long reins.

'You're sitting on a great horse,' the Pony Club instructor goes on as the girl stands with her mother's arms around her, 'who knows his job, and you didn't help him.'

'I don't think it was her fault,' Rose says cautiously, and I dart my eyes to her. 'We were right here, we saw the fall, and I don't think it was all her fault.'

The girl looks grateful for the support, but the instructor puts on a fake smile. 'Trust me, it is. I've ridden this horse myself, and he is easy.'

Rose opens her mouth, and I see her deliberate. She's not a confrontational person, and I know she doesn't want to get into a debate with this person, but she's torn, her eyes moving to the unfit pony. 'He looked like he might have done his back in when he fell,' she says simply. 'Just to warn you, it looked like he tweaked something.' She then touches my arm and says, 'Come on, we need to get going.'

'His back was already seized up,' I say when we're out of earshot.

Rose nods, looking straight ahead as we march away. 'I know.'

'That woman has no clue what she's talking about,' I say, anger building.

Rose just nods again. 'I know. Thinks she does, though.'

'But-' Too many words and feelings bubble up inside me, and I fight to make sense of any of them. 'The girl couldn't ride, but it wasn't her fault. She doesn't know any better, and neither does the horse, and the tack wasn't...'

'I know.'

I heave a breath. 'Why didn't you say?'

'It's none of my business,' Rose says simply. 'It's hard to see a horse that isn't right, but too many people overstep when they shouldn't, and I'm not going to be one of them. I made a comment about his back in the hope they'll at least have the common sense to get an osteo out, using the fall as an excuse... We're no better than them if we start telling them what they're doing wrong. There's a saying that you should never start an argument with a fool, because a passerby won't be able to tell the difference. If you tell others what to do, then you're no better. Everyone has a different way with horses, and everyone thinks they know best, and your way isn't always the right way. No two people do things the same, and there's nothing worse than telling someone else what they should be doing. I'm not going to give my opinion where it's not been asked, and I only said that about his back for the horse's sake, and hid behind the fall. Tell you what, though,' she goes on, more upbeat, 'I'm sure they'd never sell because people are always too proud and would rather a horse be wasted than see it succeed with someone else, but that little chestnut has a heart of gold, and I bet he'd be quite something ridden and cared for the right way.'

I don't realise it until we get back to the trailer, but I'm shaking, the fall and the sound of the horse hitting the fence still embedded in my mind. Gabe and our parents are hanging out by the car, keeping an eye on Ace, and they smile at Rose and me obliviously. Frodo and Eleven lie in the grass, Gabe's legs dangling off the back seat as he holds their leads.

'Everything all right?' Mum says brightly.

I nod slowly, my eyes falling on Ace. Neither of us is perfect, but I know she's a fit and happy horse. And that matters more than anything. She's healthy, and well-cared for, and I rode her well today. That matters. And I know I'm too frazzled right now to make a right choice at any fence, let alone the combination.

But there is a right choice to make.

'I'm not running her cross country,' I say, my voice catching. I glance at Rose, and she doesn't look the least bit surprised, like she knew I was never going to do anything different after witnessing that fall. 'We just saw a horse crash through a fence, and I can't...' I shake my head, tears clouding my vision.

'It was a bit scary to watch,' Rose says gently, as Mum stands up to wrap her arms around my shoulders.

'I want to end on a good note,' I say, wiping my eyes. 'I mean, I *know* we could do that course, and I'm more confident than I have been before, but I can't think clearly...'

'You don't have to do anything,' Mum says.

'You've already ridden so well today,' says Dad.

'But she's gone so well today,' I say, already regretting my decision. But I can't think straight, can't shake that fall from my mind, and I know I won't be able to concentrate over any fence, let alone that combination. Ace doesn't deserve that. If I go out there and ride her badly, then that will only take away from all the good that's already happened today.

'Then end on a good note,' says Rose. 'Only you know how you feel. If you know you're not in a state to ride, then there's nothing wrong with calling it quits.'

I nod, remembering how amazing our dressage and show jumping rounds were. 'Okay,' I say. Because I know what I want to do, have done since that chestnut horse chipped in a stride and went flying. I just wanted somebody else to tell me I'm doing the right thing, someone else to make the decision.

'You've done so well,' Mum says, echoing Dad's words, and I walk towards Ace, tied up to the trailer, pulling at a haynet.

Not getting a result doesn't change how pleased with her I am, how I feel like we've already had a small victory, how our two rounds are better than a completion. I know, deep down, that I'm doing the right thing. I know I'd only mess up the cross country now, and she doesn't deserve that. In our own way, we've achieved more than a dozen cross country rounds could. If I went out there and rode her badly, brought her home with another bad round, then the work we've already done today would be for nothing, and we'd be right back where we started.

With horses, sometimes the only way to move forward is to take a step back.

chapter 10

After my decision sinks in, and we realise I'm done riding for the day, Mum asks me if I want to pack up and head home, but I don't. Not long ago, my answer would have been a resounding *yes*. I'd have wanted to get away as soon as possible, drive away from disappointment and not have to watch others succeed.

But not today.

Today I don't feel like I've failed, even if I'm not seeing the event through. I feel like I've achieved more than I ever have before. And I don't mind telling others I've withdrawn, either. So I'm happy to stay.

Besides, I still have my friends to cheer on.

'I'm going to go watch India cross country,' I say to my parents. I've loaded Ace onto the trailer with the doors open, so she can safely eat her haylage and still see out.

It's gradually been getting warmer all morning, a degree at a time, but it's as though it's only now that the temperature has surpassed ten that I can feel the difference. The air is still crisp, the grass frosty in the shade, but the sun is shining, the sky is blue, and the promise of an even warmer afternoon hangs in the air.

Harvey's colour makes him stand out in any warm-up, and I

spot his dun body right away, galloping around the perimeter of the ring. India wears her cross country colours of light blue and white, with a quartered silk and a white shirt. The gelding is kitted out to the nines in fancy boots and an expensive-looking martingale and breastplate, but I'm not staring at the pair wishing I had the same equipment, that Ace and I were turned out like that. I'm not thinking about how lucky India is to have a pony like that.

I'm watching India steer the gelding over a warm-up fence and thinking, *I could never ride that horse. I'm going to work until I can't say that anymore. I'm going to train Ace until* we *look like that in a warm-up.*

'Four-three-four you're up in two,' the steward calls.

India turns Harvey down the long side after clearing the warm-up log, standing in her stirrups, and pushes him on, lengthening his stride to a cross country gallop. The pony responds, and India then asks him to collect his rhythm again, practising bringing him back for a combination, and Harvey sets his jaw to keep going. India slams her left hand down on his withers and takes a check with her right - pulling with both reins will only give Harvey something to fight against, and end in a dead-pull strength competition. I'm watching every action India makes, analysing it in my mind. You can learn as much watching as riding yourself if you pay attention.

The dun gelding slows his stride eventually, and India sits in the saddle to cross the near-empty grass ring, heading for her family standing by the gate.

'Can someone tighten my flash a hole. Please,' she adds, cantering Harvey right up to the trio of spectators and holding him to a perfect square halt a few paces away, one worthy of being the final movement in a dressage test.

Catherine hurries forward to do as asked, tightening the noseband a hole with efficiency. Behind her, Sophia and Mia look much as they did earlier - the oldest holding a camera, the youngest a spaniel.

'Just one?' Catherine says. 'I could go one more.'

India shakes her head. 'One. Thanks.'

'And you know how you're going to ride the trakehner, don't you?' Catherine continues, flowing seamlessly into another conversation. 'Remember what Merritt told you-'

'Mum, I'm fine,' India snaps, and before her mother can say anything else, she rides away, cantering back down the long side and repeating the exercise she was doing earlier.

While India pushes Harvey on again, lengthening his stride and bringing him back with more ease than before, I move closer to the gate, thinking of where I could stand on course to have the best vantage point. If I start at the first fence and then continue to the middle of the course, I should be able to see most of it. And then run back to the finish for the last...

'Does she know the optimum time?' Catherine asks Sophia, to my left, and I can't help but glance towards them at the sound of her voice.

'I'm sure she does,' Sophia huffs. India's sisters must take after their father, because neither looks much like India and Catherine. Sophia's hair is long and dark, hanging in a straight ponytail down her back, face angular like Mia's, features strong. The only similarity is that she and India share blue eyes, but Sophia's are darker and closer together. I haven't heard much that is good about Sophia, but she doesn't look particularly evil or spoiled shivering in a cobalt coat on the edge of a cross country warm-up.

'Harvey's often too quick,' Catherine says, more to herself than anyone, because none of her daughters seems to be listening.

My eyes drift from the human Humphrieses to the four-legged one, standing at Mia's feet. The spaniel looks up at me, eyes bright and tail wagging, and without me saying a thing, makes a beeline towards me, tugging against her lead.

'What're you doing, Troi?' Mia says to the dog, but she seems happy to be dragged by the cocker spaniel, her face friendly as she follows the dog towards me.

Catherine looks up at the sound, smiles at her daughter and dog's antics, then turns back to Sophia.

'You can stroke her if you like,' Mia says as the spaniel pushes herself against my legs

I bend my knees to rub the dog's head, smiling at her floppy ears and goofy expression. She's a beautiful roan colour, her silky coat a giveaway of how well she must be looked after. 'She's sweet,' I say.

'She's *naughty,*' Mia corrects me, ruffling the dog's neck. 'Aren't you, Troika?' *Troika?* What kind of dog name is that? 'Did you do five?'

It takes me a moment to realise what Mia is talking about, and then another to hide my surprise that she not only recognises me, but remembers the conversation I had with India earlier. *She looks younger than she is,* I remember India saying something like that before. Mia is only a year or so younger than her, but her small and childish appearance makes it easy to forget,

'Uh, no,' I say. 'I got in too close to the first jump, so I did six.'

Mia nods. 'Makes sense. I'd have done six if I was on Doris, my other pony, but Harvey likes flyers.'

Now it's my turn to nod. 'Right.'

'I like your pony.'

Again, I forget that Mia has even seen Ace, but when I remember, I smile. 'Thanks.' I nod at Harvey. 'I like yours.'

'*He* is naughty, too,' Mia says, giggling. She turns her head towards the dun gelding, and I glance at her profile while she's looking away. Like her sisters, Mia is annoyingly pretty - each in a different way - with smart clothes and a natural confidence. Her hair hangs loose to her waist, lighter than Sophia's and longer than hers and India's. I take back my earlier thought of Mia not looking like her mum, because I can definitely see a resemblance to Catherine side-on. 'He's the best, though. With Doris.'

'Is your arm okay?' I say, asking the only thing I can think to.

Mia looks down at the cast and huffs loudly. 'It's *so* annoying.' She glances over her shoulder, at her mum, then steps closer to me, dropping her voice to a whisper. 'The doctor said I can't ride, but, don't tell anyone, I *am.*'

I smile. 'Are you?'

Mia nods. 'Early in the morning. But no one knows. You won't tell, will you?'

'My lips are sealed,' I promise, liking Mia more and more. She isn't what I expected. She's privileged, sure, but like India, she doesn't come across as spoiled.

'Good.'

India turns Harvey to a roll top, lowering her seat to the saddle and waiting for her stride. The dun pony has his ears fixed on the fence, head up and quarters engaged, and the combination meets the jump on a good distance, Harvey, as always, giving it more air than necessary.

'Have you already gone cross country?' Mia asks me.

I shake my head. 'No, I've withdrawn. I…' I try to think of what to say, how *much* to say, but decide to stick to the minimum. 'She did well in the dressage and show jumping, and running her cross country just didn't feel right.'

I expect questions, and then maybe a lecture when she hears my explanation, but Mia just shrugs. 'Fair enough.'

'Four-three-four,' the steward calls.

India canters Harvey to the gate, heading for the start with Catherine and Sophia on her heels, and Mia turns to me. 'You coming to watch?'

'Uh, sure,' I say. I *was* going to watch, that's why I'm here, but quietly on my own, not with India's family I barely know. There's no walking away from Mia, though, and besides, I wouldn't want to.

When Mia and I reach the start, India is trotting Harvey in circles near the box, managing to look both determined and relaxed.

'Thirty seconds,' the steward says.

I can see Sophia's retreating figure as she disappears onto the course, the camera still over her shoulder, and Catherine is near the start box, keeping an eye on the pony.

'Twenty seconds.'

India rides Harvey closer to the start, and the pony lights up as though struck by a current, flinging his head up and rocking back on his haunches. When he threatens to rear, India pushes him into a trot, distracting his mind.

'Need me to lead him in?' Catherine asks hurriedly, jumping forward, and India nods as she comes back to walk and her mum grabs hold of Harvey's right rein. The pony jigs from side to side, buzzing to go, but Catherine looks perfectly comfortable around his bolshy attitude. *At least she can actually handle a horse,* I think.

'Five, four, three, two, one, GO! Good luck!'

India hits her watch, Catherine jumps out of the way, and Harvey flies out of the start box, attention fixed on the job at hand.

'Come on,' Mia says, tapping my arm as she start jogging farther onto the course.

The combination clears the first fence and the second and third, and Mia and I reach a vantage point on the course in time to see the fourth. Harvey lifts his head, a running martingale preventing him from sticking it vertically into the air, and India holds him a stride before releasing the pressure, safely collecting him before the fence but early enough to not cut the impulsion needed to clear the fence.

'He looks strong,' I say to Mia, my comment coming out like a question.

'Oh my god, he's *so* strong,' Mia says. 'But that's why I have *these*' - she holds up her right arm and flexes it, presumably trying to show me she has muscle beneath her coat.

'Uh-huh,' I mutter noncommittally, because I'm pretty sure I could wrap my hand around one of Mia's arms.

Though she does ride this, I think to myself as Harvey accelerates towards the next question. I've seen Mia ride him before, and did think he was a *little* tricky - or quirky - but still wouldn't have categorised him as anything but a pushbutton schoolmaster, except I'm not so sure anymore.

From our vantage point, I have a perfect view of the first combination. Even now that I'm not riding, I still couldn't settle on a line. India made it clear she's going straight…

Even before turning to the palisade, India has started to regroup Harvey, her eyes on the fence. Sitting in the saddle, keeping her leg on, collecting his stride while keeping the impulsion. When she does turn to the first element, it's nothing like the terrifying combination I watched earlier. India has Harvey between her hand and leg, his muscles rippling beneath his clipped coat, barely any sweat to be seen on him, the rider just as fit.

Everything about the stride is right, but Harvey isn't one to make things dull. He takes off over the first jump like a pogo stick on steroids, bounding into the air so unexpectedly and landing far out with such force that India loses her balances in the saddle, jolting.

I gasp, while beside me, Mia furiously mutters, 'Sit up!'

India had lined up the second element with the intention of going straight, and I don't see how she's going to manage it, but quicker than I can process the dilemma myself on the ground, she sits up, stirrupless, slams her right leg against Harvey's side, opens her left rein, and widens their line, fitting in a third tight stride. Brush fences are higher than others on course, as the rulebook allows, since horses can jump through the brush. But Harvey doesn't see the point in doing that, and he shoots upward again, tucking his knees to clear the ten inches of brush. The leap takes me by surprise as a spectator, but India is either prepared for it or just has extremely good reaction skills, because even without her stirrups, she folds to go with him, seat strong and secure in the saddle. And before Harvey has even gone two strides after the fence, she regains her stirrups, pats the pony on the neck, and carries on.

'Very good save from Indiana Humphries and Mendip Breeze as they canter on to…'

'Wow,' I say, raising a hand to my face in shock. I feel like I've just ridden the fence myself.

'Harvey's the best,' Mia says. After that, I'm more inclined to say that *India* is the best, and not the pony, but refrain from doing so.

I watch the rest of the course with Mia, the two of us running around to see as many of the fences as we can. And when India and Harvey cross the finish line with a clear round, we cheer and run up to her with congratulations. Before, when I watched somebody like India ride, even though I liked her, part of me was always hoping something would go wrong. I didn't want them to fall or hurt themselves, just have a run-out, or rails show jumping. *It's not fair,* I'd think. *They don't deserve to do well because they have good ponies and fancy tack and all the support in the world.* And while those things may be true, I also know, watching India today, that I could't have done what she did in her saddle. I couldn't have got around that show jumping on Harvey, let alone recovered during the combination on the cross country course, and I certainly wouldn't have had the initiative to change my game plan as quickly as India did. There's no denying that she and her sisters are privileged, but she still works hard, and I'm going to keep working hard until I ride as well as her.

I almost don't believe the scoreboard, and I'm sure my jaw has actually dropped as I stand and gawk like a crazy person.

Ace and I were in the lead after dressage.

I knew we'd done an okay test, but it never occurred to me we did *that* well. *In the lead...* For the first time since watching India ride, I furiously wish I hadn't withdrawn before the cross country, that I'd sucked it up and got on with it. *The lead!* When am I ever going to lead going into the last phase again?

Every time, a voice in my mind says, the same one that told me to work until I could ride as well as India. I don't know where this voice has been hiding up to now, but I like it.

A glance at the scoreboards for other sections tells me that, even with a rail down show jumping, India and Harvey have won their class. A six point lead after dressage and no time penalties cross country mean they still take the title with a couple of marks to spare, and I'm nothing but excited for her. After the rounds India put in today, she deserves it.

I'm on my way to the dressage warm-up, to watch Rose and tell her about my score, when I cross paths with Alex again. After India's cross country round, I stayed to watch Alex and Roger's, and unsurprisingly the two went clear, though it took some coaxing to get the pony near the start box. And in another twist, the Connemara jumped big into the first combination, though unlike Harvey it didn't unseat Alex, and because she was already preparing for the curving line, and would have had difficulty fitting in the three strides, Alex changed her plan and cut across the turn to jump the second element on the angle in two strides. I guess that's the thing only experience can teach you: how to react on instinct and ride by the seat of your pants, even - and especially - when it means deviating from your original plan.

'Hey,' Alex says, waving to the two people she was engaged in a conversation with. Her hair is tied messily in a topknot, and she's drinking from a can of Coke. 'How did you do?'

'I didn't run cross country.' I say the words quickly, so I can get the next bit out without having to explain. 'But we led after dressage and show jumping.'

Alex tsks. 'Must've been my plaits.' She grins, then goes on. 'Why didn't you run cross country?'

Being both brief and accurate, I explain to Alex about returning to the combination with Rose and witnessing the fall.

'Oh, I think I know which horse you mean,' she says. 'I've seen it at events before, poor bugger. That woman that's with it is a nightmare, and thinks she knows everything, too.'

'Rose and I said that!' I say. 'Rose tried to suggest they get his back checked.'

Alex scoffs. 'Yeah, it needs an osteo, all right. Of course, it'd be fine if they'd ridden it correctly in the first place. Ugh, I'm glad I didn't see that.'

'So you don't think I was stupid for withdrawing?' I say.

'What?'

'I mean, I know I should've just sucked it up and ran anyway...'

Alex shakes her head. 'Knowing when to stop is one of - if not the - most important things with horses. Knowing when to call it quits and end on a good note, knowing your and your horse's limits. I mean, sure, as time goes on, there will come a point when you do just have to keep going come hell or high water, but that's not now. I think it's good you acknowledged you wouldn't be able to do your horse justice and give her the ride she needs, and let her end the day on a high.' Alex takes a swig from the can and stifles a laugh. 'I don't know many people your age who'd have done that.'

I usually hate it when someone says the words *your age* when speaking to me, but in this case not only isn't it patronising, but it feels like a compliment.

I smile. 'So you don't think I'm pathetic?'

'Not at all! I mean, look at it this way, I know it's disappointing to think you could have won the class' - just hearing the words makes a feeling of regret grow stronger - 'but if you weren't confident you could get round and things went badly, then it wouldn't have mattered how good your test was because you wouldn't be thinking about it.'

'I guess…'

'You don't guess, I'm right,' Alex says confidently. 'Trust me, I'm always right. Look, you were unlucky with seeing that fall and all, but what you did do, you aced, and now know you can come out and do the same thing next time. Just you wait, next year you'll come out all guns blazing.'

'Hey, you live in Newmarket, right?'

I turn around at the sound of India's voice, an envelope of photos in my hand. There was a photographer in the show jumping ring, and I got an amazing shot of Ace clearing an oxer, all four feet tucked, ears forward, me not looking terrible in the saddle. Mum put up one of our last pictures downstairs, for everyone to see, but this one I'm keeping for my room, so it's the last thing I see before falling asleep and the first when I wake up.

India stands with Sophia a few feet away from me, both munching on cheese toasties and walking in the direction of the lorry park. Being faced with Sophia Humphries intimidates me somewhat, but I focus on India.

'Yeah,' I say. 'Well, not in the town, but yeah. Just down the lane from Freya.'

India nods. 'Are you going to Tatts?'

'Tatts?' I repeat. Does she mean Tattersalls? The Thoroughbred auction in the centre of town?

'Yeah, it's the sales coming up.'

'Ugh, I've had my sales fix for the year,' Sophia says, sounding much nicer than I expect her to. *Why wouldn't she be just as nice as India and Mia?* I think. Okay, she doesn't have the best reputation, but she can't be completely awful if she was raised in the same house as her sisters.

'Have you been at the yearling sales?' India asks me.

I shake my head, still trying to understand this conversation.

'Lucky you,' Sophia says with a smile.

'Speak for yourself,' India says. 'I love the sales.'

'Well, you're weird like that,' says Sophia.

'*You're* weird,' India counters, then to me she says, 'Next week is the Autumn Horses in Training Sale, which we'll be at but we're not selling anything, then we've got fifteen or twenty foals entered at the end of the month.'

I'm still a little lost, but I nod as though I understand. I'll ask Rose - I'm sure she knows what all this means.

'Anyway, if you're at any of the sales, let me know,' India says. 'We can meet up and go look at horses.'

I wonder whether I should point out that I'm not in the market for a horse, but that seems like a stupid and obvious thing to say. I think. *Just ask Rose about Tattersalls later...*

'Is it on the weekend?' I say.

'Uh, maybe one of the days, but mostly in the week.'

'Are you not at school?'

'Yeah, but I'll go afterwards,' India says. 'The sales go on till late.'

'I think people were still bidding at ten p.m. last summer,' Sophia says. 'Remember? After they've had some stupidly expensive dinner and are probably too drunk to know what they're doing. Then again, you need to have had a drink to spend a million quid on a horse.'

'A million?!' I repeat, aghast.

'And then some,' India says.

'The worst part is how bored these people look while spending millions,' Sophia says. Her voice is a lot like Catherine's - Queen's English and clipped words - but it's also less intimidating. 'I swear, this summer I saw this guy pay two-and-a-half-million for this horse, and I've never seen a person look more fed up in my life.' She smiles again. 'So if you fancy seeing stupidly rich people spend lots of money…'

'I'll talk to my mum about it,' I say. 'I'm sure she won't mind,' I add. 'She works in Newmarket.'

'Great! Shall I give you my number, then you can text me if you do go.' India passes me her phone, and as I add myself as a new contact, she goes on. 'Though if you come during foal sales, it's easy to find me because we'll be with the foals, so just go to the row of Tricklemoon Stud stables. The signs are on the doors. I think we're in Park Paddocks.'

I nod, pretending to be extra focussed on typing my number into India's phone to hide how little I understand about what she's saying. 'What date did you say the next sale starts again?'

'Twenty-ninth or thirtieth? Something like that. And then all the breeding sales begin the end of November.'

'I'll probably make those ones, then,' I say. 'The November ones. My mum's sometimes a bit funny about us going out the first week back to school.'

India shrugs. 'Whichever. I'll be there as much as I can, anyway.'

'All right. I'll definitely try to make one.'

'It'll be fun,' India assures me as she starts walking with Sophia again. 'And Freya should come, too!'

I nod. 'I'll tell her!'

India and Sophia wave as they carry on to their lorry, their voices drifting away with them. I smile, thinking how funny it is that I'm on a friendly basis with people I watched from afar just some weeks ago, and start walking back to the car, and the little mare my life revolves around.

chapter 11

'I can't believe there are already Christmas decorations everywhere. It's October!'

'It's practically November,' Mum says reasonably as she slides muffins into the glass counter case. 'Besides, I thought you liked Christmas decorations. I have thirteen years' worth of memories of being asked to put a tree up in October to go on.'

'Well, it's wrong,' I say, wiping a cloth across a table.

The café is quiet, filled only with the sound of music and tapping computer keys. I glance across the room, at Liam's straight-backed figure in a corner, his eyes fixed on his laptop screen. Since our first meeting some months ago, he's obviously got over whatever version of writer's block he was suffering from, because he's always writing now. Gabe goes over to Liam's most evenings, even though half the time, he tells me, he does nothing but sit silently in an armchair with a book in his lap, while Liam works away at his desk. Every now and then, Liam will look up and say something like, 'Remind again what colour the frog was that Amity was served for dinner when she stopped for the night in that cabin in the second book?' and Gabe will respond, 'Black and green,' without even having to look up from his book.

According to the pre-order links online, the next Amity Byron story is due out in January, which is already much later than it was supposed to be. I can't imagine the manuscript Liam is still hard at work on being a finished book in just a couple of months' time, but Liam no longer seems too concerned. He's been at the café almost every day this month, working away at a single table with a pair of headphones on, immersed in his own world, getting up only occasionally for a drink refill.

'This place needs decorating soon,' Mum says, looking absently around her. 'Do you fancy doing it?'

I shrug. 'Maybe.'

Mum frowns. 'What's up with you? I thought you loved these things.'

I shrug again. 'Not anymore.'

Mum looks like she's going to say more, but her eyes fall on something behind me, and her expression changes to one of hospitality. 'Everything all right, Liam?'

I turn around to see Liam heading towards us, carrying an empty teapot. He's recovered from the broken leg he suffered this summer, though he still limps the odd step. 'Great, thanks.' He holds up the porcelain. 'Any chance of another?'

'Sybil,' Mum says.

'On it.'

'Thanks,' Liam says again, taking a seat on one of the counter stools as he waits. 'So where's Gabe?'

'He's gone to Waterstones in Cambridge with our dad,' I say. As his coming to the event was thought of as a treat for *me*, today is Gabe's turn for a day out, and naturally my brother chose to go to a bookstore.

'I can spend hours in that place,' Liam says to no one in particular.

'Tell me about it,' Mum says.

'And back to school tomorrow?' Liam goes on.

I nod as I fill the teapot. 'And if you hear about some kid called Patrick Firwell being beat up, know I'm responsible.'

'Oi,' Mum says.

'Who's Patrick Firwell?' Liam asks.

'This boy who's been picking on Gabe,' I say.

'Gabe gets picked on?' Liam looks surprised.

'Unfortunately,' Mum says, crossing her arms as she leans back against the counter.

'Kids are the worst,' I say.

Liam scoffs. 'Tell me about it.' He glances at Mum in such a way that suggests he's talking about me, and the two of them laugh.

'I don't count,' I say, passing Liam a teapot of Earl Grey.

'Of course not,' Liam says.

'I'm not a kid.'

'No, you're not.'

Liam and Mum laugh again, caught up in a joke, only for Liam's expression to change.

'What did you say the kid's name is again?' Liam says.

'Patrick Firwell.'

Liam purses his lips, then nods.

'Why?' I ask.

He smirks. 'Leave it to me…'

The month of November is a slow one. Rose takes Ace and me cross country schooling before the venues close for winter, as we didn't run at our last event, and Ace is phenomenal. She answers every question I ask her, never refuses a fence, and makes me feel like we really could fly around an international track one day. Combined with her dressage and show jumping rounds at the weekend, it's the perfect note for her to end on, and she begins her winter holiday.

The evening we got back from the event, true to her word,

Mackenzie had Jupiter spotless. Not only had she scrubbed every bit of mud out of his coat, but his mane and tail were sparkling, his feet were oiled, and I've never seen a bed built up with so much clean straw before - and neither had Jupiter, because he took tentative steps over the luxurious bedding as though not knowing how to walk across it. Any thanks I tried to offer were shrugged off - in fact, *she* tried to thank *me* for letting her look after the gelding - and I resolved to make a greater effort to include her where Jupiter is concerned.

'Would you like to hack him with me when he's back in work?' I asked. 'With me on Ace.'

And Mackenzie has been treating me like royalty ever since.

As the boring monotony of off-season settles, the yard comes alive with jobs other than exercising horses. A vet comes out to do all their teeth, an osteo checks their backs, and the yard construction continues, which Ace is still unsure of. The weather is wet and dreary, the deep mud gone only when we're racked by strong winds, and the days grow shorter, until night falls at four in the evening. After the intensity of the past months, both on horseback and on the ground, I expect to enjoy the quieter period, to like not having to tack up when it's freezing out and I'm tired from a day of schoolwork, but nothing could be further from the truth. A few days of not riding is all it takes for me to grow bored and restless, and as soon as next year's eventing calendar is released, I start planning the season.

There are only a few days left in the month when my phone beeps with a text, and I see India's name light up across the screen.

Hey, are you coming to Tatts? Xx

'Mum,' I call, standing up from the sofa. It's Gabe's night to cook, and Mum is sitting at the kitchen table, writing Christmas cards.

'What is it?'

'Can I go to Tattersalls with India?' I ask.

'India Humphries?'

'Yeah. She's just texted to ask if I'm going. We talked about it a few weeks ago. I can walk there from the café.'

'What day?'

'Um, I think she's there all week,' I say.

'If you like, then,' Mum says. 'What exactly is there to do?'

'I'm not really sure. India knows, though,' I say, which reminds me of something. 'I think Freya's going, too.'

'That's all fine,' Mum says, her biro scrawling across a card. 'Just don't come back with a horse.'

Tattersalls is right off Newmarket High Street. The venue spans across a hill, with the sales ring situated on top, and some thousand stables scattered around it.

Since making plans with India to meet, I've been fretting about the whole thing. It's an elite Thoroughbred sales, where a single horse can top a million pounds, and I presume I can't exactly just waltz in uninvited and wander among the horses, but that's exactly what it's like. Even though today isn't a sales day, the venue is open to the public, and I walk straight in, still expecting someone to throw me out. There's grass parking either side of the road that leads you into the venue, and right ahead, uphill, I can see the glass-panelled roof of the sales ring, the centre marked by a weathervane of a winged horse.

India told me their horses would be stabled in Park Paddocks, but despite having studied a map of the premises beforehand, I have no idea where that is, so I decide to walk straight ahead, up the hill and towards the sales ring.

The sales ring doors are closed, and there's nobody around the parade ring, but there are people everywhere, wandering with catalogues in their arms and destinations in mind. Some of the most awful neighs I've ever heard ring through the air, enough to make me alarmed, but everyone else seems at ease with the panicked sounds. Stable blocks are everywhere, dark wooden buildings, each stall numbered, and the doors covered with signs informing you of the horse inside. Lot number, by so-and-so out of so-and-so and half-brother to Group 1 winner… It all goes over my head, and I can't believe I can be so involved in horses in general and not know of this whole other side to them that exists.

It takes me a good fifteen minutes of wandering around the place to find India. The first foal doesn't sell until Wednesday, but they're being pulled out of their boxes left, right, and centre. Stern faces in tweed caps, a catalogue in a monogrammed leather cover beneath their arm, inspecting each Thoroughbred robotically. The handlers stand them up, waiting for a nod from the prospective buyer, then walk them up and down. Some of the foals are impeccably behaved, showing themselves with more manners than Ace or Jupiter could manage, while others let rip and pull away, leaving a groom to hang on to the end of the lead rein for dear life as the young horse bolts.

Tricklemoon Stud is printed on navy signs in a light blue cursive font, the stud's emblem the outline of a racehorse inside a crescent moon, above each foal's details. There are at least fifteen stables that I can see associated with the stud, and handlers are all dressed in navy blue windbreakers embroidered with the name. I wonder how to set about finding India, but I'm not wondering for long.

'We need Bubble's and Middie's,' she calls to a few members of staff as she turns from a prospective buyer with a piece of paper in her hand. Standing nearby is her dad, and this is the first time I've ever seen him up close. He and India look nothing alike, and to my surprise he doesn't look much like Sophia and Mia, either, except for the angular face. He's tall and lanky, with greying hair and sunken cheeks, and he sort of reminds me of Bill Nighy.

India's eyes find mine, and she smiles widely. 'Hey!'

I step up to her, my hesitance fading away. 'Hey.'

'Dad, this is my friend Sybil. Sybil, Arthur,' she introduces briefly, and even though he looks to have a lot on his plate, her father takes the time to smile and say hello, and as smart as he looks, I find him much less intimidating than Catherine. 'You been here long?'

I shake my head. 'Not long,' I say noncommittally. I don't want to let her know just how little I know my way around. 'This place is crazy.'

'Yeah, wait till the sales actually start,' India says. 'You never been?'

I shake my head. 'Never.'

India grins. 'It's amazing, you'll see.'

One of the grooms leads a bay colt out of a stable, standing him up in front of the buyer. The foal has a bit in his mouth and oiled feet, and his coat is shinier than it should be for a horse of his age going into winter.

'Walk him away, please,' the prospective buyer says, and the groom walks the foal away from us, along the purpose-made walkway.

'That's a colt out of one of our best mares,' India whispers to me. 'Her nickname's Bubble. She only won about twenty grand, but every foal she breeds has had results.'

Only twenty grand! What is this world? The thought of a horse winning twenty thousand pounds, to me, is outside the realm of possibility.

'Are you going to be upset to see him go?' I ask quietly, nodding at the foal.

'I'm always a little upset, but not if he makes what he's worth, I won't. It's upsetting when a foal doesn't sell or fetch the price he deserves, but when a horse you've bred goes into the ring looking well and the bids go up and up' - India shakes her head, leaning close to me - 'there's nothing like it.'

'I can imagine,' I say, watching as the foal is led back towards us.

The interested party nods. 'Okay, thank you.'

'Seven-o-one,' Arthur Humphries says, beckoning the next foal forward.

The handler leads out the foal, pulling him to a halt facing downhill, and beside me, India lets out a sound of annoyance and snaps, 'For goodness' sake.'

'The other way,' Arthur scolds the handler, his voice much louder than India's. And in another second he decides to do the job himself, stepping forward to take the foal from the confused-looking lad and turning him so he stands facing the correct way.

'You show a horse on the left,' India says to me. 'That guy's useless.'

'He works for you?' I ask.

She shakes her head, then stops. 'Well, I mean, he obviously *does* for the week, but not normally. Everyone's just always so short-staffed at the sales so you hire people without really knowing what you're going to get. This foal's out of our mare Midnight, who's bred some good horses, too. We only sell good colts as foals, because fillies rarely fetch the right price unless the breeding's really popular, and if a colt doesn't stand out then you're better off waiting till it's a yearling.'

'Right,' I say, like this isn't all foreign to me.

Arthur walks the colt up and down the springy walkway, and admittedly the foal looks a lot better with him than it did a moment ago. He walks up and over his withers, with a big overtrack.

The prospective buyer scribbles something in his catalogue, then nods at Arthur. 'Okay, thank you.' And with that he walks away, on to look at the next one.

'Doesn't he say whether or not he liked him?' I ask India, and she shakes her head.

'No. Sometimes when they're interested they'll ask questions, but not really. You never know.'

'And these people are all the buyers?' I say.

'Mostly bloodstock agents. So they'll do the bidding, but they buy for other people.'

'Hey, Arthur, how're you doing?' a woman says as she walks up to the row of Tricklemoon stables. She's dressed in a tweed coat and a fur hat, and Arthur puts a hand on her shoulder to kiss her on each cheek in greeting.

'Good, Lillian, good,' he says. 'Can I get any out for you?'

'The Intrico/Dainty Steps colt,' Lillian replies, hugging an open catalogue to her chest.

'We need Bubble's,' India says to a handler, relaying the message as though translating.

Watching Arthur, I realise that the slips of paper passing around indicate whom has come to see which horse - on the one he uses now, he writes *Lillian Blackwater* and checks the box in which *Intrico x Dainty Steps* is written.

'Intrico's a horse we bred,' India says quietly to me. 'He won the July cup. We sold him after that, but we kept breeding rights, so we get free covers every year.' She says this like it's something impressive, which it probably is, but I don't understand enough about racing to know just how much.

We stand to the side as a handler - one of the better ones, I've already realised - shows the colt to Lillian, and as she walks him away, and more neighs ring through the air, I turn to India.

'Why is there so much neighing?'

'Oh, the foal sales are always like this,' she says. 'It's not like the foals have been anywhere before - well, other than when their dams were covered - so it's stressful for them.' Another cry resonates, and India pulls a face at me. 'Horrible, isn't it?'

'Yeah,' I say, watching the bay colt walk back towards Arthur and Lillian, the latter keeping an eye on the foal at all times, even as she and Arthur are engaged in conversation, and come to a square halt.

'They'll settle, though,' India goes on, crossing her arms as she stares at the colt. 'Once the sales start they'll be fine. Are you coming on one of the sale days?'

'Maybe,' I say, nodding.

'You should! Come an evening, on the second or third day - that's when the best lots go. We've got two in the best slot. It'll be fun!'

'LOOSE HORSE!' a sudden voice yells, and a foal from another row of stables comes galloping this way, expression frantic and tail straight up in the air. The Tricklemoon handler keeps her focus on the colt she's holding, which, to the horse's credit, copes remarkably well with the diversion, while the rest of us - me, Arthur, Lillian, India, and every other person nearby - hurry towards the loose Thoroughbred with outstretched arms, our equestrian-brain instincts the same.

Horses are nothing if not entertaining.

When I walk back to the café an hour later, after touring Tattersalls with India following the capture of the rogue foal, Mum smiles warmly at me, wiping her hands on her apron as she speaks.

'How was it?'

'Good,' I say, sitting down on a stool as the glass door swings closed in my wake. 'Or, more interesting than anything.'

She smiles again. 'Yeah?'

'Yeah.' I pause, thinking of how I could put the experience into words. 'I can't believe how little I know about it all.'

'Racing?' Mum asks.

'Not really,' I say. 'That's just it. I obviously know what horse racing is, even though I don't understand it all, but there are so many jobs I never even knew existed. Did you know there are people who get paid to buy horses for other people? Bloodstock agents. Their only job is buying horses! It's crazy.'

'I guess it is,' Mum says, running a cloth over the coffee

machine.

'And I'm not saying I'd want to do anything like that, but...' I sigh, still not sure what it is exactly I'm trying to say. 'It's nice to know just how many jobs there are with horses that aren't riding, and how many people are involved. Like we all speak the same language.' I think of the loose foal, of how the reaction of every person nearby, myself included, was the same. 'Like there are all these people you belong with.'

Three days later, when night has fallen, Freya and I are standing around the parade ring, leaning against the white railings, and getting covered in snow. Large flakes have been falling heavily for twenty minutes, and the foals walking around the ring are covered in white blankets. The perimeter of the parade ring is crowded, but not as crowded as the lit-up sales ring, which is overflowing with bidders whose pockets are deep enough to reach Australia.

It's freezing, and even wearing a big coat and gloves I'm getting wet, but it doesn't matter. It's all so magical - the horses, the snow, the speakers and screens. On the previously-green grass in the middle of the parade ring, men with shovels are at the ready to clear up after any horse, and I feel sorry for their sodden figures.

'This is amazing,' Freya says quietly, looking up at the sky. A wooly hat sits atop her head, and snowflakes are landing in her red locks that hang down her coat. 'At least I shut Leo in tonight,' she adds.

'Yeah,' I say, and I think of my ponies at Rose's, safe and sound from the bad weather, nestled in deep straw beds, wrapped up in thick rugs, with big piles of forage to pick at.

'I emailed Diamond's owners this morning.'

I whip my head around to look at Freya, her gaze directed straight ahead, like she's trying to act as casually as possible. 'Yeah?' I say.

She nods. 'Yeah. Just to ask how he's doing…'

'Good,' I say.

She nods again. 'Yeah.'

'He'll be fine,' I assure her. 'Just you wait.'

We're waiting for the Tricklemoon draft to go. Among the five lots they have in this evening slot are the two India refers to as Bubble's and Midnight's, and I've gathered they're the two foals the stud is counting on to make the most. So far tonight, I've seen lots make twenty, thirty, forty, even eighty thousand guineas, with some having made more since the beginning of the sale yesterday morning, and I don't think even a flying pig could surprise me at this point. How can a small, scruffy foal sell for five years' worth of income? India has pointed out various people around the site, both horse racing royalty and the real kind, and what to me is a life-changing amount of money is nothing to them.

India was with Freya and me to begin with, but she's been preoccupied since her foals came into the parade ring. The handlers are dressed in Tricklemoon coats and caps, waterproof trousers, and boots. The foals are in bridles, and were sparkly clean before the snow coated them. They get tidied up before going into the sales ring, grooms fussing over them as they wait in the in-gate, which this evening mainly means dusting snow off their backs. Since the first Tricklemoon foal went through, India has been standing between the parade ring and the sales ring, watching beside her father as the foals get spruced up, and then standing in the sales ring doors to watch them walk around. The first foal sold for twenty thousand, which I thought was good - *ridiculous*, really - but Arthur and India looked sorely disappointed by. The next went for the same, but this time they looked a lot happier. The third made fifty thousand, and they were positively grinning. It must be terrifying, not only watching a horse you've bred be bought without knowing who it's going to, but having your entire income rely on something out of your control like an auction. And now the foal India refers to as Bubble's is going through, and Freya and I hurry to the sales ring to watch, stepping around a group of men in tracksuits conversing loudly in Arabic, not noticing or caring they're blocking the entrance.

White wood panels circle the ring, with a perfectly-swept oval of straw in the middle of it. Handlers walk the foals in circles, clockwise, offering bidders a final look.

The auctioneer speaks in a rapid, chanting voice, and it's only from concentrating this evening that I'm finally able to make some sense of the words.

'Next up from Tricklemoon stud is lot 700, a lovely-looking colt by the great Intrico, out of a two-time winning mare, and dam of six winners, including the Group-2-winning Stepalongnow, and the filly Mia Isabella, who came runner-up in this year's Oaks.' The auctioneer rattles on about more of Bubble's accomplishments, and although I can't understand the significance, I realise why not only she's considered such a good mare, but why India's family has such high hopes for this colt. I know nothing, but the auctioneer certainly has a lot more to say about Bubble than he has the dams of the other foals that have sold in the short time I've been here.

'Now, who wants to start the bidding? Who wants to put me in, put me in, where do you want to start? A hundred, eighty, fifty. Someone bid me fifty thousand? I'll take thirty.' He points his gavel at somebody in the seats. 'Thirty thousand bid, do I see thirty-five?'

'Thirty thousand opening bid,' I whisper to Freya in shock.

I try to see India's face through the crowd in the entrance reserved for bidders, but she's hidden in the mass of people.

'Intrico's a thirty-five grand stud fee, though,' Freya says to me. I can understand her knowing such a thing due to not only having lived in Newmarket all her life, but both her parents being in some way involved in racing, but I'm still surprised.

'They didn't have to pay it,' I say quietly, remembering what India told me. 'She said the cover was free.'

'Yeah, but no one else knows that. So really, they've only covered the stud fee with thirty-five, and that leaves no profit margin.'

Except in the twenty seconds we've been talking, the bidding price has gone up that many thousand.

'Fifty-five thousand. Fifty-five with the gentleman on my right, do I see sixty?' The auctioneer locks on to someone straight ahead of him, somehow making out a bidder amongst the crowded seats, as does one of the suited assistants whose sole job is to look out for nods of a chin, and he extends his arms at the same time as the auctioneer holds out his gavel. 'Sixty, thank you. Do I see sixty-five?'

Every time I think the bidding is over, somebody else raises their hand. This goes on, and on, until before I can process what is happening, the hammer has fallen and India is three hundred thousand pounds richer.

'Three hundred thousand,' I say to Freya, almost hysterical. *Three hundred thousand! For a foal!'*

The next, and last Tricklemoon lot of the evening is Midnight's colt. India appears again to dust snow off his back in the in-gate, while another groom runs a wet brush over the foal's mane, flattening it on his right side.

While the colt is led around the ring, I watch one of the pretty, well-dressed auctioneer assistants weave through the seats with a clipboard in her arms, searching for the previous buyer. A - it has to be said - *bored*-looking man in a tweed cap fills in the buyer's form, while the girl with the immaculate ponytail stands beside him patiently.

Midnight's colt sells for sixty-five thousand, and my first thought is, *That's not much,* immediately followed by a second that is, *Whoa, how did that happen?* In the space of a few minutes, I've gone from thinking that paying even a few thousand pounds for a scruffy foal is ridiculous, to thinking that sixty grand is a good deal.

No wonder people get carried away in this game.

'Do you realise they've just made 455,000£ in the last ten minutes?' I say to Freya. My limbs are shaking from the shock and adrenalin. 'Wait, actually, they've made more, because that's in guineas. A guinea is 1,05£, so…'

'They have a lot of costs that come out of that, though,' Freya says.

'It's almost half a million pounds!' I say.

'And they'll probably lose that on another horse tomorrow.'

I don't see how that's possible, or why Freya is arguing the point, but we're moving out of the double doors, and there is India, hurrying out of the entrance on the other side of the horses' pathway.

'Oh my god,' I say, hurrying over to her. 'That's amazing, isn't it?'

'Yeah.' India is beaming. 'We had a hundred reserve on Bubble's, though we thought he'd go for double, but three hundred's great.'

I think I'm more excited than India is.

'Needed to go for that, though,' she goes on, 'because our last few have a crap slot in the sale, and we'll probably end up having to buy them back, anyway.'

'You buy them back?' I say.

India nods. 'Sometimes, if they don't make enough. We can put reserves on, too, but if you're going to buy back at least you can decide at the last moment.'

'And then what do you do? Keep them and race them?'

'Some of the fillies, maybe, but we usually hold them till the yearling sales.'

Behind India, Arthur Humphries walks out of the ring, his expression relaxed and happy. I'd probably look the same if I'd just made what he has.

'Midnight's went to Stanley Eddison,' he tells India with a

smile.

India's face lights up. 'Really?'

Arthur nods. 'He's gonna turn him out with Carlbrook until next year.' He taps India on the back. 'Good, huh?'

'Good,' she repeats, and I'm struck by the feeling that she and her father are way more alike than they look - composed, coolly confident, focussed, genuine.

'Stanley and I are going to get a drink,' India's dad goes on. 'You eaten anything?'

India shakes her head and clutches her side. 'You kidding? I haven't eaten all week.' She shudders, then looks at Freya and me. 'I can't, it's too stressful.'

Arthur extends his gaze to take in his daughter's friends, and he reaches into his back pocket, pulling out a folded twenty pound note. 'Why don't the three of you go grab something,' he says. 'You two haven't eaten, have you?' he asks just Freya and me, and we shake our heads. It doesn't feel right to accept an offer of a paid meal so swiftly, but then again, the guy will probably have an extra half a million in the bank by the time the week's over.

'Okay,' India says, taking the money without reservation.

'And give your mum a call, will you?'

'Sure.'

A big-bellied man comes out of the ring, looking jollier than most of the bidders here, and Arthur moves towards him, the two of them heading for the long building on one side of the parade ring. Through the windows, I can see the restaurant alive, every seat and table taken. *Who comes to an auction to spend the whole evening inside?*

'Shall we go to Highflyer?' India asks.

'Sure,' Freya says. *She* at least seems to know what Highflyer is, which is more than I can say for myself.

We head back towards the stables, passing the row of Tricklemoon boxes on the way. India detours from our route to run to the stables of the five foals that just sold, whispering farewells to each, especially Bubble's colt, whose door she opens to give him a big hug, and I swear I hear her cough back a small sob. When she comes back out of the stable, there's a tear running down one of her cheeks, and she laughs as she sees Freya and me notice, wiping it away.

'This always sucks,' she says, laughing more tears away. 'I'm too much of a soft touch. He's gone somewhere good, though,' she adds, more to herself than us.

'The tall guy with the grey hair, yeah?' I say, though I realise this describes almost every bidder here.

India nods. 'He's a big bloodstock agent for one of the main studs.' India names said stud, but it means nothing to me. 'Still,' she goes on, shrugging. 'It's still hard.'

While we walk down the hill beyond the stables, India calls her mum. Her phone's volume must be on high, and Catherine's voice carries as it is, so I can hear every word the latter says through the receiver.

'That's amazing,' I hear Catherine say. 'Fantastic. Well done everyone. What time will you be back?'

'Uh, I dunno,' India says, as the path we're walking down gets steeper, the thin layer of snow crunching underfoot. 'Dad's gone off for a drink with Stanley.'

Catherine groans. 'So, you're never coming back?'

Freya and I stifle a chuckle, and India grins. 'Fine by me.'

'Shall I come pick you up? You do have school tomorrow.'

'No, please,' India says. 'Freya and Sybil are here, and we're going to Highflyer for something to eat.'

'Oh, that's nice!' Catherine says, and she sounds so earnest that I warm to her slightly, even though I'm basically resolved to dislike her on principle. 'I don't want any moaning tomorrow morning, though.'

'I won't. And it's not like Dad can drink much, anyway,' India says, 'because he has to drive.'

'He'd better remember that. I'll text him.'

'Okay, I need to go,' India says as we reach a car park at the bottom of the hill. Beyond it lie more stables, most with the lights off, and I can't imagine where we're actually going.

'If you change your mind and you want me to come pick you up, let me know.'

'Okay.'

'Okay. Have fun. Drive safe.'

At the end of the car park is a building, a sign reading *Highflyer Café,* and the warmth is a relief when we step through the doors. I shake snow off my boots and coat, revelling in the comfort of being indoors, and follow India and Freya to the short queue.

'Ooh, I'm going to get chips and a hot chocolate,' India says, eyeing up the salty potato wedges being served into paper trays. 'Perfect.'

I glance at the menu board, then back at the food being served behind the counter. 'Actually, I think I'm going to have the same.'

Freya smiles. 'Me too.'

A few minutes later we're seated at a table in the café, each huddled over a tray of chips and a paper cup of hot chocolate. A TV screen on the wall plays soundless live footage from the sale ring, with the lot numbers and prices flashing up at the bottom of the screen.

'I'm so starving now,' India says, pulling off her Tricklemoon cap and dunking a fat chip in ketchup.

'These are so good,' I say, shoving a small chip into my mouth.

India nods. 'The food here's the best. Well, I think so, anyway.' She swallows a mouthful of hot chocolate, then lowers the cup to the table. 'How are the horses?' she asks, looking at both Freya and me.

'Leo's good,' Freya says, nodding.

'You both looked amazing last month,' India says.

I nod. 'You really did.'

Freya smiles shyly. 'Thanks.' She glances briefly at me, like we share a secret, then looks at India. 'I think I'm getting the hang of him now.'

India scoffs. 'Please, you always have had. Seriously, I'd put money on it you're heading to Europeans next year.'

Now it's Freya's turn to scoff. 'No way.'

'Yes way.' India looks at me. 'Don't you think?'

I nod again. 'For sure. You both could be.'

'We'll see,' Freya says, looking down.

'I doubt I will be,' India says. 'I'm not that bothered either way to be honest, because I don't see the point in having Europeans as a goal when I have no control over being selected.'

'You've both got three years left, anyway,' I point out.

'Only two for me,' India says. 'I'm fourteen December 31st, so as of January I qualify as fifteen.'

'Oh, yeah, I forgot that,' Freya says.

India shrugs. 'I really don't mind that much. How are your ponies?' she asks me.

'They're fine. On holiday until the first. Well, Jupiter will be back in work a bit before because his holiday started earlier.'

She grins. 'Same as ours. They get four weeks holiday, and that started the beginning of October, so I've already got Otto and Fendi hacking. And Mia's already had to bring Harvey back into work because he starts jumping out of his field if he gets too long off.'

'Her arm's healed?' Freya asks.

'Oh, yeah, she's fine.'

'I like her,' I say. 'Mia. She seems really nice.'

'Ugh, try living with her.' India inhales another chip, then shrugs. 'She *is* nice, just tiresome. She needs an *Off* switch.'

'Sophia seemed nice when I met her, too,' I comment. *Words I never thought I'd say.*

'Yeah, well, she plays the part well. She's nice to other people, just not us.'

'How's Last Encore?' Freya asks, and the name rings familiar as that of Sophia's Junior horse.

'Mason's always fine,' India says. 'That horse wears a halo, I swear. He has a heart of gold.'

I swallow another mouthful of chip and wipe my greasy fingers on a napkin. 'So Otto and Fendi come back into work next week?'

'Yeah. Well, probably after the Mare Sale, 'cause I'll be here most of the time, but after that. And we're going to St Lucia over New Year's, so they'll get a week off then, too.'

'The Caribbean?' Freya says, saving me from asking where St Lucia is.

'Wow,' I say as India nods.

'My mum likes to go away for New Year,' she says, looking slightly embarrassed.

'No, it's good,' Freya says, trying to put India at ease.

'Trust me,' India says, 'I'm looking forward to the event season *way* more!'

'Yes,' I agree, nodding reverently. 'Second that.'

'Yep,' Freya says.

'What's your goal?' India asks us.

'Novice and Pony Trials, I guess. And maybe Brand Hall Pony Champs?' Freya says, then looks embarrassed to have voiced such a thought. 'Maybe. I dunno.'

'For sure,' India says. She looks at me. 'Is that your goal, too?'

'My goal is to actually complete an event with Ace,' I say, turning slightly bitter. I take a swig of my hot chocolate, trying to wash away the feeling of jealousy. *Don't,* I think. *It's not worth it, it doesn't solve anything.* 'Novice would be amazing, though,' I go on, looking down at my hands. 'Maybe with Jupi.'

'Definitely,' Freya says, and when I look up, both she and India are nodding confidently.

'He and Ace can do Novice no problem,' India says. 'I haven't done a Novice yet, so we can work towards it together.'

Your ponies have, though, I think. But I'm not doing this - not making excuses for others' success and feeling sorry for myself. I smile. 'Deal.'

'And we can all do Pony Championships at Brand Hall,' Freya says.

'Oh, and go to Haras du Pin in August!' India adds, referring to the International Pony Event in Normandy, France.

I laugh. 'You two, maybe, but I doubt I will.'

'Got to dream, though,' India says. 'Right?'

I nod. 'Right.'

And in that café, huddled over cups of hot chocolate, as the snow falls outside, that's what we do.

chapter 12

Ace and Jupiter come back into work in time to prevent me from joining a cult out of sheer boredom.

I don't know how some people can live without horses.

I really don't.

There hasn't been a day I haven't been up by seven and at the yard before school to take care of the ponies, as well as every evening, and I'm *still* bored.

All the times I pined for a morning off, for a few days of lounging around doing nothing like most people my age - or most people full stop. That I imagined a life without responsibilities, free to be as lazy as I like. No staying outside all day, no heavy lifting…

That never really crosses my mind anymore.

I like rising before the sun. Like sitting in the kitchen with the dogs, my hands around a cup of tea, while the world outside is still asleep. Like walking to the yard and seeing my ponies snug inside their stables. Like knowing they're being cared for properly. I can't think of a catalyst, a defining moment where I went from wishing I didn't have to do the work that goes with riding to actually enjoying it, only know that I never wake up wishing I didn't have to go to the yard anymore. Sure, some mornings, when my alarm clock is ringing on my bedside table, waking me abruptly, I wish, for a moment, that I could close my eyes and go back to sleep, that I could stay under the covers and not go out into the freezing weather. But instead of cursing the horses for being the cause of having to get up, I remember the horses and they make me *want* to get up. They make me silence the alarm and switch on the bedside lamp. They make me swap pyjamas for clothes and boil the kettle. They make me slide my feet into boots and pull on a coat and walk down the country lane, because once I'm in the yard, and I see those two familiar faces look out at me over stable doors, all those other things are forgotten.

Jupiter comes back into work after a full month off, and not a moment too soon. He's never been cold-backed, never been funny about being tacked up after some time off, and I have no qualms about throwing a saddle straight onto his back. The winter fitness schedule Rose has advised me to tackle involves two weeks of walking, and I don't waste a moment.

The sky is clear, the temperatures freezing, and with a Newmarket rug over his quarters I lead Jupiter into the stable courtyard, check my girth, swing onto his back, and ride him straight onto the country lanes. To think I used to be afraid of hacking him regardless of the situation, and now I'm taking him onto the roads, alone, after over a month off. I don't know which one of us that says most about, but I do know I feel safer on his back than just about anywhere. I'm relaxed, and Jupiter feeds off that, walking in a relaxed manner, reins loose, as we circle the block.

'There's walking and there's *walking*,' Rose has said to me many times, because letting a horse plod along with his head in the air isn't going to do anything in the way of gaining muscle and fitness, but for this first ride, I allow Jupiter to walk on a loose contact, not asking too much of him. The same way I know I'll feel my muscles tomorrow, he needs to be eased back into things, too. But in a few days I'll collect him, shorten his frame to a correct outline, and make him march, moving forward into the bridle and stepping under himself.

And it doesn't feel like a chore, even when the wind is nipping at my cheeks and turning my toes numb, because there's nothing I'd rather do than work on improving my horse for the event season to come.

* * *

'Do we have any more tinsel?' I ask Mum, stepping back from the Christmas tree.

Mum walks out from behind the counter, places her hands on her hips, and frowns. 'Really? You think it needs *more?*'

I whip my head towards her, then look back at the tree. 'What? You don't like it.'

'I never said that. I just think it's very…'

'Perfect?' I venture.

'Tinsel-y,' Mum says. 'I'm not sure you need any more.'

The Norway spruce stands against the glass shopfront, so that it can be seen from outside. It's nearing seven p.m. now, has been dark for hours, and the twinkling lights I've spent a good part of the evening untangling are shining back at me in the window. Silver baubles, decorated cookies, and, because this *is* Newmarket, wooden racehorse ornaments hang from the branches, evenly separated apart. And, yes, okay, there is quite a lot of tinsel wrapped around the tree, but I had to make up for the few number of ornaments, and I say so to Mum.

'It looks too bare otherwise,' I add.

'You know I'm only teasing.' She gives my shoulders a squeeze before turning back to the counter. 'Thank you, it looks great. Homey.'

'It *does* look homey.' I stifle a yawn, stretching my arms

overhead. 'Are we gonna be much longer?'

Mum shakes her head. 'No, we can go in a sec. We'll be ready sooner if you made a few coffees to go.'

I frown. 'Why do-' I cut myself off, realising what Mum has in mind, and start moving towards the coffee machine. 'Okay.'

She doesn't seem to notice my hesitation, her focus on the muffins left in the counter case. 'I'll just box these up,' she says, 'and then we can go.'

For as long as I can remember, Mum has bought extra coffees and baked goods in cafés, even when we couldn't really afford to. As guilty as I am to admit it, it embarrassed me when I was little. Never could we wander into a coffeehouse without coming out with breakfast for others, the expression on my mum's face unreadable as she carried a tray of coffees and bags of muffins - individual bags, she always requested, and baristas would execute the demand with annoyance, thinking Mum was just another precious customer with unnecessary requests, when nothing was further from the truth.

Everything my parents did was embarrassing to me, and I was too young to know that feeding the homeless shouldn't have fallen into that category for longer than I care to admit. It wasn't until a year ago that I realised my mum's compulsion to help, to do something small that could make a big difference to somebody else, was something to be proud of, and not one of the many traits I found annoying. And not only has she always handed out hot drinks and snacks routinely, as though it would never occur to her *not* to, but she never looks proud when she does it. I've heard others brag about good deeds in ways that totally diminish them, because they do it purely to enhance their own self worth, but Mum never looks self-indulgent when she hands out sustenance, her expression neutral, because it's just something she thinks *should* be done, not something she does for good karma or to make herself feel good.

Newmarket has far fewer homeless than Cambridge, but Mum still makes the effort.

'Aw, can't we take the lemon ones home?' I say as I watch Mum lift the leftover lemon and poppyseed muffins into the paper box.

'Oh, selfless child,' Mum sing-songs.

'You've already got five chocolate ones,' I point out.

'Then the lemon ones must be better if there are only two left.' She closes the box with a flourish. 'Honestly, Sybil,' she mutters, shaking her head. 'What am I going to do with you?'

'You know I didn't mean it,' I say, and Mum scoffs. 'Hey, you're pretty lucky,' I go on. 'At least *I* didn't buy a horse at Tattersalls without asking for your permission. Or, actually, buy a horse with your money.' I laugh, just thinking about the incident.

Yesterday was the last day of the Mare Sale, which, according to India, is the worst slot of the sale. Freya and I went after school, and admittedly there were fewer people at the venue, though the horses looked no worse than the ones that sold on the previous days. Not to me, anyway.

'It's not that the horses are bad,' India explained, 'it's just that they have no page - their breeding isn't fashionable - or they're consigned by small studs or individuals that nobody's heard of.'

This didn't stop Arthur Humphries from buying, though, because in the half hour I'd been there, I'd seen him raise his hand for three different lots, ultimately securing two of them for far less money than any of the horses he'd sold here himself. India said he was looking for bargains, cheap horses with nice-but-not-fashionable-enough-to-be-expensive breeding and good conformation.

'Your best bet is to buy an unraced filly for minimum bid, obviously that looks nice and with okay breeding, and put her to a good stallion. You'll sell a foal out of an unproven mare more easily than one out of a loser.'

I wasn't sure what Arthur saw in the two lots he bought, because they didn't stand out from the others in the parade ring to me, but he seemed happy with the purchases, and India was already rattling on about plans to send them to this stallion and that one, caught up in the world. Seeing her at events, I'd always taken it for granted that she planned to event to high level, that that was what she wanted to do with her life, but watching her in this environment, caught up in the excitement of Thoroughbreds, I wondered if I assumed wrong.

Freya and I were about to leave, to get a lift back to finish off the horses before darkness settled at the ridiculously early time of four p.m., when India stepped between us, seizing each of our arms, and nodded at a horse being led up to the parade ring.

'*That,*' was all she said, and she released us to open her catalogue and search the number indicated by the sticker on the horse's rump.

Siren Sounding, the page read. Unraced. Filly.

'She's only three,' I said, looking at the filly's birthdate.

'Four next month, though,' India pointed out, her eyes staying on the mare. She was a vibrant red chestnut, the same shade as Freya's Leo, though her coat was fluffier from living out and not being clipped. The mare had a white star in the centre of her forehead, and a white sock on her left hind. She was of a chunky build - in fact, she looked nothing like a Thoroughbred, and I wouldn't have believed she was one if I hadn't known for certain. She stood around fifteen-three, walked around the parade ring as calmly as a cob, and had a mischievous glint in her eye that wasn't mean, but certainly promised a stubborn character.

'I need it,' India said simply, staring at the mare with an open mouth.

While the chestnut was led around the ring, India leaned against the railings, her upper body dangling in the ring, and spoke to the handler every time they passed near her with an ease and confidence that gave away just how many times before she'd done this. I could hear neither what she asked nor what the person leading the mare replied, but after three exchanges like this India nodded, her expression clouded by a poker face, and made her way back over to Freya and me.

'No vices. She's come from up north. Was in training, but matured late and they never got around to racing her. Claim she's sound.'

I frowned, confused by the comments. 'So you're asking because you want to ride her?'

'No, of course not,' India said, as though the thought of riding any of the horses in this ring was absurd, but she didn't intend it meanly. 'Just asking to know. She's by So Much Noise, who obviously isn't popular, but I like him, though granted his stud fee's not that expensive.'

At this point, after the past week, I didn't dare ask what India considered "not that expensive".

'So what would you do with her?' I say. '*You* want to buy her?'

'Well, no, I'm looking for Dad. She's got good conformation, and she *is* out of a Nureyev mare, so if we put her to something fashionable then the foal could sell all right.' India bent her catalogue and held out Siren's page towards us. 'See here? Her dam won a race, and has had three winners from five runners, which isn't bad. A foal out of her' - she nodded at Siren walking around the ring - 'could do well. And, you know, it's the last day, it's a crap slot, and that's what you're taking advantage of. She'd make a few grand easy on another day.'

There were four lots to go until Siren Sounding, and Freya and I followed India into the near-empty sales ring, where her dad was sitting in one of the seats near the entrance, his face morphed into a bored expression as his eyes darted from the catalogue on his knee to the horse in the ring.

'One-three-one-eight,' India whispered to him, bending low as she spoke, and Arthur wordlessly flipped his catalogue to that page. 'I really like her. She's in the parade ring. I spoke to the handler - no vices, late to mature. Good feet, plenty of bone.'

'The name sounds like a bad omen if you ask me,' he muttered, but I still saw him read the page carefully, giving the horse a fair chance. 'So Much Noises aren't doing much at the moment.'

'But they look nice,' India countered. 'Put her to something good, and you could have a decent foal. Her dam *does* have a page.'

The two batted words back and forth like this, and it was all noise that had little meaning to me, but finally Arthur pulled a face and shook his head.

'I just got two, we don't need another, and certainly not one that's such a gamble. Even if she did have a nice foal, it'll be two years until we see any money from it. And there's still the February sales yet.'

I wouldn't have pegged India as one to fuss when she doesn't get her own way, but she was clearly getting agitated. 'Just look at her,' she said, her voice more patient than I expected it to be. 'Trust me, she's good.'

When Siren walked into the ring some ten minutes later, following lots that only made between 800 and 3500 guineas - which was pretty meagre compared to the numbers that had been flying earlier this week - Arthur eyed her up critically and shrugged with a nod of his head, which I took to mean he conceded that India was right, the mare *was* good.

'She's not bad,' he whispered to India, 'but there are plenty more like her. We don't need her right now.'

It took some coaxing, but the auctioneer managed to get an 800 guinea bid, which was the minimum sale price. As he continued his incomprehensible speech, trying to entice new bidders, India repeatedly nudged her father's shoulder, trying to get him to raise his hand for the mare.

'Last call and I sell to the lady by the doors for eight hundred.'

India thumped Arthur in the arm again and snapped, 'Bid!'

Arthur began to shake his head and mutter, 'India,' but he barely had the word out before the auctioneer turned towards us, pointed a finger, and said. 'One thousand bid. One thousand, do I hear one-five?'

'India,' Arthur snapped as his daughter lowered her arm.

'I'm doing you a favour,' India whispered.

'All done at one thousand? Selling at one thousand?' The hammer dropped. 'One thousand buys, thank you, Arthur.'

At first I was surprised that the auctioneer had taken India's raised hand as a serious bid, but of course he knew she was with Arthur of Tricklemoon Stud. Then I expected Arthur to protest, to tell the auctioneer there had been a mistake, if that was even possible. But when one of the ponytailed and suited girls made her way towards us with a clipboard and pen, Arthur merely shrugged and filled out the buyer's form.

'You owe me,' was all he said to India as he handed back the piece of paper. 'If she's a bugger, you're looking after her.'

'I will, I will,' India assured him, giving his shoulders a squeeze. 'Thank you.'

'Uh-huh,' Arthur said, feigning annoyance, but I could see a smile tugging at the corner of his lips. Almost as though he was proud his daughter had just bought a horse on his behalf, even after being told no.

India led us out of the sales ring as soon as the form was filled and towards a stable beside the vet offices, where Siren had been taken. All horses were brought here in case the new buyers wanted any tests done on them, she explained. We followed Siren back to her stable, where India proceeded to feed the mare Polos and make a fuss of her - she loved the mints, and was less bothered by the latter. But she was sweet, and seemed easy enough to handle, so I reckoned India was maybe right about her.

'I still can't believe you did that,' Freya said after we shut Siren's stable door, shaking her head. The handler who had led the mare around had only her entered in the sale, and had already left to drive back to Yorkshire, freed of his responsibilities.

'Your dad wasn't even angry!' I said.

'Why would he be? I *know* he liked her. She'll probably breed a big winner and make him really successful and he'll have me to thank.' The mare pushed her nose up against the grid on the door, and India scratched her top lip, beaming. 'I love her.'

'So, you know,' I say to Mum now, pushing thoughts of India and Siren to the back of my mind, 'you should count yourself lucky.'

Mum passes me a tray of hot drinks and swings her handbag onto her right shoulder. 'I'm sure India does a lot that you don't do.'

'What does that mean? That if I did more I could go out and buy a horse - with *your* money - without your permission?'

'It means that they live a life that is very different from ours,' Mum says patiently, stepping around the counter with a box of baked goods in her hands, 'and that I'm sure India is involved enough with the stud work to make such a call.'

I scoff. 'Please. There's no way you wouldn't go mental if I got another horse, even if I did work all hours of the day.'

Mum sighs, clearly bored of this conversation. 'Hit the lights.'

I hit the light switch when Mum reaches the door, the café illuminated only by the twinkling lights of the tree. 'You're only changing the subject because you know I'm right.'

'I bet India doesn't lecture her parents, either.'

'Only because they don't lecture her,' I counter.

After we saw Siren in her stable and headed back up to the sales ring, Catherine Humphries appeared from the direction of the car park, yet to know what India had just done. I'd still never really had an actual conversation with her so much as heard her speak to others, still thought her stuck-up and irritating, and was prepared to see her have a meltdown when she heard what India had done.

'Hi, girls,' she said warmly, smiling as we approached. Her face was made-up and her hair immaculately blow-dried, looking blonder than usual against a Barbour jacket. Up close like this, able to look at her face clearly, she looked older than I thought she was, closer to fifty than forty. 'What're you up to?'

'Hi, Caddie!' a passerby called in a foreign accent, waving, and Catherine smiled and waved back. Like Arthur, she obviously knew a lot of people here.

'Oh my god, you have to come see the mare we just got,' India said, grabbing her mum by the arm and spinning on her heel, heading back towards Siren's stable. I didn't know how people navigated this venue without already being enrolled in a serious fitness regimen, because I was exhausted from the constant back-and-forth, but followed with Freya nonetheless as Catherine was led away. Sore muscles weren't going to keep me from seeing this reaction…

India babbled all the way to the stable, telling her mum about seeing Siren in the parade ring, rattling off facts about her pedigree, not even denying that she put her hand up on Arthur's behalf to secure the bid, all of which Catherine listened to with her usual expression, like this was nothing out of the ordinary.

'Oh, she is nice, isn't she?' Catherine said when we reached the stable, and I felt like throwing my arms in the air and crying out for a witness, for somebody to please confirm that *this* was not how parents are supposed to react to their thirteen-year-old daughter spending their money on a horse without permission. As it was, I had Freya beside me, and when I glanced at her, she looked just as baffled.

'She's really friendly, too,' India said, hitting the kick bolt with the heel of her boot. 'Hey, Ren-Ren, c'mere.'

Ren-Ren? I thought.

'Ren-Ren?' Catherine said, her expression turning to one of mockery.

'She's called Siren,' India explained. 'Siren Sounding.'

Catherine's eyebrows shot up. 'Well that's a steer clear sign if ever I saw one.'

I stifled a laugh, not wanting to warm to the Catherine Humphries I'd built up as a villain in my mind for so long, and watched as she stepped into the stable, beside India.

'She's friendly,' India said again as the chestnut mare stepped forward towards Catherine. 'Isn't she cute?' The Thoroughbred's ears were forward, but I didn't find her as adorable as India did. It wasn't that she wasn't nice and friendly, because she was, but there was also something brutish about her that just couldn't be described as "cute".

'She *is* nice,' Catherine admitted, putting her handbag down in the gravel outside the stable door. 'Hey? Are you sweet?' she cooed to the mare, scratching her forehead.

Freya and I soon had to bid our farewells in order to make it home to our ponies before dark, and as we walked back to the café, where Mum would give us a lift, two thoughts stuck in my mind: How could India's parents be so cool about what she did? And that maybe Catherine Humphries wasn't as bad as I thought. *Caddie* Humphries, that's what everyone seems to call her to her face, but I'm not sure I'll ever be able to bring myself to refer to her so casually.

'I'm sure India gets lectured plenty when it's called for,' Mum says, the cold wind that hits my cheeks when she opens the door knocking me out of my daydream.

'I doubt it.'

We step onto the pavement, still illuminated by streetlights, lit-up storefronts, and headlights, and Mum frowns as she turns to lock the door, balancing the box of muffins against her chest. 'So let me get this straight. You're now trying to tell me that the Humphrieses, whom you've spoken about as though they were these millionaire villains-'

'I never said that-'

'-are now *too* nice for your liking?'

'I never said that, either,' I say crossly, fiddling with the tray of coffees. 'It's just that Catherine's always seemed awful at events, and I'm surprised to see that she's actually somewhat decent, and also that she lets India get away with so much.'

'Well, events are stressful,' Mum says. 'Trust me, as an event mum, it's very hard for us to be nice to you in those situations.'

'Oh, thanks,' I say sarcastically.

'And besides,' she goes on, 'haven't you said that both India's sisters are nice, too?'

I think back to the conversations I had with Sophia and Mia, who both seemed like decent human beings, and just as easy to get along with as India. 'Yeah,' I say, voicing it more as a question than an answer.

'Well,' Mum says reasonably, turning away from the locked door, 'if all the kids are nice, then surely the parents are all right.'

I groan. 'Why do you think that parents can do no wrong? Why can't we be all right on our own, even with bad influence?'

'Sybil. You know what I mean. Of course India and her sisters could be nice without their parents being so, but from what I've seen they're happy girls with good manners, and that's got to come from somewhere.'

I'd be happy and polite too if I had their lives, I think. *Stop thinking like that,* I scold myself. 'I guess,' I concede out loud. 'It's freezing,' I add, holding the tray closer to me for warmth.

'It is,' Mum says, looking down at her box of baked goods. 'Just think how lucky you are you're not sleeping out in this.'

The next two weeks leading up to Christmas pass both slowly

and quickly - quickly because I feel like we only just moved to Newmarket, like Ace and I only just crossed paths and yet suddenly the year is coming to a close, and slowly because I manage to achieve a lot in these last weeks. The building work is complete, the yard now boasting four extra stables, a new overhang for hay and straw, and a six-horse walker. Ace is back in ridden work - following two days of being lunged in just a rope halter to not catch her in the mouth if she pulled away, another few days of being lunged with tack on, and a couple of cautious ridden sessions in the school, making sure I didn't get thrown off before winter training had even begun. The mare was spooky to begin with, like she had been when she first arrived at Rose's, seeing imaginary ghosts she wanted to bolt from everywhere, but she also settled very quickly, and I was pleasantly surprised when I was able to start walking her along the roads and bridleways within ten days of her coming back into work.

Rose's fitness program comes to twelve weeks in total, three months until the ponies are competition-ready, and the plan is to get some dressage and show jumping outings in before they start eventing. I can't wait for it to all kick off again, for it to be next year so I can compete every weekend, to be plaiting manes until my fingers are numb, cleaning out stud holes until my back aches, to be trotting down a centre line. This time last year I didn't even know Ace, and I only rode Jupiter sporadically, competing the odd weekend for the fun of it. I envied those with serious event prospects and giant setups and competitive parents, and yet I never thought I actually wanted that myself, and I still don't, but I do like the hard work side of horses more than I ever thought I would. I wanted to ride Jupiter in a Pony Trial, wanted to get him up to Novice level, but I didn't really know how much I'd have to commit myself to make that happen so much as it was just an idea.

And I'm not just looking forward to it happening.

I'm looking forward to working for it.

chapter 13

Dad gives me my Christmas present early, because my present is tickets to Olympia, a week before Christmas. I have two tickets, so naturally I invite Freya, and we spend Saturday evening in London, watching the Christmas Tree Stakes, and then go to Dad's for the night.

'Those jumps were ridiculous,' I say to her that night while I'm sitting in bed. Dad's flat only has two bedrooms, so Gabe and I have to share one with twin beds, and Freya is in my brother's, across the room from me. It's nearing midnight, but neither of us is tired, still full of adrenalin from watching the jump-off.

We're each sitting up in bed, speaking quietly to avoid waking Dad in the other room. Outside the window, London is still alive with streetlights and car horns, and I think how I don't miss living in a town in any way at all.

'I could never show jump,' Freya says, shaking her head as she eats from a bag of chocolate buttons.

'Me neither,' I say, taking a handful from my own bag. 'I'd love to know how high I could jump, though. Just to know.'

'You mean, like, do a puissance or something?' Freya says.

'Yeah. I'd probably fall off, though,' I say, which reminds me of something, and I sit up further. 'We could do one ourselves! I remember India said she and Mia did a puissance once.'

Freya frowns at me mockingly. 'Yeah, that's why Mia's arm's in a cast. Great idea!'

'But that was just unlucky,' I say. 'Besides, you've seen Harvey jump. Anyone would fall off him. But we could do our own puissance.'

'Leo's still doing fitness work, though,' Freya says. 'Even if he wasn't, I probably wouldn't risk it.'

'That's exactly why you *should*,' I say. 'It'd be fun.'

'Fun?' Freya repeats.

'Yes,' I say adamantly, putting my bag of chocolate buttons down on the nightstand. 'There's no point in having horses if you don't have fun sometimes, right?'

* * *

'Sybil, can you get the door?' Mum says, her hands covered in flour and the kitchen counter in some flattened pastry.

'Come in!' I yell over the sound of the dogs barking, and Mum glares at me.

'See, that wasn't what I had in mind.'

I shrug, and before I can see who is opening the front door I hear Liam's voice telling the dogs to hush.

'Hello, Liam,' Mum says warmly, dusting her hands on her apron.

'Hello,' Liam says back, closing the door behind him. Ever since he finished editing his book earlier this month, he's looked a lot less like someone who sleeps on the streets and more like the type of person you'd expect to live in his grand house. His brown hair has recently been cut, and he's dressed in a Ralph Lauren jumper, clean dark jeans, and suede shoes. He steps towards the kitchen, cradling some items in his arms. 'Things look busy in here?' He phrases it like a question.

'Well, you know what it's like,' Mum says, rinsing her hands beneath the tap and shaking off the excess water before grabbing a tea towel.

Liam nods, and I glance at him quickly, his eyes meeting mine for just a second, and I know we're silently communicating the same thought: no, he *doesn't* know what it's like, because he's a childless guy who lives alone, and has never had to deal with last minute Christmas Eve cooking and preparations.

As I look at him, Liam lifts his shoulders in a shrug so minor that you'd miss it if you weren't paying attention, expression blank, and I look away to suppress a laugh.

'A lot of people coming tomorrow, then?' he goes on swiftly before Mum can notice our exchange.

'Uh, no, not really,' Mum says, opening the oven door to check on her red cabbage. 'My mum and her partner are coming from Gloucestershire, and Sybil and Gabe's dad is coming up for a bit, too.'

This last part was a great surprise to me when it was announced a couple of days ago. With all my fretting about the upcoming holiday, never did it occur to me that my parents would actually be spending the day together.

'Dad's spending Christmas here?' I spluttered when Mum told me and Gabe this. 'But you're divorced!'

'I know we're divorced, Sybs,' Mum said, 'but we still both care about you, both of you, and want to spend the day together.'

'But you're divorced,' I said again, unable to comprehend what Mum was saying. 'How can you spend the day together?'

'Your father and I are perfectly capable of spending a day in the same room. Just because we're not together, doesn't mean we're not still friends and care about each other.'

'So he's driving down for Christmas lunch?' Gabe asked, though he seemed much less perplexed by the ordeal than I was.

Mum nodded. 'He's eating here, then driving on to your grandparents'.'

'What are you doing, Liam?' I ask.

'Oh, not much,' Liam says, clearing his throat. 'Drinking some mulled wine, listening to the Queen's speech. The usual.'

'You're not spending the day with family?' Mum says, her brow creasing with concern.

'No, no,' Liam says, smiling reassuringly. 'My folks are up in Scotland.'

'You could drive up,' I point out.

He shakes his head. 'I'm not big on Christmas, to be honest. I'd much rather stay here with the cat. Besides, my sister has the *most* annoying kids.' I start to laugh, and Liam goes on. 'They're five and seven, something like that, and I only have to be around them for a minute to get a migraine.'

'I didn't know you had a sister!' Mum says, which I think is sort of a silly thing to say, because why would any of us know about Liam's family?

'Two. Matilda and Rachel.'

'Older or younger?'

'Tillie, who has the kids, is the oldest, and Rach is a few years younger than me. Don't get me wrong, I love my sister Tillie, but her husband's a bit of a pr - a bit up himself,' he corrects, purely for my benefit I think, 'and their boys are spoiled rotten. I went up for the holidays last year, and when I fell asleep on the sofa they drew on my face!' he says, sounding genuinely scarred by the experience.

'Christmas is about enduring that sort of thing,' Mum says.

Liam shakes his head again. 'No, not happening,' he says, and he doesn't even sound like he's joking.

'They're just kids,' I say.

He scoffs. 'Easy to say when you're not the one who had to spend eight hours on a train with Harry Potter glasses and a lightning bolt drawn on your face in permanent marker.' I try to stifle a laugh, as does Mum, but neither of us is very successful, and Liam pretends to look wounded. 'You think I'm exaggerating? The train was packed with kids, and every ten minutes I had one run up to me and snicker, "Hogwarts is the other way!" or "You got on at platform 2, not platform 9 & 3/4" before running off.'

Mum and I are still laughing when Gabe comes down the stairs, frowning at us all. 'What's so funny?'

'Liam's nephews drew Harry Potter glasses on his face in permanent marker and he had to spend a whole train ride like that,' I say.

'Did you get made fun of?' Gabe asks.

'Yes.'

'You were on a train? Did someone make a Hogwarts joke?'

'Yes,' Liam says again, unamused.

Gabe snorts. 'Good, or else that would've been a waste.'

'I don't know why you don't like kids, Liam,' Mum jokes, holding out a hand towards Gabe, 'they're great!'

Liam smiles subtly, one corner of his mouth tugging upwards. 'Nah,' he says, glancing from me to Gabe, 'these two are all right. Anyway,' he goes on, shuffling the items in his arms. 'I just came to drop off a few things for tomorrow.'

'Oh, you shouldn't have,' Mum says as she accepts a bottle of champagne, but I know she has a gift for Liam waiting beside the tree in the form of whiskey and shortbreads.

Liam puts a large, flat box of chocolates down on the table, revealing two more items cradled against his chest. 'Now, they aren't wrapped,' he warns, speaking to Gabe and me, 'but I thought you might like these, too.'

I gasp, and Gabe practically squeals as Liam holds out finished copies of the next Amity Byron book. The thick hardback book is covered in a beautiful dust jacket, the lettering embellished with foil, the cover art detailed and in keeping with the previous books.

'Oh my goodness, Liam,' Mum says, looking adoringly at the books.

'Oh my god,' Gabe says, flipping the book open to the first chapter, only to flip back a few pages. 'Did you sign it?'

Mum glares at Gabe, but Liam only laughs. 'I did. You two own the only signed copies in the world. I only got the box of finished copies yesterday.'

'That's very generous of you, Liam,' Mum says. 'What do you say, kids?'

'Thank you so much, Liam,' I say, and I mean it. I read the first books in few sittings, and have been dying to know what happens next. Despite Liam's willingness to have Gabe and me over at his house and to discuss the already published stories, he's refused to reveal anything about the latest instalment.

'Liam,' Mum goes on, as though just struck by something, 'why don't you join us for lunch tomorrow?'

'Oh, no, I couldn't-'

'Really, I mean it. It's low-key, and we have way too much food, anyway.'

'You have your family-'

'Really,' Mum insists, 'we'd love to have you.'

'Yes, please come!' I say, and Gabe echoes my words.

'You don't have to decide now,' Mum says. 'We'll be eating around one, and there'll be a seat for you at the table if you want it.'

Liam nods, looking genuinely touched. 'That's very kind of you.'

It isn't until some minutes later, after we've waved Liam off and returned to our own activities, that I really focus on the book, flipping through its first pages. As Liam promised, the copy is signed, *W. J. Heathcote* scrawled in black ink, but that isn't what catches my attention as I turn to the dedication page.

'Oh my god,' I whisper.

For Gabe and Sybil,
He who has a pen need never raise a fist.
(Apologies again for not resembling a wizard)

* * *

Later that evening, I walk along the icy road, wrapped in a thick coat, tucking my chin into my scarf. It was so cold this morning that I brought Ace and Jupiter in after only a couple of hours in the field, so I only have to feed and skip out now, but there's something else I want to do first.

'Freya!' I call, spotting my friend in her pony's paddock as I walk along the road.

Freya turns her head at the sound of my voice, a shavings fork in her hand, and she rests it on the barrow at the sight of me, abandoning her poo-picking.

'I'm frozen,' she says when I reach her.

I nod. 'Me too.'

Freya looks over her shoulder, at the tidy-but-muddy field, and Leo looking out over the half door of his stable, rugged up to his ears. 'C'mon. Let's go inside.'

The kitchen of Willow Tree House is warm in both senses of the word - the Aga fills the room with heat, and the tartan blankets and smell of cooking apple add to the cosy lived-in feel. Through the open door to the snug I can see flames roaring in the fireplace, and can smell the old seagrass carpet. Stripes trots up to greet us, and I scratch his spotty head, admiring the silver tinsel wrapped around his collar.

'Crumpet?' Freya says, holding up a packet, and I nod.

'I'll put the kettle on,' I say, because Freya's is one place I'm more than comfortable enough to jump up and boil water.

Freya carries the present I've brought her to the tree in the sitting room, returning with one for me, and I laugh as she hands it to me.

'Nice wrapping.' The present is covered in brown paper that smells of oats and molasses, the inside of a horse feed bag, and tied with baling twine.

Freya shrugs, trying not to laugh. 'I might as well do something with the feed bags. Save the environment.'

'No, I like it,' I say. I'd never have thought to wrap my own presents like this, proven by the very colourful paper and silver ribbon Freya has just been given, but I wish I had.

'*Brown paper packages, tied up with strings,*' Freya sings.

'Fair enough.' I jump back up as the kettle switches off, and pull two mugs from the overhead cupboard.

Having known Freya as long as I have, I knew there was a reason other than Christmas spirit that she asked me to come inside so eagerly, and it's when we're seated with cups of milky Earl Grey and plates of crumpets slathered with butter and blackberry jelly that I discover why.

'I got this last night,' Freya says, leaning back in her seat to pull a piece of paper from the crowded buffet top behind us.

At first I'm not sure what it is I'm staring at, confused to be faced with a photo of a pony that looks like Diamond, then I realise it *is* Diamond, pictured with a small rider on his back and a large rosette hanging from his bridle. Above the photo is an email, from a Diane Edgerton, and I read the words.

Dear Freya,

So sorry for not getting back to you sooner!! Time got away from me this month, and I wanted to make sure I wrote you a proper message.

Diamond is everything we hoped for and more. Hettie took him to Pony Club camp this summer and had the time of her life! The two have really started to form a partnership, and I have no doubt they will do great things.

They have been to three shows so far, and placed at every

one.

Diamond is part of the family. Hettie is mad about him, but I think I am even more so. He's a member of the family now, and always will be.

Here's a picture of them winning their last Hunter round. As you can see, he's still terribly fond of his food! I'm hoping to keep Hettie in a ring for a little while longer, but she's been cross country schooling and is desperate to start eventing Diamond like you did!

Hope everything's going well for you and your new pony! If Diamond's anything to go by, any horse is lucky to get you as an owner and rider.

Please wish your parents a Happy Christmas from us, and don't hesitate to come visit Diamond anytime you want.

Diane and Hettie xxx (And Diamond!)

'He looks so good!' I say, lowering my eyes back to the photograph. The spotted pony has one ear pricked and the other cocked to the side, as though listening to his rider. Little Hettie looks like the quintessential showing rider, her stick legs clad in cream jodhpurs, her torso covered by a tweed coat, and bright blond hair beneath a velvet riding hat. As the email said, Diamond clearly hasn't missed a meal since he's been away, looking as chunky as ever, muscle bulging through his chestnut spots.

'He does, doesn't he?' Freya leans across the table to look at the printed-off email again, smiling to herself. 'And they sound like they really love him.'

'They do,' I say reassuringly. 'He's probably thrilled, getting fed as much as he wants, spoiled rotten, and only having to trot around a show ring.'

Freya laughs. 'Yeah, probably.' She looks down, at her half-eaten crumpet, then raises her eyes back to me. 'You know how he was nothing when I got him?'

'Literally,' I say. Not only was Diamond a scruffy, unbroken pony, but he was seriously underfed, all his ribs showing.

Freya smiles. 'Well, I kept feeling like I'd failed him by then selling him, and I still do, in one way… but, like, then I think of what he'd be like now if I *hadn't* got him. If he'd never been treated right… You know?'

'You gave him a chance,' I say. I know those are the words Freya was looking for, but she still looks slightly unsure.

'Yeah?' she says.

I nod. 'Yeah. Absolutely.'

'Like you did with Ace,' Freya adds, never one to keep the conversation revolving around herself.

This time it's my turn to be uncertain. 'I dunno about that. She wasn't exactly badly treated.'

'She was misunderstood. Okay, she was fed and well enough looked after, but she wasn't *happy,* and she wasn't actually doing anything.'

'She *was* in foal,' I point out.

'Yeah, but she was only in foal because she'd been given up on. And now you've made her into something.'

'Rose rode her too -'

'You know what I mean.'

My next argument dies on the tip of my tongue, and I think of Ace, of the flighty, angry bay mare that came off the lorry at Rose's six months ago. Has it really been that long already? Almost seven months, even, which is crazy to think. It feels like yesterday I used to dread riding her, and didn't really know what I was going to do to win her over. But I did. Sort of.

'I guess,' I concede, swallowing a mouthful of tea. I lower the mug back to the table, and my eyes are roaming absently over the room when I spot a new photograph. 'Hey, I haven't seen that one,' I say, jumping up to inspect the picture propped up on the piece of furniture behind Freya. It's a cross country shot of Leo, the words printed in gold on the paper frame indicating it was taken at the last event, and I stare at the photo in awe.

It's not a jumping shot, not some copybook bascule over a fence that seems massive to me.

The photo was taken between fences. It's a close-up shot, cut off at Leo's withers. Freya is leaning forward in a two-point seat, her face determined, and the chestnut pony just as much so, his ears pricked, eye relaxed. Freya's left hand is forward, mid pat, against the gelding's neck in encouragement, and Leo is responding by carrying on, eye on the job.

They look like a team.

'I like that picture,' I say, staring at the photograph. I still don't have any cross country pictures of Ace, but maybe I'll get one half as good as this one someday. The two of us working together, the moment captured perfectly.

Freya gets up from her seat to stand next to me, eyes fixed on the photo. I turn my head to look at her, and for once her face gives away what she's feeling, lips tugging into a genuine smile and her eyes full of emotion. 'Yeah,' she says. 'I like it, too.'

'Merry Christmas, Maggot,' I whisper, letting myself into her stable. It's not even seven a.m. yet, the rest of the world still asleep beneath a night sky, but despite it being Christmas Day, I woke up this morning with only one thing on my mind, and it was being at the yard as soon as possible to give Ace a hug. I thought of Jupiter too, of course, but not in the same way. I've spent other Christmases with the grey gelding, but this is my first with Ace.

The bay mare is standing at the back of her box, her silhouette only just visible in the dark. I could turn on a light, but I don't want to disturb her or the other horses.

'You all right?' I say. The light shining into the box from the moon and stars is enough to make the white heart on Ace's forehead shine, and I walk straight towards her head. In the half-light like this, I can't make out her expression, can't watch for pinned ears or bared teeth, but it doesn't matter, because I trust her.

'I love you, little one,' I say, my fingers finding the space between the front of Ace's rug and her neck cover. I slide my hand beneath it, checking her clipped body for warmth, and step nearer, wrapping my arms around her neck. 'You're happy, aren't you?' I carry on quietly, mulling over Freya's words yesterday. Ace has never been mistreated, never been deprived of anything, but there's a big difference between being alive and living. Plenty of horses get the bare essentials, get a field to roam in, the odd slice of hay, and a cover in winter, but that's not the same as being happy and cared for.

I lean into Ace's neck, staying very still, and the mare snorts, slowly releasing a breath in a way that makes her sound like a dragon. I wonder if I should move, if I should step away and leave her in peace.

But then Ace surprises me.

She stops me from moving.

Because suddenly her head wraps around the side of me, and she's resting her weight against mine.

When I step up to our cottage a couple of hours later, after turning out and mucking out the ponies, and being force-fed Christmas cookies by Mackenzie, my entire body frozen, I don't expect to see Walter sitting on the chair by his front door. Seriously, this guy has three-hundred-and-sixty-five days of the year to sit outside, and he manages to choose the two coldest. I haven't seen him since the first time we officially met, and am not too sure what to say. After what Rose told me about him, I want to make an effort to speak to him every now and then, but I also don't want to get stuck out here today of all days. He doesn't have a newspaper today, but a large leather-bound book.

'Good morning,' I say politely, walking up to our front door.

'Good morning,' Walter says, his hands shaking as he lowers his book. 'No day off?'

I shake my head, wondering how brief I can be without being rude. 'Not with horses.'

'Tell me about it,' he chuckles. 'One thing I don't miss. How did your event go?'

'My event?' I say, forgetting Walter even knew about it, especially since it already feels like so long ago. 'It was okay. I withdrew before cross country, but she went clear show jumping and led the dressage. What?' I add boldly, seeing Walter laugh. I don't need to talk to old people if they're just going to laugh at anything I say.

'You said "she",' he says. 'Most riders these days don't give the horses credit.' *Oh.* 'That's nice to hear.'

'Well, Ace definitely wouldn't do something just because I want her to,' I say. 'She's not exactly going to let me take all the credit. The vinegar worked,' I add. 'Cleaning the bit.'

Walter's smile widens, and he nods slowly. 'Always does the trick.' He looks down, at the book on his lap, and taps one of the pages, holding it out towards me. 'See this here?'

I cross the garden, stepping over the plants between the two cottage fronts, and see that what Walter is looking through is a photo album. The page he holds open shows a photograph of a racehorse, crossing a finish line with his nose in front.

'Bought this horse for eight hundred guineas, I did,' he tells me proudly. 'A few years later and a million couldn't have bought him.'

'That's amazing,' I say, and turn around as I hear a door open.

'Sybil?' Mum says, stepping over the threshold. 'I thought I could hear voices. Hello, Walter. Happy Christmas. Oh, don't get up,' she adds as Walter begins to stand from his seat.

'I'm not dead yet,' Walter jokes, standing up despite Mum's protests, putting the photo album down where he was sitting. 'Happy Christmas, Ms.' He then takes a step back, gesturing at

Mum and me. 'Now don't let me hold you up. I was just boring your daughter here with stories from my racing days.'

'I doubt that very much,' Mum says. She steps nearer me, hugging her cardigan tight to her chest, and I see her gaze drift to Walter's home, searching for an extra car in the driveway, or some movement behind a curtain. 'Do you have plans for the day? Any family coming round?'

Walter smiles and shakes his head. 'Just me. I have a roast chicken and a Christmas pudding to myself.'

Even though Walter is trying to make light of being on his own for the day, it's obvious he doesn't want to be, and I know what Mum is going to say before she even says it. I knew the moment she saw the lack of activity in the cottage.

'Well, would you like to join us for lunch?'

'Oh, no,' Walter starts to protest. 'Don't worry about me, I wasn't fishing for an invite.'

'No, you weren't, I'm inviting you,' Mum says.

'It's a family holiday, you don't need an old nuisance like me imposing.'

'Nonsense! We only have a few family members coming, and you know Liam' - she points behind her, at Liam's big house farther along from our semi-detached cottages - 'well, he's coming, too. It's very casual.'

'That's very kind of you to offer, Ms,' Walter says.

'Please, call me Maya.'

'Maya.' Walter nods. 'Well, I really don't want to impose on you, but I much appreciate the invite.'

Mum smiles. 'You are more than welcome. We're eating at one, so I'll leave the ball in your court, but we'd be very happy to have you at our table.'

My grandfather passed away a few years ago, and the day after his funeral Gran took off on a round-the-world trip. She'd never travelled before, and she didn't know what else to do with herself, so for a year she lived off Grandpa's life insurance. She saw the Northern Lights in Iceland, went on a safari in Africa, walked the beaches of Thailand... For a year she moved from one country to the next, sleeping in basic lodgings and never staying in one place longer than a few weeks. I remember asking Mum, after receiving a postcard telling about almost being stung by a sting ray, whether Gran had gone crazy, to which Mum responded that she thought this was the most sensible thing Gran had ever done.

A few weeks before she was supposed to come back to the UK, Gran made a final stop in Jamaica, and that's where she met Glenmore, and the two have been together ever since. Five years her junior and originally from Montego Bay, Glenmore couldn't be more different from Grandpa, but we all adore him. He makes the best curry in the world, and taught me and Gabe to play poker, which I'm pretty sure he lets us win at, because I've won enough playing against Glenmore to cover an event entry fee or two.

Gran and Glenmore arrive at twelve o'clock, and the hour until lunch is spent catching up, passing in a blur. Glenmore asks about Jupiter, and I tell him all about Ace, as well as try to explain, again, what exactly eventing is, because he can never remember the particulars and not for lack of listening.

The first knock at the door comes at five to one, and I swing it open to reveal Liam, holding a bottle of wine.

'You look nice,' I blurt, surprised to see him look so smart. He's dressed in a blue blazer over a shirt of the same colour, his trousers brown and his shoes leather, face clean-shaven.

Liam frowns. 'Are you saying I don't look nice the rest of the time?'

'Uh-'

'Oh, thanks,' he deadpans, then grins, and I step aside to let him into the house, Frodo and Eleven rushing up to greet him.

'This is Liam, our neighbour,' Mum introduces as Gran and

Glenmore stand up to greet him

'Pleasure to meet you,' Liam says, stepping forward to shake Gran and Glenmore's hands as Mum takes the bottle of wine from him.

It's a few minutes later that the door knocks again, and I expect it to be Dad, but it's Walter who stands on the doorstep. Despite Mum telling him lunch is casual, he's gone to the effort of putting on a suit, one that doesn't look like it's been worn in a while, and he holds a bouquet of flowers.

Liam jumps up immediately, offering Walter the most comfortable seat and fetching him a drink, and soon we're all seated around the small table in the even smaller house, laughing and eating pigs in blankets. Walter and Liam both start conversations easily, Walter and Glenmore currently engaged in a discussion on horse racing while Gran is eager to talk literature with Liam.

'I'm a Jane Austen fan,' she tells him, swallowing a mouthful of champagne. 'You know Maya's middle name is Elizabeth after Elizabeth Bennet.'

'No, I didn't know that,' Liam says, glancing at Mum with amusement.

'Can't say it's ever come up,' Mum says brusquely. To Gran's disappointment, Mum has never been a fan of *Pride and Prejudice*.

'And Maya after Maya Angelou, of course,' Gran says.

'Of course,' Liam repeats, trying to hide his amusement at Mum's embarrassed face.

We're all engaged in conversation when the door opens and Dad steps in, twenty minutes after lunch was supposed to start. He doesn't knock, so no one expects him to step in when he does, and there's a bit of an awkward silence, but it's quickly recovered from, and Liam and Glenmore are among the first to jump up from their seats, followed by Walter.

'I didn't think there'd be any traffic,' Dad says, putting down a bag of gifts and taking off his coat, 'but everyone was trying to get out of London.'

'I know I would, if I lived there,' Liam says quietly, and I stifle a laugh - you tend not to live in the countryside if you're a fan of London.

There are greetings and introductions, and I can tell Dad is somewhat surprised to see two faces he doesn't know, but he's polite nonetheless.

'A toast,' Walter says when another bottle of champagne is opened, raising his glass. 'To good neighbours, and new friends.'

Gran raises hers. 'Hear! hear!'

After an afternoon of eating, laughing, playing charades, and all listening to the Queen's speech, I make it back to the yard, eager to be with the ponies. I used to find having to look after Jupiter on Christmas Day a hindrance, even with Mum's help. I'd wish I didn't have to go out, that he could be ignored for just one day, but not anymore. I *want* to look after Ace and Jupi, want to spend this day - even just a small part of it - with them.

'Merry Christmas, Jup,' I say to the grey pony, feeding him a carrot over his half door. He crunches it greedily, orange pieces falling from his mouth as he tries to take too much in one bite, and I smile at him. 'I know we all talk about Ace a lot,' I whisper to him, scratching my numb fingers against his head, 'but you're still my number one. You always will be. You know that, right?'

Jupiter nudges my shoulder, and I pull another carrot from my pocket, feeding it to the gelding before turning around, resting my back against the stable door. The sky is grey, and the frost I woke up to this morning has never melted, still covering the grass like a thin layer of icing sugar. The lights are on in Rose's farmhouse, and smoke drifts from the chimney in a plume. She's sure to be out again so, bundled up for evening stables, probably dragging Mackenzie out with her to lend a helping hand.

'You happy here?' I ask Jupiter, looking over my left shoulder at him.

The pony turns his head towards me, nudging my arm for more treats, completely oblivious. His ears are pricked, eyes alert, silver mane peeking out from beneath his neck cover.

'Yeah,' I say, as Jupiter nudges my coat sleeve with his upper lip, my eyes on the stables around us, and the frost-covered world beyond. 'I'm happy here, too.'

chapter 14

'Have you got to page 204 yet?'

'Huh?' I spin around from the staircase - or, more specifically, from the jacket hanging from a coat hanger on the bannister. I couldn't believe it when I opened my present from Mum this evening to see a navy blue show jumping jacket reveal itself in my hands. I must have made some offhand comments about my tweed coat, because I hadn't even thought to ask Mum for a new jacket, but clearly my yearning hadn't gone unnoticed. She'd asked Freya to help her choose, she explained, and I'm glad she did because my best friend couldn't have chosen a more perfect jacket. I've barely taken my eyes off it since it fell from the wrapping paper.

'Have you got to page 204 yet?' Gabe repeats urgently, walking up to me with Liam's book in his hands. With long drives ahead of them, Gran, Glenmore, and Dad all left well over an hour ago, while Walter and Liam stayed a tad longer, both too caught up in a discussion with Mum to end the evening quite yet, and Mum escorted them out the door twenty minutes ago, but the chatting hasn't stopped. I can hear three laughters drift through the closed door every so often.

'Uh, no, not yet,' I say. There's been no time for reading today.

Not long after getting back from looking after the ponies, the landline rang, revealing an overseas number, which was my cue to speak to my real father, our annual conversation - or biannual, as we sometimes speak on my birthday, too. It's an awkward two minutes of talking to a stranger who shouldn't be a stranger at all, in which holiday greetings are exchanged, and he always repeats the same two sentences: How's school? And, You're welcome to visit anytime.

After hanging up, we opened presents, and I've been too consumed by the jacket since then to notice much else.

'Why?' I ask Gabe.

'You're not going to believe this! So Amity has-'

'Hey,' I snap, covering my ears. 'Don't spoil it for me! I just told you I haven't read it yet.'

'It won't spoil anything, promise. Amity-' Gabe cuts himself off, shaking his head. 'Okay, never mind what happens exactly, except there's this really annoying guy, a total bully, and, anyway, Amity plays this prank on him and he ends up stranded in the woods in his underpants, where these wolves chase him down, and he doesn't die or anything, it's just really funny-'

'Gabe,' I interrupt. 'What's your point?'

My brother steps nearer me, opening the book to where his finger guards a page. 'Look at the guy's name!'

I lower my eyes to the page, not sure what the meaning of this is, but then I see it.

Patrick Firwell.

And I remember the words of Liam's dedication, suddenly making perfect sense. *He who has a pen need never raise a fist.*

'Sit straighter through your body. Good. You've just lost the rhythm, you're not going anywhere, so get her moving.'

Rose nods as I apply her corrections, as I squeeze Ace on with my leg, squaring up my shoulders and sitting straighter, making sure I contain the energy and don't let the mare's stride flatten.

'That's it. Good girl. Now go down the long side and turn up the centre line to do a left half-pass.'

I sit up through the turn, my eyes already on the middle of the school, visualising my next movement. Ace tries to bend her head to the inside and swing her right shoulder out of the ten-metre turn, but I'm already prepared for that, guarding her outside shoulder with my leg and ready to ride her straight, to keep her straight for a stride before asking for left bend and pushing her in that direction.

And when I curve her to the left and touch her with my right leg, there's no resistance. Ace's right hind steps under her, the left fore extends, and we're moving towards the track. I go through a mental checklist in my mind, making sure Ace's body remains straight, that she's not over-bending, that my own position isn't in her way.

'Don't let her get away at the last minute,' Rose corrects me as I hit the track. 'Don't get within two metres of the fence and let it fall apart, keep the half-pass right up to the last stride and then ride her straight, but the rest was super.' She gives a decisive nod. 'Again.'

I repeat the exercise, careful not to make the same mistakes again, then ask for a half-pass on the other rein. At some point in her life, even before Rose got her, Ace was well-schooled, because she knows all the basics of flatwork, and doing lateral movements on her is easy. *She* makes it easy. She teaches me.

'All right, let out your reins and leave her on that,' Rose says, and I lengthen my reins, Ace lowering her nose to the sand.

I trot her a few circles like this, reins at the buckle, allowing her to stretch out her back, as Rose gives me some hints on how to improve the exercises we worked on.

'Good girl,' I say to Ace as she comes back to a walk, mouthing her bit happily. 'You're the best.'

'She *is* the best,' Rose says, stepping up to the mare to scratch her forehead. 'Who'd have thought we'd ever be saying that?'

'I bet she did,' I say, scratching Ace's neck. 'I can't wait to start jumping her again.'

'Not long,' Rose says. 'You know, we could probably start some pole exercises and trot jumping now. Won't do her any harm, and she hasn't exactly lost any fitness.'

This latter statement is true - unlike Jupiter, who came out of his winter holiday looking as though he'd swallowed a whale and blew like a train after every ride for the first couple of weeks, Ace has held her condition and already looks event-ready. Jupiter even had a two-week head start, but you'd never guess it looking at them.

'Okay,' I say, and I smile as I remember a conversation with Freya some weeks ago, then shake the thought away, but not quickly enough for it to escape Rose's attention.

'What?' she asks, grinning.

I shake my head. 'Nothing. It's just... I was thinking about this thing Freya and I were talking about, about having a puissance one day, to see how high Ace can jump.'

'The top of the stands, I bet.'

'No way?' I say.

'Of course,' Rose says, scratching Ace's head again. 'I'd put money on it there's not much this pony can't jump.'

'Maybe,' I say, lost in a daydream of Ace clearing the Olympia wall.

'Well, shall we find out, then?'

'Huh?'

'A puissance,' Rose says. 'Sounds like fun. Give her another week or two of work, and she'd be fine.'

'But she's not supposed to start jumping till February.'

Rose shrugs, a smile tugging at her lips. 'You've got to break the rules and have fun every now and then, right?'

'I guess…' I start to say, but my words are cut off by Rose's ringing phone, which she pulls out of her pocket and frowns at.

'I missed a call from this number yesterday…' She hits the answer button. 'Hello?' She frowns again as she listens to the voice at the end of the line, and I think that she looks more tired than usual. Leah, the only yard help Rose has, has been flaky lately, leaving Rose with the bulk of the yard work, and it shows.

As she holds the phone to her ear, Rose's expression turns to understanding, presumably realising who's speaking on the other end, only for her to look confused again, and she excuses herself to continue the phone call elsewhere.

I swing out of the saddle and run up the stirrups, Rose forgotten as I focus on Ace. 'Let's get you out,' I say to the pony. 'I have to go see Freya…'

Freya texted me last night, asking if I could come over today as she had something to show me. Since Christmas, it's snowed three times, and water still covers sections of the road from the last thaw. I've never known it to snow so much in such a short period of time, and for the first time in my life, I've been crossing my fingers that it *doesn't*. I used to love snow, but now it's just something that gets in the way of riding, and I'd much rather be schooling the ponies than building a snowman.

When it hasn't been snowing, the temperatures have plummeted below freezing, and there have been days we haven't even been able to take the horses out of their stables because the whole yard was iced over, too dangerous to walk across even after emptying half a dozen bags of salt over the concrete. I turned the ponies out in the snow, because the ice had already kept them cooped in a day, and was surprised by just how much Ace loved it. She walked around the paddock with her nose on the ground, burrowing through the snow as she moved, utterly enthralled.

Jupiter, on the other hand, stood in a corner of the field,

pretending to shiver beneath his combo turnout rug, and stared at the gate until I relented and brought him back in. When I went back for Ace an hour later, it had started to snow again and she was still happily amusing herself. A dozen seagulls were perched on the top rail of the fence, huddled together, and when Ace looked up at me from beside them, her heart-shaped star visible through the flurry of falling snow, I knew the moment was one that would become a memory that would never fade.

As I walk along the country road, thinking back over the past weeks as my eyes fix on the thatch cottage and paddock beside it in the near distance, I can't help but feel that something is... *wrong*. Or off, anyway, because nothing looks bad, but something isn't right. I can see Leo grazing in the field, his vibrant chestnut mane, except he doesn't look right. His mane is too long, his body too short...

For a second, I think it's Diamond, that his new owners who claim to be so enamoured with him have changed their mind and given him back to Freya, but this pony is chestnut, not spotted, that much is clear even with his turnout rug on. It *must* be Leo, except the mane really does look too long. When did I last see him? Could it have grown that much in that time...

The smell of smoke lingers in the air from the cottage chimney, and as I step up the pathway that leads to the paddocks and stables, spotting Freya with a haynet over her shoulder, I think I must have imagined it, that Leo looks the same as always.

Except then I see Leo, in the stable building with the half door shut, and he lets out a low whinny at the sight of me, his ears pricked, and the pony in the field answers.

Freya spins around, putting the full haynet down by the stable door, and at my puzzled expression, she straightens up and shrugs.

I shake my head in disbelief, eyes going from one pony to the other, trying to process what is going on.

'I know,' Freya says, a faint smile on her face.

I shake my head again. 'What-'

'You know my dad was taking some horses down to an auction in Malvern yesterday? Well, he had to wait there for the whole sale, in case they didn't sell or something, and so he was waiting in the bidding ring, because there wasn't much else to do, and the meat man was there as always, buying anything cheap, and then this pony comes into the ring...' Freya shakes her head. 'Eighteen years old, schoolmaster, been there done that, a little kid leading her around, and she was about to go to the meat man for sixty pounds.'

'Oh my god,' I say, eyes darting to the pony in the paddock. She's in a rug I recognise as one of Diamond's, but even that is too big, falling less than an inch above her knee. She looks sweet, though. *Normal*, not like there's any reason she should be turned into dog food.

'He couldn't bear it. He *claims* he was just going to drive the bidding up, and the meat man bid a couple more times, but nobody else did...'

'So he bought her,' I say.

Freya laughs. 'Kinda. Imagine what Mum and I were like when he called yesterday afternoon to tell us to get things ready for another pony.'

'You annoyed?'

'You kidding?' Freya huffs. 'I would've been mad if he *hadn't.*'

I look towards the paddock, at the little pony picking at the sparse winter grass as though she's been here her whole life. 'What's her name?'

'Isabel. I'm going to call her Izzy.' Freya turns to her grooming box, picking up a catalogue balanced on the lid and opening it to a marked page. 'Here.'

Compared to the Tattersalls catalogue, which was as thick as a Bible and probably contained just as many words, this one is a leaflet. I lower my eyes, scanning the page, and spot Izzy's description.

Lot 11 - The property of Mrs L Pollard
ISABEL, CHESTNUT MARE, 18 YEARS, 13.2HH APPROX.
Sire: Jumping Jack Flash
Dam: Wishful Plum

Isabel is a fantastic child's 1st pony who has done cross country, show jumping, dressage, Pony Club, and pleasure rides. Fabulous to box, shoe, catch and clip and a real pleasure to own. Has also had a foal.

'You read it?' Freya asks, looking over my shoulder.

I nod, handing her back the catalogue.

'Doesn't it just make you sick?' She puts the catalogue back down on her closed grooming box. 'I mean, this little pony has given her whole life to families, teaching kids, and as soon as she's no longer wanted, they actually sit back and watch her go to the meat man. Dad said he only bid at the last second, and if he hadn't then she'd be at the abattoir right now, after everything she's done.'

'It's not right,' I say.

'No.' Freya crosses her arms.

'But she's safe now,' I go on.

Freya nods, her gaze elsewhere. 'Yeah.' She snaps her head towards the fields, then looks back at me and opens the gate to the occupied paddock, which connects to the second stable door. 'Wanna go see her?'

Izzy lifts her head and pricks her ears as we approach her. Her head is delicate, fine and dished, with a small white stripe the length of a pencil starting at her forehead. Her ears curve upwards at the tips, and her eyes are bright. No wonder Craig took pity on her.

'She's so sweet,' I say, walking with Freya up to the mare.

'She is.' Freya stops walking, and I halt beside her. 'Izzy,' she calls to the mare a few paces away. 'C'mon.'

Izzy walks up to us happily, ears always staying forward, the tips almost touching. She goes straight to Freya, who scratches her head, then turns to me with the same air of trust. I hold out a hand to stroke her neck, and am met by a ridiculously silky mane.

'She's so clean!' I say.

'Yeah, she's been coated in coat shine. Wait till you feel her tail.'

Izzy is adorable. She's friendly, and sweet, and when Freya leads her to the stable, by the neck of her rug, and puts a head collar on her to remove the cover, I see that her conformation is just as nice as the rest of her. Her age shows, in the way her back is just starting to dip and her coat is flecked with grey hairs, but she's still gorgeous.

'Has she met Leo yet?' I ask as the gelding behind us kicks his stable door.

'Only with me holding him, but he seems to like her. I know Olivia only turned him out on his own, but I texted Leni this morning, and she said she always turned him out with others and that he's a pushover, so I think they'll be fine. I'll turn them each out in a different paddock first so they can meet over the fence.'

I almost make a comment about Freya reaching out to Leni, Leo's first rider, something that surprises me, something I'm sure she'd never have done a few months ago, but decide against it. Some things are better left unsaid.

'I think it'll be nice for him to have a friend,' Freya goes on. 'I mean, I know he can see the horses across the road, and he goes hacking with Ace and Jup, and sees other horses all the time at competitions and lessons... but I think he'll like having a field buddy.'

'Especially one as nice as *you*,' I say to Izzy, planting a kiss on her outstretched nose. She's the cutest thing I've ever seen, and the thought of her ending her days in a slaughterhouse makes bile rise in my throat. Even if she *weren't* nice to look at, it wouldn't be right, not after all she's done. 'But what are you going to do with her? Are you going to try to sell her or something?'

Freya shakes her head immediately. 'You don't *sell* an eighteen-year-old, that's what makes me annoyed. You're just getting rid of the responsibility and basically giving her to someone else to die. I think you should put an old horse down yourself above rehoming it, where you have no idea how they'll end their days. It's irresponsible.'

I frown. 'What are you going to do with her, then? She could live another ten years.'

'Well,' Freya says, pulling two carrots out of her tack trunk, 'I did have an idea.' She hands me a carrot to give Izzy, and walks up to Leo with the other. 'The catalogue said she's already had a foal, so I thought maybe I'd have her covered later this year.'

I watch Izzy crunch the carrot, picturing a smaller version of her by her side, and butterflies flutter in my stomach. 'Oh my god, yes.'

'Maybe I could put her to something about fifteen hands, and get the perfect fourteen-two and produce it as an event pony.'

'Yes, you have to do that,' I say, caught up in the excitement of future foals.

'Or put her to something bigger and breed the perfect small eventer. I don't know. I wouldn't have her covered until May or June, anyway, so I've got time.' Freya strokes Leo's delicate head as the pony stretches his neck over the half door, resting his head against her waist and nibbling at her coat pockets.

'Yeah, you have time,' I echo.

Izzy steps forward through the gateway, towards Freya and Leo, and stretches her nose out, the picture of innocence and elegance. Freya smiles at her, reaching out a hand to scratch her head, and Leo copies, trying to touch noses with Izzy. The little mare flickers an ear, sniffing him, and lets out a tiny squeal, stomping her left fore, which terrifies Leo, and he jumps back in his box, making Freya and me laugh.

'Pushover, all right,' I say.

Freya grins, turning back to her chestnut gelding. 'Watch out, Lion. She's going to put you in your place.'

My mind is whirling with thoughts of Izzy when I walk back into the yard some time later. If I were paying attention to my surroundings, I'd notice that Rose's lorry is gone, but I'm not. I glance absently towards the farmhouse, wondering if Gabe is still here. Since I told him about Jemima being a fan of Liam's books, the two of them have formed an unlikely friendship, and are the only two members of the unofficial Amity Byron Fan Club. I saw Liam the other day, and he said he'd receive a formal email from them requesting his presence at a meeting.

I don't know that Gabe and Jemima would be able to maintain a conversation if they didn't have Amity Byron in common, but I'm just glad he has a friend he enjoys spending time with, however long the friendship lasts.

Ace and Jupiter are in the paddock, with Cinder and Pheasant, and before going to bring them in I wander around the new stables in the hay barn, admiring the solidly-built partitions, and glancing an eye over the distant horse walker.

One of the stable doors is open, pinned back to the wall, with a deep straw bed down, and a freshly filled bucket of water. I wonder about this for a second, but then I remember Izzy down the road, and my thoughts are taken over again.

It's twenty minutes later, when Ace and Jupiter are standing in their stables with hosed off legs, while I'm rubbing Jupiter's fetlocks dry with a towel, that I hear the approaching rumble of the horsebox, and remember it wasn't here when I arrived. Slowly my mind connects the dots, between the missing horsebox, a missing Rose, and the bedded down stable. Is there a new horse coming? Did she go to get it? Must have.

Bolting Jupiter's door behind me, I walk across the courtyard, twisting to try to wipe some of the wet mud off my jodhpurs. I always forget about my muddy wellies when I sit back on my heels to dry the horses' legs, and mud is caked to the back of my thighs. Combined with the splatters that hit me when I lead the ponies in, their footfalls spraying me with every step, I'm something of a sight. Why do show jumpers and dressage riders never look this dirty? I swear they always look clean.

The horsebox has pulled up by the hay barn, and I watch Rose climb down from the cab, her expression distant. Behind the building, the farmhouse door opens, and I see Ben walk out with Mackenzie at his side.

'Don't let the dogs out,' Ben tells her, and Mackenzie wrestles the door closed as the exuberant Flopsy and Florence try to sneak out.

'You've picked up a new horse?' I ask Rose, hurrying to her side to help unbolt and lower the lorry ramp before Ben and Mackenzie reach us.

Rose looks surprised by my voice, as though the smallest thing surprises her. Her expression is still distant, her eyes glassy, and for a terrifying moment, I think something is wrong, but then she smiles, and I hear her breath catch.

'Not a new horse…'

We lower the ramp, Ben and Mackenzie reaching the lorry as Rose jumps up to undo a partition, and I step back, trying to get a look at the horse inside. A pair of white ears stick out from behind a haynet, and as Rose swings back a partition a matching head follows. It's a horse as opposed to a pony, about sixteen hands, and if his almost-white coat is anything to go by he isn't young. *Really* old, even. In his twenties, I'd say if I didn't know any better.

I'd expect Rose to tell Mackenzie to move out the way when she's about to lead a random horse down the ramp, because if the horse were to misbehave, Mackenzie, right by the ramp as she is, would be in the firing line, but Rose doesn't.

'Come on, Ri,' she whispers, leading the grey horse down the ramp.

Ri…

The horse plods down the ramp without a care in the world. A fleece covers his body, but his angular frame confirms that he must fall under the older age bracket.

Ri…

Rose halts the horse at the bottom of the ramp and wipes her eyes with her sleeves, as my mind connects the dots all at once - an old grey horse, the name on his leather head collar…

'This is Orion?' I say, hardly able to believe it. Rose's horse of a lifetime, the one she sold because she was made an offer she couldn't refuse, the one that allowed her to buy the yard she is in now.

Rose nods, wiping at fresh tears again, and Ben wraps an arm around her before stepping near the horse.

'Hello, old man,' he says quietly, running his fingers down his head. 'Long time no see.'

Mackenzie is all over the place, rattling on to me about Rose receiving a phone call from Orion's owner saying he was ready to retire for good, and having promised her many years ago that they would offer him to her when the day came, though Rose never believed it would really happen. And rushing to get him right away, driving straight to Sussex, not wanting to waste a second…

'I can't believe I'm actually meeting Orion,' Mackenzie says, bouncing into the stable behind him. The grey horse is not the least bit perturbed by the tiny figure jumping all over the place, though that could be because he remains by Rose's side the whole time, as though he's never forgotten her the way she's never forgotten him.

'I can't believe you've got him back,' I say, leaning against the stable door, staring at the white horse picking at a pile of hay with gusto.

Rose shakes her head, still looking as though she's just seen a ghost. 'I can't, either.'

'He can't do anything, can he?' I say. 'I mean, he can't be ridden or hacked or anything like that…'

Rose shakes her head again. 'No. He's twenty-two or twenty-three this year, I can't remember. He's showing his age, and being grey, he has a few melanomas, too. He's living out his days now.' She smiles, as though something's amusing. 'He'll probably cost more to feed than any other horse here, not to mention future vet bills and what comes after he passes.' She laughs. 'And he's taking up a stable slot that is supposed to earn…'

I frown, confused by what Rose is saying. 'You wish you didn't have him?'

'Of course not.' Orion turns his head towards Rose, nudging her shoulder, and she leans into him to rest her head against his neck. 'That's what you do.'

* * *

'Okay,' Ben says, stepping to the side of the jump stand, holding up the tape measure. 'One-twenty.'

I rest a hand against Ace's neck, feeling as though I'm about to be sick. I glance to my left, at the two combinations beside me. On Leo, Freya looks more relaxed, and Leo looks positively bored, like this is all too easy, while my grey pony looks so excited that I almost laugh. Rose wasn't going to take part in the puissance, said it was a game for the younger generation, but then I had the idea of her riding Jupiter, and we both found it so amusing that she accepted.

Except I'm wondering if I chose the wrong pony, because Rose and Jupiter are making this all look way too easy.

'Mum first,' Mackenzie calls from Cinder's back. The bay mare rattled a rail at a metre, which I think Mackenzie was secretly pleased by, even if she won't admit it, because she looked pretty scared to have got that far as it was.

'Go on, Rose!' Mum calls from the side of the ring, leaning against the railings with Nell at her side. 'I'm sure you can get Jup to do it.'

Rose grins at them. 'All right, just you watch.'

Jupiter has finally lost his winter weight through the work he's done these past ten weeks, and he strikes effortlessly into a rhythmic canter, Rose sitting lightly in the saddle. There is dry mud on his hocks and caked to his ears, because forty hours in the day wouldn't be enough to allow me to get it all off every day, but the parts of him covered by a rug when he's turned out are clean, and I'm amazed by how good he looks. He's moving forward into the hand, his neck flexed, head carriage still, quarters engaged. Rose makes him look like a top event pony, and I think that maybe, just maybe, that's what he'll end up being.

Ben steps back as Rose turns Jupiter to the metre-twenty upright. The grey gelding lifts his head through the turn, eyes locking on the fence with excitement, but Rose stays quiet in her seat, containing Jupiter's stride, slowing it right down and yet building more impulsion than I could ever achieve with him myself.

She waits, waits for the stride she wants, and Jupiter launches into the air like a Grand Prix show jumper, tucking his knees, and my jaw drops as I watch him fly over the fence, Rose looking like she was made to ride him, and unsurprisingly, they land clear.

'You were saying?' Rose quips, grinning at the spectators before trotting Jupiter over to Freya and me, patting the pony's neck and bringing him to a halt. 'I think I have my next Advanced eventer here.'

'I think Orion has a better chance of coming out of retirement than Jupiter going Advanced,' I say.

'He could be the next Teddy O'Connor,' Freya says, naming

the famous fourteen-two event pony - who even had Shetland in him - that competed at four-star level.

I doubt this, but Jupiter is certainly looking good, and showing more skill than I ever thought him capable of.

'Come on, Freya, you're next,' Rose says.

Leo looks beautiful, and Freya keeps her eyes on the fence at all times as they circle at one end of the school. His head is up, balance on his hocks, and they canter down to the upright and clear it as though it were a mere cross rail.

'Go on, Sybs!' Mum calls.

'Come on, Maggot, you can do this!' Rose cheers.

Ace strikes off into a balanced canter, and I slowly release a breath, trying to calm my nerves. *We can do this,* I think. *It's just an upright.*

When Ace comes out of the corner, she starts to rush with anticipation, but I remain calm, and this in turn calms her. I make sure to keep my leg on, because I have a habit of taking it off when I'm not rushing towards a stride, and before I know it, we're landing clear on the other side of the fence.

Ben raises the fence to one-twenty-five next, and in the same order, all three of us clear it with ease, and my nerves fade to excitement. A metre-twenty-five! I've never jumped that high in my life, and Ace makes it feel easy.

'Okay,' Rose says, raising a hand, 'I vote we call it a day at one-thirty. I don't fancy going any higher on a fourteen-two, though I'm sure he can do it.'

'Agreed,' I say, and Freya nods, too.

Rose goes first again, and I feel as nervous for Jupiter and her as I do for Ace and myself. She shortens the pony's stride until he's almost cantering on the spot, gathering the energy she wants him to explode with over the jump. Jupiter's stride rocks with anticipation, right up to the base of the fence, and then Rose lets him loose and he's flying. His knees tuck, his whole body stretching in a bascule, and all I can think is, *That's my pony*. That pony, the one I objectively thought was an average lower-level schoolmaster is actually mine, and he's anything but average.

Mum and Nell whoop, and from Cinder's back, Mackenzie cheers.

'I love this pony,' Rose sings, leaning forward to shower Jupiter with praise.

Leo shakes his head as he picks up the canter, and Freya steadies him on a circle again before tuning to the fence. He starts to rush away from her leg, the anticipation too much, and she steadies him, though they still get to the fence a bit deep, but Leo pushes off his hinds with everything he has, and they land clear, the impact jolting Freya on landing.

'What are you feeding him, Freya?' Mum jokes, and Freya laughs as she wraps her arms around Leo's neck, the pony looking ready to jump again.

'All right, Maggot,' Rose says, taking her feet out of the stirrups and crossing them on Jupiter's neck in front of her. 'Show us how it's done.'

I'm either going to be sick or shriek with excitement, I'm not sure which. Ace strikes off into a canter when I barely touch her with my outside leg, and I let out a long breath, eyes searching for the fence. It's huge, seriously huge, like the size of a four-star show jumping track. And then I weirdly think that if I can jump this, I could go four-star, which is ridiculous because I have no desire to ride Advanced or gallop around Badminton, but the thought crosses my mind, and I shake it away just as quickly, focussing on the task at hand.

Ace's head comes up out of the turn, her ears framing the fence, and I try to keep her calm, while also making sure I have enough impulsion to clear the upright. Her stride comes up beneath me, building with momentum, and as we get nearer the fence, I realise I actually have to look *up* to see the top rail, higher than I am - or, at least it feels like it is - which is more than a little terrifying. But Ace keeps moving beneath me, as though she has wings and wind is gathering beneath them, and before I know it we're launching into the air, soaring.

I release with my hands, allowing Ace to stretch over the fence, the cold air nipping at my eyes and blurring my vision. A metre-thirty, we're actually doing it. We *can* do it.

Ace lands clear, and I let out the biggest breath of relief as I hear cheers behind me. *We can do it. We* did *it.*

I lengthen my reins as Ace canters on, patting her neck and grinning from ear to ear. If we can do that, I feel like we can do anything.

And we're going to come out prepared next season, ready to nail it. All guns blazing.

about the author

After years of living in France, Grace currently resides near Newmarket, where she works with horses full-time.

https://www.facebook.com/GraceWilkinsonWrites

gracewilkinsonwrites@gmail.com

Printed in Great Britain
by Amazon